Murray Pomerance

Savage Time

Copyright © 2005 by Murray Pomerance

All rights reserved: no part of this book may be reproduced in any form or by any means, electronic or mechanical, except by a reviewer, who may quote brief passages in a review to be printed in a newspaper or magazine or broadcast on radio or television.

We acknowledge the support of the Canada Council for the Arts, the Government of Ontario through the Ontario Media Development Corporation and the Government of Canada through the Book Publishing Industry Development Program for our publishing activities.

Some of the stories in this book have appeared before, in somewhat different forms: "Decor" in *The Paris Review*, "Honeymoon," "Koi" and "Death in Venice" in *Descant*, "Sand" in *The White Wall Review* and "Rite de Passage" in *Prairie Fire*.

ISBN 0 7780 1275 1 (hardcover)
ISBN 0 7780 1277 8 (softcover)

Cover art by Winslow Homer
Book design by Michael Macklem

Printed in Canada

PUBLISHED IN CANADA BY OBERON PRESS

Contents

Part 1

Decor 8

Armistice Day 16

Petit Mal 38

Honeymoon 59

Koi 71

The Cereal Hour 83

Part 2

Sand 102

A Matter of Definition 116

Death in Venice 128

Tabula Rasa 151

Rite de Passage 165

Always to G.G.

•

Only the ephemeral is of lasting value—Eugene Ionesco

PART 1

Decor

"Listen," Trudy Kay had Ettie Savage on the telephone and she was breathing somewhat more forcefully than normal. "About your living-room. You'll remember I was talking to you the other day. I want you to know I haven't forgotten. I've been thinking. I've been turning it over in my mind. We've got to do something about that room. We absolutely have to. Do you know what it's like now? It's depressing. I get depressed when I go in there. It's cramped and tight and you can't figure out where anything is. Do you remember when we were designing it with Ed? Do you remember? The whole idea was to have *space*—" After saying *space* she paused and gave a forceful breath, as if to create space over the telephone. Then, when all Ettie could do was insert a tiny "Well," she carried on: "The furniture. We have to do something about the furniture. Because nobody in his right mind can find a place to sit down. And I'll tell you another thing, there aren't enough ashtrays, but that's something else. But you have to be able to sit *down*. I don't know how you can live there. I don't understand where you sit. It was originally intended—don't you remember what Ed originally intended?—there'd be plenty of incidental activity going on, but I don't know how you can do it. Everybody's afraid to sit. *I'm* afraid to sit. Ed didn't expect people would be burning holes in the sofa with their cigarettes or cutting holes with scissors or letting the dogs do their, you know, *business* on the chairs. You know.... And the piano, you see what I mean? The piano. And the plants. And the pictures. It's all gone wrong, it's all gone *meshugge*. You know what I mean, *meshugge*?" Ettie coughed a little, in a genteel fashion although she knew perfectly well how to avoid gentility. "I can't believe you like it that way. Tell me. You like having everything all over the place? Because *I* couldn't tolerate it. *I* just die when I'm in that kind of situation. Robert Keneally's coming out. He comes out, you know. He's coming out anyway so I thought I'd just get hold of him and we'd go over the place with a fine-tooth comb. If you're talking decoration there isn't anybody else,

I'm sure you know that. Trust me. He'll take one look at your place and it'll be pure creativity." When Ettie put the phone down and looked around the room it seemed fine, it was as it always had been, so she thought she'd better have a look with her glasses but trying under all the magazines she couldn't find them.

•

On a day when there was nobody home, and when the dogs had been boarded and the plants watered and the bird feeders on the patio filled to capacity, Trudy Kay gained access to the house. She rolled into the gravelled drive in her 1971 Ford Fairmont with the clutch that stuck. She waited. A 1979 Honda Civic rolled in after her, as grey as the grey translucent sky. Robert Keneally got out. He wore maple-coloured corduroy trousers, a burgundy velour shirt, a pair of slippers. They stood for long minutes in the gravelled drive and she pointed and he nodded and she pointed up at the yawning oak trees and he looked away. They came into the house as if perhaps she would sell it to him—"Isn't it wonderful?" "Isn't it spacious?"—and his eyes were rolling over the hibiscus and the poinsettia and the tumbling jades, the spreading lawns of violets, the Boston ferns blocking the light like jungle growth. She gave him the long tour, so that before they arrived at the living-room they passed all of the bedrooms, and the four baths, and the study, and the parlour, the kitchen, the basement, the wine cellar, the sauna, and the nook where breakfast could be taken beneath a poster of a Toulouse-Lautrec. "Ahhh," said Robert Keneally, "Yes, yes, yes, yes, yes, yes, yes."

•

Next to the living-room, and six steps above it, was a parlour, and in the parlour were picture windows, and through the picture windows drizzled a light that was even and melancholy and blue. Robert Keneally stood there for long minutes, turning his face from the window to gaze around the high, small room. The room filled him with a sense of pleasure. Then he stepped down the stairs to the lower space, where in the corner there was a canvas by Willem de Kooning and a Steinway concert grand on the lid of which two dying pink amaryllidaceous flowers sat. He ran his hand over the surface of the piano, ebony, needing polish. He was tall, and slender as a poplar. "I think," he said softly, "This...there." And his aquiline nose and eyes as dark as coals gave onto the parlour. "Where the window is." He stepped away, and stepped back, and stepped away. "With the keyboard ...against...the window." Tiny Trudy Kay was watching every move he made. It had never occurred to her that there was a dancer in him. "Against the wall? You mean against the wall? All the way over there?" He lowered his voice as she waited and his answer rang out in the silence like an incantation. "The window," he moved back and forth along the keyboard, "is here, you see. Here. The keys...are beside...the window...in the window light...."

•

She sat herself on the sofa that would need to be recovered, that had cigarette burns and puncture wounds from scissors all over its surface, and over the top of the television listings from the *Times* she scanned the wall where he was standing. There was the de Kooning, and then a Prohaska, and then a Motherwell and a Dash and a very small thing by Lee Krasner. "You know," she said, and her voice had an insistent buzz, "I don't know why, but that wall doesn't do a lot for me. I think the panelling can go." Beneath the row of paintings, glowing amber in the late afternoon light, was panelling. "I think the panelling can go because, search me, it doesn't give me that satisfying feeling. Do you know what I mean, Robert?" He was moving very quietly with a folding ruler. He had the ruler folded out to six feet. He was using it vertically and horizontally on the wall in question. To no-one in particular he murmured, "Bookshelves." "Brilliant!" she said; "Bookshelves would be very nice. And I think the panelling goes, wouldn't you say? It definitely doesn't speak up for itself." Keneally moved his ruler. "Why?" his voice was softer than ever, directed only at himself although he stared at her while he spoke. "Why? We're covering with bookshelves. If we're covering with bookshelves why play with the panelling?" And she thought for a moment, squinted up her wrinkled eyelids, lit herself a cigarette and puffed it zealously. "It's just me, you see. My idiosyncratic taste. But in my place when I did the walls I used rosewood, not this stuff, and my walls have stood up considerably better than these if you ask me. But rosewood does that, doesn't it, Robert—stands up? Tell me, don't you adore this ceiling?—" He was moving slowly around the room, squinting at the windows, placing the extended ruler along the fronts of the chairs and whispering to himself. "Robert, don't you think this ceiling's marvellous? Ed didn't come up with that on his own, you know. Do you know who suggested that to Ed?" He looked at her openly. "Me," she said, "It's one of the only things in this place that hasn't gone to the dogs, if you'll pardon the expression. I'll tell you, Robert," she doused the cigarette, "The more I think about it the more I'm convinced—that wall has to go. It's an eyesore. You walk in here and you look at it and immediately you want to leave." He was moving along the wall in question, skimming the air with his finger. "Bookshelves...here...I think...," and his palm was clasping and unclasping itself over the surfaces of the Krasner, the Dash, the Motherwell, the Prohaska, the de Kooning. "A de Kooning from the early eighties—my God!" Then Trudy Kay gave a peremptory little sigh and spoke with a wheeze that was sinister. "Robert—although I have to admit the bookshelves are brilliant, I have to say: one way to look at this is that you're solving the books problem. And the other way—is that you're creating the pictures problem. Isn't life delicious!"

•

"You'd think," said Trudy Kay, "she'd keep some crackers here. I'm fainting. All she has is saltines. What's saltines when you're fainting? You'd think she'd have some decent cheese biscuits. Do you suppose she has any cheese? If I have to eat saltines there might at least be some cheese. She probably hasn't bought any cheese in months. The refrigerator is probably full of exotic cheeses she bought three months ago. You see, it's that kind of a family, Robert. We're trying to get the living-room right for a bunch of people who sit around eating saltines. Do you see what I'm trying to say? See, we could do the kitchen over again, too. There'd have to be a new refrigerator and new cupboards. The oven I know she put in just last year. We'd have to take the counters apart completely. You know it doesn't take much, sometimes I think even if I had a little piece of cheddar I'd be satisfied."

•

He had wanted to make a map on a piece of paper that had blue lines and he had asked her for a pencil. "Pencils everywhere and none of them have a point," she said. "Isn't it perfect? Isn't it exactly what you'd expect? That's how they live here, without pencils." So she had gone out to her car to get him a pencil and in the silence he had taken himself to the windows that gave onto the patio. There was an aviary of sorts out there. The cherry trees, the wild pear, were laden heavily with feeders, and the pine was heavy with feeders, and the birds were fluttering and jousting from perch to perch in the silvery light that was shooting in shafts through the branches. He did not know how to name them, but the artist's eye in him was held unmeasuring and shuddering with joy at the manifold finches, the gold finches and purple finches; and the reckless blue jays swooping and scattering; and the cowbirds who strutted haphazardly; the grackles who poked; the crows poking with the grackles; the indigo buntings, one turned fully turquoise and one moulting; the cardinals, male and female, singing from flaming beaks, "Chew, chew"; the doves swirling along the patio pave like aging waltzers at the Waldorf; woodpeckers pecking at suet and orioles with blazing wings and tawny-breasted towhees, black-capped chickadees, proud and prancing pheasants craning their ringed necks both curious and terrified, terrified and curious as they caught his eye and strode away. There were a dozen garbage pails, battered, some lettered so that he could read them: "Bird mix," "Blk sunflr sds," "Thistle sds," "Cracked seed," "Millet," and others in a row behind now, as a cloud moved, shining with a radiance of pure silver. "The money they must have to do this!" he whispered to himself, and he held a great sigh within his chest, and then she was back with a pencil from the car but it turned out to have no point so he was reduced to using a pen with blue ink to make lines on the paper already covered evenly with lines that were blue.

•

As he sketched, Robert Keneally hummed. He hummed "Top Hat" and "S'wonderful, S'marvellous That You Should Care for Me," and then "Cheek to Cheek" with a little shift of his hips. Trudy Kay took his place at the window and gawked at the birds feeding. "Isn't it something, those blue jays?" she was rather loud. "They're such criminals. He's got them all over, you know. The property is covered with them. Did you know—he's a naturalist. He's always been that way. Well, you can see by all the trees. Look at that blue jay! The blue jays are just pigs, you know, they just dive in and eat everybody else's food. I'll tell you what I think—if ever there was a bird who couldn't mind his own business, it's the blue jay. Look, look—" she was cackling, "They take from everybody!" The decorator was standing back from the scene of his imaginary creation to a moment of imaginary evaluation. His eyes screwed tight. His fingers spread out in front of him. He paused and took a slender cigarette and inserted it between his lips. "Mmmm," he said. "It's going to be lovely." And he moved, ahead, back, to the side, ahead, back, to the side, and his hands were limp at his sides, and he seemed to know where the paintings would be rebirthed and to see the wall covered with books and the furnishings re-established. "Do you know what I have?" said Trudy Kay. "I have sparrows."

•

They had moved out to where the cars were parked and were conferring a last time on the gravel. "Let me tell you what I think we should do, Robert," she said. "I'm honestly not exaggerating, not that I would ever exaggerate, but I really do get a sense from the place...and you have to remember I know what Ed had in mind when he did the original designs, I mean, I know everything...that it should be...another place altogether. The two of them had a long conference with Ed, believe me, and I was there for all of it. Because who do you think brought Ed in in the first place? Who do you think got them Ed?" He looked into her eyes. "Right. Because we go back a long way, Ed and I. We go back to Provincetown." "My God," he said softly. "Sure—we go back to Provincetown, and you know what it was like in *those* days. So I made the connection for him. Well, I made it for all of them. And I know what they were talking about. I understand the spirit of the thing. You know what I mean by spirit, Robert. That wall, the panelling, really should go. Really. The whole damned thing, once and for all. And we'll do the bookshelves, which is your idea. It's a terrific idea, Robert. We'll do the bookshelves. And then we'll put the piano somewhere out of the way, maybe in the parlour. But, you know, we'll have to leave the parlour window free because they let the dogs in and out there. You know they have dogs—I'm sure I told you. Little dogs. Pekingese or Balinese or terriers or something. They're coming in and out all day long. A thing like that would drive me crazy. I'll tell you what else. We could think about redoing the floor, because I'm not wild about the floor she's got in there if you want to know the truth. The dogs are always, you know, crapping on it and the whole thing is just generally out of the question. And the more I think about it the more I'm convinced we should take that panelling out and maybe—we're getting pretty adventuresome here, Robert—expand the room outwards over the patio. Do you know what I mean, on the far side, where he's got that bird stuff? Because the only thing out there is the birds, you know. We can dispense with them if we have to. It's just blue jays, isn't it? They'll find somewhere else to eat. Or we could relocate the whole thing, the feeders and everything, inside the garage, a kind of bird schmooze-house. That would be charming. And it would give us double the living room. Can you imagine the view! See, Robert—do you know how long I've known Ettie? Thirty-five years. That's a hell of a long time." "It certainly is," he whispered. "That's a hell of a long time and I know the way she thinks. You have to respect the way a person thinks, that's my bottom line. I'll tell you how she thinks. She's not happy with this. She tells everybody she's happy because she doesn't want to upset—him. Because why? Because he's very sensitive. I should have told you, maybe it's very important, but he's sensitive. She's never for a minute been happy with the kitchen and she doesn't like the piano down there. Since the piano's down there she never plays it anymore. She used to play it all the time. She used to play it forever. And the blue jays—they're driving her crazy. She wants shelves for books. That was a fabulous idea, Robert, really. But fundamentally she's not happy, she's not fulfilled, which is my bottom line. She wants space, that's what she wants. She wants freedom. I think if we could just clean the place out and start over again she'd be a lot happier." He saw what she meant. He took his piece of blue-lined paper on which he'd made a blue map and he folded it and stuffed it in his hip pocket. He gently touched the handle of the door of his car. "Do you really want to know what I think of that panelling?" she was half turning away from him, lowering her voice so that no creature hiding in the trees could overhear. "How long did I say I've know them, 35 years? For 35 years every time I go into that room I think I'm at a funeral."

•

Their two cars were parked beside one another on the gravel driveway, the driveway shaped like a half moon that opened doubly onto the street. Her car was facing one direction, his was facing the other. At the steering wheels, with their windows down, they could be conversing in a kind of intimacy. "Robert—you'll let me handle it with her, right? There's no need at this level for you to be getting involved. I've known her for 35 years." They drove away from one another and he mused as he drove along the majestic dunes that it was, in all truth, one of the most beautiful houses he'd ever seen. He put a cigarette to his lips. He thought about an interesting new design for bookshelves that would let the magnificent panelling glow through.

•

Ettie stood in a still posture with Doc at the window while the finches and orioles and doves quibbled for their food and the scrambling dogs yelped with joy to be home from the kennel, and while Trudy Kay, in her bathtub, dreamed of pulling out the garden Ettie had planted and replacing it with Japanese bonsai, and while Keneally made careful drawings of the grand piano by the blue window light of the parlour, guiding his hand in a meticulous silence but hearing in his thoughts Ettie sitting at the keys and playing, perhaps from memory on a sombre afternoon, Chopin.

Armistice Day

"I'll tell you a thing about women," the old man said, getting up from the table to brew himself another cup of tea. And then as if, as a tactic, this were nothing but questionable, "Wellllll..., maybe I won't." Finally, after a good long pause, until the sun had come out again from a hideout in a cloud shaped like an anvil, "I'll tell you something *you don't know* about women. There anything you don't know?" He didn't wait for an answer. "They cherish, above all things, the admiration of other women. It's basic to their nature. They want other women to gaze at them. And the only thing a woman really loves about a man is that a man can attract those other women for her to pose to. A lot's been said about the way men control women. Yes, yes. There's that British fellow, says men control women by looking at them. But he has it wrong. It's not men who look at women, it's women who look at women, that's my point, and that British fellow's crazy. Women find women fascinating." He puttered around while he said all this, and these comments, as he moved like a feeding crane, seemed to come out of nowhere. "*Fascinating*, I mean in the original sense. Know what *fascinating* means? Comes from the Latin, *fascinum*, means evil spell. Witchcraft. It's what women do with one another, from morning until night." The old man had taken a seat and had been observing the purple finches hopping and chatting on the branches of the great spruce. Now he stood and let his jaw sag, opened cupboards hunting for the Earl Grey teabags—"The Jackson's of Piccadilly Earl Grey teabags..."—filled the water purifier, stuck a peanut butter cookie in his mouth. He rearranged some tomatoes artfully in a great flat glass bowl, he poured the purified water into the kettle, flipped the kettle on. And now he waited. It is surely the technique of the therapist to wait, but waiting had never been accomplished as musically as this. "It's a great mistake to think that women like men *intrinsically*, in the same way that men like women." The kettle nagged with a shrill whistle and then shut itself off in embarrassment—one of the many curious luxuries that had been imported to this house from England—and he made his tea weakish, as only an American will, toying with a slice of lemon to slide into it but then abandoning the slice to the sink along with shrimp shells from last night's dinner and unmonogrammed spoons. He went for the milk. He slopped milk onto the counter when he poured it. "A little less viscous than I counted on," he whispered, "a little less viscous. Life is a hazardous business." Then with something of a limp he came back to the table, where Owen had 30 more seconds by a stopwatch to finish the New York Times crossword in record time, and put his tea down to cool, and stared outside at the birds. It was true that he never really wanted to drink his tea, he wanted to manipulate it. He wanted an excuse to fondle it. When the tea was cool enough it would be suitably undrinkable and he'd be able to stand up and make another cup of tea. "I'll tell you all about women, unless you know everything already. Do you know everything already?" Owen was old enough to know, but not old enough to know much. Owen said, "Six-letter word beginning with d, means 'unpleasant.'" They were silent together, and finally Doc said, "Women without women are like fish out of water. When you finish that thing, we'll go fishing."

•

They went in the Rover to Goff Point. Just outside of Sunday a BMW turned rabidly out of the IGA parking-lot, missing them by inches. Owen felt his lunch come up. "Should be charged with reckless driving," he said, craning his neck to see the car, burgundy and not very clean, disappear back around the station curve. "That what you think?" Doc was chewing something, "That the way you see it? See, I wouldn't say that was reckless driving. That was attempted murder. Yes yes. We take everything too lightly in this society. That's why crime is everywhere. You go into a restaurant and the food's tainted so they get a summons from the health department. Ridiculous. It's attempted manslaughter, and anywhere else, where there was reason, that's how it would be seen. They oughta pick up that driver, put him in jail for 25 years, that's the end of it." Owen found himself staring rather too intently at the stands of scrub oak sliding by on the ocean side of the car, then across the road at the LIRR track like a straight lance stretching out under the chrome yellow sky to the eastern horizon. Life was sharper now that he knew somebody had been trying to kill him.

•

When they reached the walking dunes Owen jumped out and adjusted the axles, Doc calling to him over the purr of the engine, "Just rotate that nut in the centre of the hub clockwise a quarter turn. Right right! And just go around to the other wheel. Right. And that's great. Right right! Because I'm too old for this kind of thing and it doesn't bother you, does it." Owen didn't see the point of answering. But when he got back into the cab, not feeling at all today like a sapling, he said, "I've had headaches." They were pulling forward in lurches now, onto the beach, and then skimming the waterline. "Mussels aplenty out here," Doc sang. "Once upon a time you couldn't get people to take mussels for garbage. Now they're *moules*. What do you mean headaches? More than one at a time? General headaches or pointed headaches?" Doc Savage was writing a book on headaches. Headaches fascinated him more than fish, though it was true that at five o'clock, and it was five o'clock now, fish were Doc's religion for an hour. "Predictable headaches? Spontaneous headaches? One-sided headaches? Headaches that seem to come in patterns?" Owen didn't know how to answer all this, but he was leaning on his hand which was supported by his arm which was supported by his elbow on the window sill of the bouncing Rover. "I see you're cradling your face," Doc said. "That where it hurts? Do you think it's the face that hurts, or the expression on the face? When we get back you can try some paregoric. It's out of style by 75 years but we'll try it. Lots of useful things are out of style. Ever try putting your hands under running warm water?" Owen hadn't tried it. "Ought to try it. Ever lose your sense of space and position? Ever get lost? Some people can't tell their left from their right when they're migranous. 'Course a lot of these people get treated as if they're just stupid. I suppose I've gone without saying that in my supposition you are a migraneur. Yep yep. That's what you are in my supposition." The water was shimmering in the crisp amber light, blue-black, and the sun was keeping its distance. Gulls careened in low flight paths toward the dune grass, so did a tern. The shadows of Owen and his arm, sticking out of the shadow of the Rover, were long and soothing. The Rover swooped around the long sickle of beach that closed Napeague Harbour—it's a gull's beak facing west at the end—and then came to the point of the thing, where the land terminated, and rounded it upon huge beach stones, until they were on the Bay side of the promontory. The beach sand was bluer here, and the seaweed more copious, and a hundred yards further along the tide had made a twenty-foot channel where they could cast amiably. "You ever sit and talk to Ettie?" Doc wanted to know, opening up the back, unloading the rods and the tackle box and a little silver flask. "You ever yap about anything with her? By the way, don't throw too far out. They like to come in, here. I'll be interested to know if fishing helps your headache. I ask because Ettie likes to yap more than I like to yap." Fishing didn't help Owen's headache, and no, he hadn't talked to Ettie, not really, and it was pleasant to stare, now toward sunset, at the purple stretching shadows of the waning light upon the water as he gave a little lift to the line. Fishing didn't at all help. "Ettie takes herself out for lunch with that Ophelia Goldman. That one gives me a headache, not to be pejorative. Or, as I prefer to put it, *peej*-ra-tive. Not to be *peej*-ra-tive, she gives me a royal pain. Yep yep. At least, it would be, if I were royal." Owen thought maybe he had something. He decided to wait, not to tug. "'Course if you don't like paregoric you can drink jasmine tea, there are many who advocate that. Or ASA. ASA's a myth, though. ASA helps people because they believe it will help them. Ettie goes out for lunch with that Ophelia Goldman and they shmoo-shmoo their faces off about politics. That's all she wants these days, is to go to lunch and put her nose together with Ophelia Goldman's. Gives me a royal headache, and I know something about headaches. You ever see the two of them together?" Owen realized the tugging was gone and the line was quiet. They weren't catching anything but the beach was firming up to the vision like so much crystal, and the light was itself a sort of diamond, when Doc started hitting the flask. "Not natural," said Doc, "if you want to know what I think. All this shmoo-shmooing. But see—well: you *don't* see, do you. If you saw, I wouldn't have to say all this. What I'm saying is, she's a seductive one, that Ophelia Goldman, and she's not unintelligent. She's educated. She went to Sarah Lawrence. You ever meet her?" Yes, said Owen, he had met her; and he would have said what had happened at her house, but at that moment Doc definitely did get a bite, what he called a "distinctive" bite, and it was a snapper just barely right-sized, which he took and flipped into a plastic bucket, and then Doc got another bite, and a third, and he started to chuckle. "You tell me," he said. "You tell me. The minute I have a taste of Highland Scotch, the snappers find me attractive." "I'm not getting anything," Owen said, as if to corroborate. "I'm not getting fucking anything." Doc smiled broadly into the sunset. "Hazardous business, life. Hazardous business."

•

What had happened at the house that belonged to Ophelia Goldman, who was 62 and thus two years older than Ettie (at least insofar as anybody ever seemed to say, because in general, it was agreed, Ettie was beyond description), was what Owen, who was 23, *could* call seduction; though he did not call it that, and did not in open fact call it anything. His silence, in open fact, was the clue that, in the mysterious calculus of maturity, gave Doc the complete picture. Owen had been telephoned—it was still possible to remember this—at the Savages', where he was helping Doc build a wooden shed to hold the trash bins: where everyone in town knew he was helping Doc because he was always helping Doc and nobody else ever came to help Doc and Doc was always in need of help. Could he come to Ophelia Goldman's as soon as possible, because she was having trouble with an outside light? "You go, you go," said Doc. "Make Ettie happy if you help the other one." The other one provided a ladder and a new light-bulb, for it was not the fixture but the bulb within the fixture and the fixture was upon the soffit, and that was that. "I really cannot begin to tell you how grateful and how impressed I am," she began, sounding, yes, very educated, very Sarah Lawrence Sisterhood blah blah blah. "You are a saviour. You are a genius. You are a magician. I express my gratitude to a lot of people, it's natural when you're running a political party, but this is something different." Owen would not have known what to say to these walnut eyes, these pomegranate lips, had he in fact accomplished something; but for changing a light bulb, in a manner quite unrelated to politics—! "I absolutely insist!" she said, clasping his hand, and when she stood back he felt that there was something crisp resting in his palm. He looked down and almost lost his balance, had to catch himself. It was a $50 bill, new from the mint. "I absolutely absolutely absolutely insist. You are a dream. I cannot begin to tell you. And you mustn't try to hand it back to me because I only touch fresh money." He allowed her to make a cup of tea, for which she had no milk in the refrigerator. "It's amazing how I always forget to buy milk. Walter Savage would have something fascinating to say about that, I'm sure, some kind of theory of repression of my mother. In fact, I suspect I do repress my mother; although we get along; or we avoid not getting along. I have a very good memory, there are some things," she seemed to drop her eyes upon him, "that I simply never forget. But milk!—" He dashed out to the IGA and came back with a quart and—he was never able to explain this—the current issue of *Gourmet*. "See! You're also a mind-reader! You're a gift from above! I will make you dinner from this!" She sat beside him on the divan and asked him, in a very motherly way, about his studies at NYU. She put a cigarette in her mouth and looked at him with his jade green eyes, but he didn't reach for matches so she did. "My husband Marcus was a great enthusiast. Art was his whole life. He had so many books you would have loved to see. I gave them all to the library. I had to do something, they took up a wall. Fifteen years he's been dead, it's unbelievable! We used to pick up *Gourmet* at the IGA and make dinner from it once a month. I can cook elaborately, you know. I'm not just interested in who gets elected to the Town Board. I'm a complete person." Owen, whose head was throbbing, had the curious thought that if only he'd been studying art history he could have been floored to learn that this was the home of the famous Marcus Goldman, author of *American Art in the Twentieth Century*, but then he remembered, with a twinge, that art history was precisely what he was studying and he became suddenly nervous, as if eyes in the walls were judging his every move. Something took shape under her cleaver on a very limited countertop, and he allowed himself to doze a little, and to repair the fraying picture wire behind one or two of the Jasper Johnses canting on the wooden walls. The $50 bill had to go beneath his plate at dinner, he knew that, but now she said, "Listen, I'm flat on cash. Take the money I gave you, be a darling, and go buy a decent bottle of wine." Peter the wine man, who was almost closing but who was not quite closed, and who smiled perhaps a little too much but always knew, somehow, by the look on your face what to recommend, said that for the money a 1966 Puligny-Montrachet was just about as good as you could get, and he had one chilled, but Owen kept telling himself he should walk out the door and go back to Doc's without looking behind him. He took the bottle and Peter gave him a nice little green plastic corkscrew. "I met Marcus when he was about your age," she said, pouring out the Puligny-Montrachet. "We had adventures together. Everything was an adventure. Thinking about it makes me feel young again." Owen didn't tell Doc anything about this, because Doc would certainly tell Ettie and Ettie would repeat it, twisted as a dream, to Ophelia Goldman, and Doc would say, too, as Doc always said, "You spend too much time writing scenarios, inserting ideas into other people's heads. I told you, the only thing women want is other women. What you were there for was: get the wine, fix the light-bulb, admire the frogs' legs, finish the ice-cream."

•

The deal was, Owen came out to Doc's one weekend a month and worked for food, bed and fat-chewing, and this had been going on, it was true, for years. Doc had guest-lectured at NYU and Owen had asked a bright young question and that was that. But the next month, on the appointed day, he was so sick he couldn't turn to face his shaded window. The only relief, and it was hardly that, came from sandwiching his face between two pillows, but he could feel the throbbing from his shoulders to his pelvis. "A thing about that," Doc said four weeks later. "Little thing—" Owen was handling the Herculean task of putting the hundred thousand free unsorted screws into the 60 little screw drawers in the fancy new apple red screw cabinet in the garage. "Don't fight a migraine, because a migraine is yourself. It feels like every other object in the universe, I know, but it's you and only you." Owen looked up, both as if Doc had said something in a foreign tongue and as if Doc had touched his soul. "I find," said he, "that if I go to a class where they're showing anything painted after about 1920, I get a big one. Say, 1928; John Sloan's 'Sixth Avenue and Third Street' or Matisse's 'Seated Odalisque': bingo. I'm fine with the modernists, up to the Nabis, but beyond that, bingo. My head comes off and floats around the ceiling." Doc took a step toward him and squinted, gave him the diagnostic gaze, and said, with a little syncopation, "We should talk one of these days about sex."

•

But before anything at all could be talked about, Owen had a full-blown attack. He decided it would be nice to write out the details, or at least the details of the anticipatory phase, because in his many years on the island (his many pilgrimages) he had learned to be cognizant of what was happening to him. (He had, of course, many times before written out the details of his attacks on pieces of paper, but he had lost all of the pieces.) It was Doc who had helped him learn to be cognizant. "A great deal of false diagnosis is produced," said Doc, "by the misarrangement, or artificial arrangement, of cognizance." Accordingly, and so that Doc would have something to read later on, he put some paper into the old automatic typewriter Doc had used for writing outlines before he bought himself a fancy new automatic typewriter for writing outlines on. Owen started to type ISLAND ATTACK, with the date, but on ISLAND the ribbon ran out. Laboriously he changed the ribbon. Then there was ink on his hands so he had to go into the bathroom and wash the ink off ("Out, out, damned spot!" he bellowed in his thoughts, washing first the left hand and then the right, then the right again and then the left) and there do a complete repetition of the on-off routine with the taps, this time *prestodigitato*. He was out of breath, then, and he felt perspiration at the back of his neck. He sat down and typed ISLAND ATTACK but he had trouble with the date, he had a lot of trouble, because it was 1977, or was it 1987? Or 1877? Or 1897? Or 1798? Or 1777? Or 1999? Could it have been 1999? Had 1999 come yet? Somehow he thought 1999 hadn't come yet but he couldn't *establish* that 1999 hadn't come so he told himself, "Put 1999," so he put 1999. Or 2001? It *wasn't* 2000. Or *was it* 2000? 2001? 2002? 1992? ISLAND ATTACK, JUNE 1999. Or was it June? June was up on the wall calendar next to the refrigerator, but that was June 1990. What to make of this? He removed the paper and on a new sheet typed ISLAND ATTACK, JUNE 1990. June, June, June, 90. Nine-oh. Three lines of description started out fine, but he quickly found that there was a Thing, a Gnarled Entity, call it a ganglion, between his shoulder-blades (except that they didn't feel like *his* shoulder-blades, they felt like *the* shoulder-blades) that was getting in the way of the syntactical commands to his left fingers (which felt like *the* left fingers, or were they right fingers? No, he could somehow see without disturbance now that they were left fingers, *the* left fingers); so that he was making systematic errors with the "s," the "r," the "t," the "g," the "e," and the "a." He was also typing the word "*and*" when there was no call for it ("I and was on and the and island and"); his left fingers wanted to go ahead with the "a" and his right hand seemed to be taking orders from the left and shoving in the "n" and so on, and then the left followed the right and finished off with the "d," all completely against his volition. "Don't, don't," he kept saying to himself in fact, "Do not write *and*." Frequently Owen wanted to make things plural but his left fourth finger wouldn't type the necessary "s" so the report came out obliquely in singular. And the upper case was sticking once in a while (once iN A WHIle) and dropping down without warning (mortification). And more. Owen, for the life of him, couldn't imagine sentences that had a beginning, a middle, and an end because everything, all the meaning in the universe, seemed to hang in front of his face like a Cumaean Sibyl that wouldn't let itself be touched. He threw off half a ream of garbage paper, then surrendered altogether, deciding he should feed the cats, but the electric can opener wouldn't do a proper job so he had to venture to pry the lid of the kidney and bacon up with a fork. The cats wanted out but the sliding door caught. Working on the door he broke his fingernail. The cats crept off in opposite directions (He wondered, would they ever meet? Would each go all the way around the universe until they came back and bumped into one another?). It was now too dim, he needed light. Turning on the switch he blew a bulb. *And.* At the hardware closet he suddenly remembered the clothes in the dryer from what might have been a hundred years ago. *He suddenly and remembered and the clothes and in the dryer and from what might have been a hundred and years ago.* He checked them and discovered the popped circuit-breaker and the stuff lingering moist in a heap. Wasn't it T.S. Eliot, the most quoted poet in world history, who wrote, "The end of all our exploring/ Will be to arrive where we started?" Wasn't it, it wasn't, wasn't it, it wasn't, wasn't it? *And.* If it wasn't—but it was—did it, now, matter? Outside in the late afternoon the cardinals and the woodpeckers—two woodpeckers—were going mad on suet and he thought it would be nice to take pictures of the rosy glow on the hibiscus leaves and on the Lady Belinda daffodils and on the Gloire de Dijon roses that Ettie had planted because Doc liked to read that poem, "When she rises in the morning/ I linger to watch her," so he went out with his Polaroid and something went wrong with the batteries in the film pack so the film wouldn't come out and the motor kept repeating itself with a wheeeeeeeze and a wheeeeeeeze and a wheeeeeeeze and a wheeeeeeeze. He felt a sudden obligation to put on the television. The reception was, of course, faulty, but it was possible to get the news, all of which was morbid, was killing and decapitation and bleeding and depression and poverty and killing and decapitation and torrential rains. The pressure, the implantation, call it the ganglion, between the shoulder-blades was easing now. Easing now. He knew that the pain would be next, the grand pain, *La Grande douleur, il dolore stupendo,* followed by the pervasive disconnection of all of himself from all things.

•

Just before the worst part of the pain, the part that was like being cooked and being carved up simultaneously, or like being eaten, or like breathing through sand, Doc came in redder than a poker. "Damn! Damn to hell! Damn interference! Where are my scissors? I can't redo this outline without scissors. Everything in this damn house is where you won't find it! Damn it to hell!" Was this really Doc or the phantom of Doc, because Doc was with Ettie in England! Was this Doc? This was like the tattoo of the drummer before the parade. Owen felt himself reeling, his head heavily falling. And ringing through his head: *Sssssssssssssss!* Doc was certainly in England. Doc cut pieces out of his outlines and made collages with glue on new paper, purple paper, "reassemblages" he called them, but Doc was in England where they had buried T.S. Eliot, most quoted poet in the world. Doc said, "Keep those cans filled with seed. Those cans, keep 'em filled. You gotta see to it that the seed doesn't run out in those cans." Doc and Ettie took off in a limo, for England, with Doc singing like a bird, "Chew, chew," gasping for air, gasping for air, his lungs going, but now Doc couldn't find his scissors, he couldn't reassemble, and the text he had written would go all rotten and would never be finished. He would never get the book finished. And Owen couldn't find Doc's scissors, and Owen was Doc, and Owen was also Ettie, and Owen was flying to England, right now, right here, looking through the plate glass at the cans that weren't full of seed. Peter Pumpkin-eater was looking at Owen, and they were little boys trying to climb the back yard fence in perfect unison, as twins should, and "Poor Owen," Peter said, "Poor, poor Owen."

•

His twin brother, Peter: was *that* why he saw equivalents wherever he looked, because he was a twin?: Peter who was half an inch taller but otherwise seemed identical to him, even though Peter was always the one people thought would become a politician, the one people listened to and thought dignified. Suddenly he thought, "I am Peter and he is Owen. Owen there, Peter here." He couldn't tell if he was as serious as his brother, or whether while his brother climbed into the limelight he was going to fall into nothingness. Peter had certainly had girlfriends, although he couldn't seem to keep one long, but Peter had certainly had them, and there were all those afternoons in the apartment in the West Village with him naked and writhing under the covers, writhing and audibly moaning; while Owen was strapped with the knowledge that girlfriends were sadly out of the question, although he wanted a girlfriend more than he wanted sanity. Out of the question. But girls always seemed to be laughing at him, and for Peter, girls came like squirrels to peanut butter. Was Peter in fact better than he was? A better mouth, a better prick, a better potentiality? This brought up the issue of comparisons, a riddle that would drive Owen into a great flat rubber band of pain that wrapped around his eyes and made them pop like lichees. Whereas normally all things arranged themselves neatly in a hierarchy, one thing always preferable to another thing, now all things were laid out as on a lawn, a trimmed lawn, flat, perfect, indecipherable, equal, alarming. PETER (OWEN), OWEN (PETER), but now what did his brother look like or what did he? What did anybody look like? On a table beside his elbow were Kiwi spray shine for shoes and a tin of household oil. SPRAY SHINE (HOUSEHOLD OIL). His eyes flicked back and forth between them. The shine was in a brown tin. The oil was in red. BROWN (RED). And beside the red oil tin was a green box of envelopes. TIN (BOX). RED (GREEN). Ettie came in and said in her chirrupy voice that he looked like he needed a hot drink, did he want coffee or tea? COFFEE (TEA)? TEA (COFFEE)? And somehow when it was decided that she'd brew coffee it wasn't clear whether he wanted it with milk or without. WITH (WITHOUT)? MILKY (MILKLESS)? And he noticed soon, in fact instantaneously, that she had the steaming mugs in her hand and that she was standing as if she weren't certain whether or not to sit. SIT (DON'T SIT).

He saw Doc's cold cigarillo sitting at the edge of the table, where there was a hole in the tablecloth shaped like a rabbit. TO THROW IT OUT (NOT TO THROW IT OUT). "I ought to throw this cigarillo of Doc's away," Ettie said in her chirrupy voice, and she did, she threw the cigarillo into the fireplace, as Doc would have but with more gentility, and at once a razor blade sliced down between Owen's eyes. She reached out to give Owen his coffee unaware that as his fingers touched the mug he was thinking, "Take...Don't take. Don't take...Take. Take, don't take, don't take, take." The ring of the telephone snapped him away just in time. Was it Peter, with his sweet potato voice? Was it Peter, his twin, his first love, his oneness, his world? "Yes," said Ettie into the telephone in her chirrupy voice, "Yess, yessss. Yesss, yesssss. Yes, yes, yes, yesssss." Very James Joyce, yes yes. James Joyce my lovely brother my twin my happiness.

•

And now that Peter had grown up and found Elizabeth—or that Elizabeth had found Peter, because it was she who was the fisher and he who was the fish, that was a certainty—now that Peter *was with* Elizabeth, in Elizabeth's care, under the domain of Elizabeth: would Owen continue to be an attachment? More frightening: would he have to become attached, too, to Elizabeth? She hadn't in any way fished for Owen, with her misty eyes looking through walls, and indeed Owen was not, and never would be, the sort of creature Elizabeth would notice in life, let alone consider and bait a line for. He was a stutterer of sorts, call it a gestural stutterer, because he was never certain, but she was all fluencies. That was why she adored the handsome Peter, who never doubted even though he never understood, and who was always a pillar, while Owen was a chameleon who climbed pillars, winked at you from pillars. Peter would marry Elizabeth and they would float off forever in a bubble of perfection, and Owen, who was a twin, would be split away. There: map of the future. Already now with the Savage rooms swirling around him, and the Savage birds outside fluttering in and out of view like ideas half thought, he felt himself diminished, receding, becoming a point and then an atom and then subatomic and then, in the great galactic ocean of birds and stars and teacups and histories, lost.

•

"Owen—Have you noticed?—gets an attack every time he comes out here," Doc said. "Bang. Once a month." Ettie, casting on something golden and angora, said yes, she had noticed. She said, yes, she had noticed with some distress, and was it us did he think? "*Us?*" said Doc, "*Us?*" "I've noticed it's worse all the time," she said, drawling a little and singy-songy, "and I've thought it could be *us*, in the sense that you and I are disturbing something in him, and that he is responding to *us*." Doc paced up and down with his jaw open. He kept pacing up and down. "Get a cracker," he muttered. He paced up and down. "*I know* something about this," he announced, his head in the air. "*I have knowledge*. It's not *us*, it's *him*. *We* don't provoke a migraine in Owen. *Owen* provokes the migraine in himself when he's here." Ettie had a lot of casting on to do because this was going to be a shawl. She kept casting on and she said, "Is there a difference, dear?" Doc stood at the sliding glass door with a kind of grimace, as if he were out there and winter were settling comfortably in here.

•

The next month great things had changed. The story came from Ophelia Goldman, who was ahead of Owen in line at the IGA and who was feeling, of course, disposed to confide. "You've noticed, there's no Ettie." The boy shook his head, dumbed, because he hadn't shown up at the ramshackle house by the beach yet and so hadn't noticed anything. "See, there it is, the politics of everyday life. Ettie has vamoosed." This was distinctly more than unbelievable, because Ettie, in Doc's conversation if not in person, was a fixture. "Walter won't tell you what happened but I will. Two weeks ago she came back from a meeting—of our committee, I might add, though I hardly see how it's relevant, but Walter will certainly cast a light upon it—and she noticed a car pulling rather cunningly out of the driveway. Cunningly, I tell you." Owen suddenly noticed how wrinkled the old lips were. "She went inside and said who was that and Walter just told her to mind her own business. He's really so completely imperial and also so perfectly narcissistic. She went looking around and in the bedroom she smelled something. What's that smell in the bedroom, she said, and he just stood there and bang, it slapped her flush in the face. You haven't been around long enough to know this, but he was having an affair with Mallie Sedgwick who used to be one of his patients—this was around the time he was also treating what's his name, I can never remember, the one who was in *Citizen Kane*. Or was it *Casablanca*? They're the same to me. Whatever. Walter had an affair with Mallie Sedgwick and that smell that Ettie smelled was Mallie Sedgwick's perfume again. Have you seen her movies? I haven't seen one of them." Owen had seen all of Mallie Sedgwick's astonishing performances, had been in love half his life with Mallie Sedgwick like every other American boy, because, after all, in a certain category of movie star, Those Who Live Only In One's Dreams, there was Jessica Lange and there was Mallie Sedgwick, period. "Ridiculous on both sides," Ophelia Goldman picked something off her tongue, "and Walter old enough to be her father, for heaven's sake. Ettie just packed up and now she's in New York and he's out there alone, except that Mallie Sedgwick comes by when she's not shooting. You'll probably see her when you get back over there. I'm in touch with Ettie every day, in case there's anything you should want me to pass on. In my opinion," and here she raised her voice to its best podium capacity and her consummate nostrils flared, "it's a sad and a very pathetic thing. This is what happens, though, you see. This is what you get. When I see Walter at the fish store he looks through me as if I were made of glass." Owen, who was buying a Mars bar, saw that the covers on all the magazines racked next to the register were printed with Mallie Sedgwick's face. Ophelia Goldman's bill was $277.85; and she'd forgotten milk again.

•

"There are actresses," Doc said calmly while Owen sipped his soup, "and there are Actresses. In your generation, when all they do is take off their clothes and sit around staring at the camera with lard on their lips, you wouldn't be in a position to know. Mallie here is an Actress. Wouldn't you say that, Mallie, speaking honestly about yourself?" Mallie Sedgwick, in the flesh, who was pouring actual Dubonnet over three actual ice cubes in three actual glasses, looked up with eyes like planets and kissed the air as she spoke. "Well, I certainly feel unreal," she said. She had a very plain voice, not like on the screen, and a great deal of charm, too, because she didn't use her face to seduce and she looked directly into you when you were the person she was speaking to, quite as if she had known you for years. "I admit I work hard. I don't work harder than other people, but I don't have any trouble sleeping. I put in a day." To Doc she added, softly, "You are one of my big fans." Whether or not it was true, Doc seemed proud of the thought. He was certainly devoting himself. He had gone, of his own accord, and as a testament, to fetch the stepladder which was necessary for obtaining the fish poacher from the top of the kitchen cabinets. He had sent Owen for something in the four pound range and bassy. He was making a little show, with a nappy new shirt on and a red string tie and his undomesticated hair slicked back à la James Dean. The bouillon had with the greatest affection to be drawn up from scratch and, clicking his teeth, he drew it: water, Chablis—a very great deal of Chablis—peppercorns whole, sprigs of thyme and tarragon from the garden—Ettie's garden—chunks of carrot, parsley, celery, quartered onion. The steam from this was intoxicating. And the bass was laid upon the rack, its blue eye accusing upwards, then wrapped round and round with cheesecloth. "Never a bubble!" Doc cautioned—to whom?, the movie star or the art student? "Nary a pucker!" Slowly, at any rate, the fish went in, with Mallie's stabilizing hand at one end and Owen's at the other, and it sat under its steam cloud while Doc yagged at his wristwatch like a certified neurotic. "Twelve minutes the pound. Twelve minutes the pound." They talked about what three people can talk about when they all know that two of them are secretly lovers: the President of the United States; the New York Yankees; how it is that Jerry Lewis is funny to some people and not to others; how to grow gigantic tomatoes; Piet Mondrian; goldfish; the way the IGA is beginning to look shabbier and shabbier with the new management; hurricane probabilities; what is eaten in Thailand. "He tells me," Mallie announced rather splendidly to Owen when Doc stepped over to the stove to polish his creation, "that you are the perfect friend, 'Yep yep'—" she did a wonderful imitation of the way Doc used his voice, "the very best assistant he has ever had." And then, because Owen didn't reply, it being the fact that she was so close to him he could smell her lipstick, and because a cue that has been missed should always be covered, she added, "So hello and thank you, my very good friend, for keeping him sane for me!" Music had been playing on the stereo, the Polovtsian Dances of Borodin. The lyric choral theme came up, the one that had become "Take my hand, I'm a stranger in paradise." "Shall we dance?" said Mallie and she took Owen around the room while Doc broke up rosemary twigs. Owen thought it was strange but she felt like any other girl he had ever danced with. She was wearing a cardigan precisely the colour of the stormy sea. In dancing with her he felt himself move away into another world. Surely this wasn't mere excitement but Owen had been lifted off the earth, and feeling Mallie Sedgwick's warmth against him, and smelling her hair, he forgot where he was and who he was and dreamed, standing, that he was on a beach under the stars and that he wasn't a human anymore. Doc, gawking through his bifocals, was prodding the fish with a tongue depressor.

•

But after the remarkable dinner—Mallie had made lemon *pots de crème*—there was a great tempest. "What's the goddam game, Goddamit!" was Doc's side, and Mallie's could be summarized in, "I love you. Don't doubt me. I love you." They weren't, clearly, seeing eye to eye, and they didn't come out seeing eye to eye, and Doc said to Owen they'd have to have a little man-to-man talk later about how people don't see eye to eye and what you should do when you're looking in on two such people, and Owen went out and looked up through binoculars at the million stars. The night was frigid, wonderful. There was—there! swift!—a shooting star, and Mallie came down for hot milk and smiled, and Doc came down for a cigarette and did not smile. In the morning Mallie was gone and Doc said to Owen, "Wellll—, some do, some do not. There's a great deal she doesn't understand about men. There's a great deal they all don't understand. Way of the world."

•

All round, the blackberries were daily dropping. The pheasant lost his feathers and a hurricane wind established itself to twist the very roots from the trees; and then, like a phantom, disappeared. "Yes yes," sang Doc. "Yes yes yes." Doc said out of the clear blue sky, walking up and down the length of his baronial dining table, "I affirm that it's a difficult life." He had a way of looking around, as if for a cigarette or a package of paper clips—though he didn't want to smoke and he had no papers to put together—with his spectacles dangling around his neck like a sommelier's spoon. In his slippers and baggy corduroys, his checked viyella shirt, he looked the picture of the country gentleman at home. He got a chair and stood on it and with a grunt from the top of the cabinets where the wine glasses were kept (dusty) he drew down a monstrous sealed jar in which for seventeen weeks he'd been marinating his apricots. It was a thick glass in the jar and a heavy lid sat upon it, the jar was a veritable *bocal*. Doc would have been the first to tell you this if he felt like telling, *le gros bocal*, come all the way from the south of France, twenty inches tall, twelve across; but he grunted now instead and looked down with a squint, giving over the jar to Owen and climbing to the floor with a huff and a puff. "We'll try these. These will rectify. Yes, yes." He took a cloth to the whole thing in the kitchen and then moistened the cloth and did it again. He gave the top little taps with a ladle. He lifted it off. He was a big man, so that he seemed to pre-empt the available smelling space as he yawned over the opening of the maceration. But suddenly he drew back, straightfaced. "Funny. Not funny-comical, funny-peculiar." He ladled out two bowlfuls and led the way back to the table. "Funny-unanticipated." There was something quick about his movements and quick, too, about the way he dropped into his seat, that made Owen want to race to eat. He spooned some apricots in the direction of his mouth. The ambrosia was at his lips. "Don't!" Doc said. Owen wasn't sure if this was one of Doc's rituals. Doc was sniffing, squinting, looking off through the window to the grackles going mad in the pear tree. "Botulism," he said then. "Smell it?" There was the thing about Doc Savage: nobody on earth is supposed to be able to smell botulism, botulism isn't supposed to produce a smell, but here he was smelling it, in the apricots he'd coddled for seventeen weeks with Armagnac and God knows what else. Maybe that was why they all said he was a prodigious diagnostician. "You don't have to believe me, of course. Life is a hazardous business, yes yes!" He kept saying that over and over as in a golden cataract he poured the volume of apricot juice into the kitchen sink and sloshed the marvellous fruits into the plastic garbage pail. "Then again: if one thing doesn't get you, another thing will."

•

Ettie was back, or at least she was leaning against the kitchen sink sipping a cup of tea, when Owen came in, four weeks later. "Hi, dear," she said somewhat unemotionally, and, pointing, added, "Water's hot." Owen looked around, and the place was as it had always been. "Out in the garden," she said. "At the picnic table. Waiting for you, I suspect. Says he's got a new idea. Of course he's always got a new idea, which is why he doesn't finish the old idea. For supper, I thought fluke, if you want to pick some up. Or I'll get it up and you can cook it, there's a deal. You're the chef." Out under the pear tree Doc was finishing off a cigarette and a sentence together, but the sentence, whatever it was, didn't please him because he stroked through it and wrote something beneath that took twice the number of words. Owen closed his eyes and smelled the pears dangling above. "Tell you," Doc said, "We'll pick some pears and we'll macerate them with something and put them to soak for a few weeks. Chartreuse, maybe. Some people find Chartreuse nauseating. It's good with pears. I think we can get to the heart of those headaches of yours today. Been waiting a long time to. Both of us. Getting to the heart of a headache, at any rate, is what I call education. We'll pick some pears and we'll get to the heart. Actually, we won't pick pears. We'll put a blanket down and you'll shake the trunk and we'll let the pears surrender. Surrendered Pears, that's what we'll call it. Getting to the heart of a headache is one of the great puzzles, yes yes. You got somethin' you're holding in. Don't know what it is. Could be lots of things. It's in there, and you're packing it tight. Those headaches: that thing you got in there wants to come out, but letting it out would be a real problem for you. People don't go making real problems for themselves if they can avoid it. So you're avoiding it. Perfectly natural. The headache is a detour." Owen, who had driven out on the Long Island Expressway where today there were detours all the way from the Sagtikos to the William Floyd, looked at the old man with his hands limp on the table next to the writing pad. "You think I should talk about what it is, assuming I know?" Doc gave a flash of grin and shook his head. "Talk won't do a thing. Talk won't let it out. It can't come out because it's in. In is where it is, see. Migraines are coming precisely because you're trying to let it out. Stop trying. Just relax. Let it stay in there, your great sexual secret." Owen felt his throat seize. "It's sexual 'cause—what else could it be, you gone and murdered somebody? So just keep it to yourself and don't think about sharing it anymore." Owen thought of getting in the car and high-tailing it, but he didn't want detours again, he wanted to sit and look at the peonies, and Doc was already turning his attention away to a piece of driftwood lying on the grass. "There's one thing I'll tell you, and then you can go make some tea and re-file all the index cards on the chair near the television. Here it is: the migraine is helping your life. It's helping your life a lot. Sometimes I think, it would be nice if I could get a migraine. But, of course, what I have instead is all this." He looked around at the estate, the grass, the birdbath, the house, Ettie inside on the telephone, two pheasants back near the orchard gate picking this moment to start a war.

•

At four o'clock Ettie was knitting in royal purple and Doc was flicking cigarette butts into the fireplace while Owen was finishing up alphabetizing the books in the library. Doc looked up at him through the aperture that had been designed in the library floor. "We go fish for dinner, boy?" Owen raced to finish, threw himself into the Land Rover. "I hope we catch something you can poach," he said as they were jouncing along the stretch that leads out of town. The taste of that bass! The lemon pot de crème! Whole minutes went by without a response, Doc lost in creative thought. Then, from nowhere, "Poach?" said he; "I don't practise poaching." Owen thought semantics had intruded. "You know what I mean, in the liquid, in the poacher, with the carrots and stuff." Doc stared forward with a squint, swerving when cars came against him. "I don't know at all what you mean, not at all. I don't poach. I haven't ever poached. You're getting another one of your fancy notions. See, I've always told you you're creative and you have daydreams. But fish don't get poached by me. I couldn't poach a fish to save my life." "It was the best fish I've ever had," Owen said, not at all aloud, "the one you made, four weeks ago, for me and—" Doc sliced him with a glance that was all axe-metal black and gravitational. "I suspect," he gave a cough, "you're a little confused," he gave another cough, "about that. I don't think your memory's working correctly, at all." They came to Goff Point, perhaps a little too early. The sky was bright. The water was oddly calm. They threw out their lines for a good two hours, and they grunted at the wind, but nothing came in.

•

"See...," Ettie said. It was very late. Doc had been in bed for an hour. The embers were shivering in the fireplace. Peach pie was half-eaten on the table. "Let me show you something." There was a cabinet not far from the fireplace, which had glass doors. The eighteenth-century Sèvres plates were in there, the Sèvres egg cups, the Sèvres teapot and the compote and the two cobalt blue Sèvres swan candlesticks. From a centre shelf, where it was nestled among them, she took down with two hands a mercury bowl. It had been etched with horses and inscribed with the name that had been her name until she traded it for the name Savage. "I can't think of anything more fragile," she said, "than this. The Sèvres is steel by comparison. This needs only the slightest pressure, something cramped against it too tightly, the smack of a fingernail, and it's gone forever. It gets a hairline crack and nothing can make it quite the same. You know what it reminds me of? Masculinity." Owen was lost. "I'll explain it to you. Walter's in many ways a child. He's like you. All of you men are, somehow, children. You want what you think you want. And then you try to get it, because the mind, of course, is one of the first things to develop. But to take it so seriously! To think you can *think* about want! Well! I just had to show him that business is business, you see. You understand that better than he does, in some ways. You have an independent life, and you make a contract, and you have every reason to expect that if you hold up your side of it——." She seemed to lose track, staring out into the darkness and softly, repeatedly, inhaling. Owen thought he could see now, or that he was beginning to see, a colossal arrangement, a choreography. "One has a right to have expectations," she said. "One has a—Here—." She went to the sideboard and fished out a slim envelope. She put it on the table next to his coffee mug. "It's a cheque. Take it. You ought to get more out of this than a few words of his wisdom, though I'm absolutely sure they are words of wisdom, and my bad cooking. There's a kind of contract here, Owen, and he's been abusing you, too. He's been having his way." It was not a huge cheque, but it was a substantial one, and at first he didn't know whether to accept it. Then he recollected that she hadn't really offered it with the opportunity to do anything else. Owen lay abed that night upon the sofa in the living-room, with the moonlight dripping through a skylight over his head, and all he could think of was Mallie Sedgwick, in her sea-green cardigan, because she—he could not explain this—was the only part that wasn't somehow bargained for. She had talked to him. She had met him and held him in her arms. She had been, distinctly, incomprehensibly, a sensation. As for the rest, it was all clearer than he had ever thought it could be; too clear; and cold; and desperate. He wondered whether it was time to think about going away to graduate school.

Petit Mal

The arpeggio that Prince Andrei Bolkonsky demanded was C-sharp minor, an impossibility as far as Adam was concerned. His pudgy little hands, for one thing, were beyond the pale of cooperation; and his little mood was scarcely, now in baseball season, sympathetic to arpeggios or to the whole of music or to the sharp impenetrability of the forbidding Prince Andrei Bolkonsky. This gentleman, 27 years old, slender, magnificent as royalty, was not really a prince, of course, nor did he think of himself as a prince or behave in what princes would regard as princely ways. He was an autocrat of sorts, and he had Russian ancestry—so that Cowrie was in no way hindered in inventing for him an epithet drawn from Tolstoy—and gave piano lessons—or what could pass for piano lessons—and he played the piano. He played the piano in what pianists regarded as *almost* princely fashion, with a sumptuous technique and a mastery, here if nowhere else, of his own emotion. Perhaps his fingers did not quite permit themselves to sing. He played Chopin. He played—it need hardly be said—Rachmaninoff. And he expected his pupils to do the same, or to wish they could. So he had been torturing Adam, who was nowhere near Rachmaninoff, into brave arpeggios, and Adam had been whimpering and repositioning himself bravely upon the little bench while Cowrie and Jodi sat on the sofa with their hands folded upon their laps. Prince Andrei Bolkonsky smoked Gauloises. He lit one now. Cowrie thought, for some strange reason, "Flowers," when the smell of it hit her. He said, "One day I will be off to play in Bruxelles." He could have said Brussels, Cowrie told herself, and then she repeated it to Jodi, "But he chooses to make a certain representation. He chooses a form in which to fit himself." Jodi was dreaming of Prince Andrei riding through the woods on a horse and so she wasn't listening but Adam was soaking it up like a sponge. "I will be at the Palais des Expositions. I will replace our lessons when I come back. *If* I come back." It was not merely Rachmaninoff that the Prince played, but the Études Tableaux, a form in which one could have fit quite anything and seemed marvellous. The Prince bent over Adam and changed a hand position, then stood up to take his full posture. With his dark hair and his thick lips, his glowering young eyes, his lengthy fingers, he was a beast. Jodi, who was fiddling with a locket at her neck, took a peek at him and carefully watched her mother peeking at him, too.

•

"What is it that's attractive about males?" said Jodi, splashing her bath water. "I'm eleven years old. I should know." Cowrie had very often found it imperative in her life to do small business, and she did it now. She made a neat row of the hairbrushes on the shelf beside the sink. She took some toilet paper and carefully wiped off all the bottles of shampoo one by one. "*Attractive?*" "Sexually," said Jodi, who was examining a nipple. "Is it their *thing* you're turned on by, because I think it's hideous." It wasn't at all that she was being confronted by a daughter that stunned Cowrie, it was that her daughter was another human being. And she could only say, "Well, what exactly are you referring to? I mean, why exactly are you bringing this up?" Jodi was completely honest when she said, "I really don't know." But then she made a discovery. "It's him," she said. "It's Princie. The way you were looking at his you know." "I was not"—Cowrie instantly regretted that she had committed herself to making a headline of this—"looking at his penis." Jodi was reduced to a hysterical giggle and purple cheeks, and she ended, "His...*penis*...is big. Much bigger than Daddy's," with a certain tone stockbrokers often use when encouraging the purchase of stocks.

•

Marlowe, who was something of a stockbroker, indeed a fabulously successful stockbroker and therefore one who scarcely needed to spend long hours at the office, was taking the day off and having a seizure. He had ensconced himself on the softest of the seven sofas, the one in the dayroom, and he had started up a CD with Jacques Brel singing something frantic and rhythmical that only a person who understood French would understand. Now the petit mal was setting in quite firmly, and he found his spine pressed back against the cushions and the bookshelves on the facing wall turning from colour into black and white. "Cowrie?" he tried, but already it was going for his jaw, and he knew that if she were upstairs she wouldn't have heard him. He told himself he was going to have to get the cellphone battery fixed. The room was disappearing and he hoped he wouldn't swallow his tongue. Jodi found him quite a while later, almost half an hour, at the point where it looked as if he were asleep. He was not ostensibly breathing and she went quietly for Cowrie, not knowing how she felt about this horror but knowing it was a horror, convinced that her father was dead and wondering how one made arrangements for a funeral. Cowrie came running. His skin was cold but she got him sitting and his eyes came open and he smiled dilutely. "Marlowe, Marlowe, Marlowe," she whispered. She got him tea. It took another hour and he was himself. "Daddy has petit mal," Cowrie told Jodi and Jodi, knowing a little French, thought some reference had been made to parts of her father she oughtn't to speak of, in order to humiliate her. "Oh, Mother!" But she went upstairs and looked it up in her dictionary, thinking all the while it was a very curious way to speak of the male, petit mal, and found it was his brain, indeed, that had been spoken of. Marlowe came and put a hand on her shoulder—that made her shudder—and said, "If you ever find me passed out like that, it's just a seizure. You just try to keep me warm, and you try to lift me up. And it passes. It's like anything else unpleasant in life." This last confounded the poor girl, because when you are eleven there is a great deal that is unpleasant in life. "How are your piano lessons?" he concluded, and he had a very happy, even relaxed smile, a smile that subtracted a decade from the way he looked. "Fine until Adam takes over," she answered. "Adam takes all Princie's time, and Adam doesn't care at all about music." Jacques Brel was still singing downstairs, because the machine was accidentally on repeat. *"Bien sûr nous eûmes des orages/Vingt ans d'amour, c'est l'amour fol...."*

•

The songs of Debussy have a tendency to be intoxicating, particularly if one performs them with a little brandy, as

Stephen Sergov now did in front of 500 dry-mouthed sycophants, with his wife Jillian singing. They had what romantic little girls would certainly have found a puzzling marriage. The intimacies were expressed as modulated diminuendoes, as prolongations of cadence, as fortuitous choices of tempo rather than as ticklings, frictions, the productions of love bites. Indeed, for a young man of 27, Stephen was exceptionally sedate in his physique, preferring to sit and read with a cat upon his lap over monstrosities of gourmandise, exacerbations of drink, hilarity of manner. He almost never laughed. Jillian practised her songs, mended her dresses, read Agatha Christie. Why her mother should ever have been inspired to think of this gentleman as a Prince bewildered Jodi, but she was beginning to realize—in the way that eleven-year-old girls begin—that she had cultivated a regard for him herself. Next to her bed was a photograph of him, for example, scissored from a publicity brochure. On pieces of coloured paper strewn into her desk was his name, copied a hundred times in a struggle of penmanship. "Stephen Sergov. Prince Andrei Bolkonsky. Prince Stephen Sergov." For her, he was all panache. He wore only blue jeans, and T-shirts of baseball teams. His eyeglasses were tortoise-shell and most often in his mouth. He kept rubbing his fingers on his thighs. Everything of his pose was sensuality, and all of her regard for him was dream. She thought she saw the skin of his shoulders. She thought that perhaps one lazy afternoon he had told her he desired her, though she had no further intimation of what this could mean. She had learned, from one of her teachers, a recipe for sexual practice; and this had been elaborated upon, almost Talmudically, by one of her friends, Daphne Himmelfarb, whose mother was a writer who had published scandalous romances under the pseudonym Veronica Vales. But there was a gap between what Jodi knew for fact and what she could bring herself to imagine. And he would always be her Prince, there was no point denying this, and she denied it. Therefore she could not take her eyes off him. He had a dry look, tinkling away for his very short little wife, and she opened her mouth very wide when she sang. While he played, he flattered his youth by entertaining fantasies of pulling the panties off an older adolescent girl named Felicity, who had no talent for playing Brahms. Jillian missed a note and it was a moment before he noticed that she had stopped. They went back. She touched his shoulder. After pulling off the panties what could one do? It was true that Jillian had a voice for which many pleasures had been sacrificed, a disciplined voice. "I thought perhaps," she whispered when the song was done and the applause came at them like gunfire, "we might have Chinese food for dinner."

•

The Prince did not know it but he possessed in the clockwork of his marriage a jewel in common with Cowrie and Marlowe. That marriage had been contracted in an unorthodox fashion. He had come to the city with Jillian, who had been visiting her parents in the lower bowels of Manhattan. She had brought along what her mother, at least, had long desired to see her possessed of, a lover, in the person of a talented young musician from four generations of Russian nobility. They had been intimates for some year and a half, and had accomplished together in that time the full range of gyration and intertextuality possible for experimentally minded persons of moderate inhibition and vocabulary. In short, the beaches of the isle of boredom had become discernible upon the horizon. He had brought her to dine at an Italian joint in Brooklyn and they were driving back toward the Lower East Side on the Williamsburg Bridge. "Look," said Stephen—he had not yet been crowned a Prince—as they began to make the metallic part of the roadway, and struts flashed past their peripheries like thundering premonitions, "Let's be preposterous and make a deal. There's a light where Delancey Street meets Clinton Street on the other side. If it's green when we get to it, we'll get married next weekend. If it's red, we'll go our separate ways." Her sense was thrown into the pit of her stomach when he said this, and when she saw that he hadn't taken his eyes even by a fraction from the road, but she falteringly agreed, thinking, "I love him, and I will trust to everything that he wishes." She was certain, looking ahead to a long line of cars and barely sighting a light that looked green, that he slowed a little when it wasn't absolutely necessary. But when they arrived it was green again, having been red at least four times in the interim, and so they married, and went to Shreveport, Louisiana for a honeymoon (where he had a little recital to give, playing Dohnanyi). And they lived happily in their marriage, which is to say, each of them forgot the story of the bridge and behaved exactly as if they were destined to be with one another for all time. With Cowrie and Marlowe it was virtually the same, though more inexplicable. They had been dating for less than nine months, in college, he at Columbia doing Business, she at Barnard forgetting Anthropology and memorizing English. Marlowe had been one of those mastering types who show on the first date every manifestation of prowess and no intimation of delight. He had driven her, she remembered, in a white sports car to see the première of *The Sting*, during which he had kept muttering, "Brilliant!" Sex with him had been a deep satisfaction, not in part because she had tired utterly of masturbation and had not been with a man for over a year. She told herself he knew a great deal about wine. He certainly did know something about money. They talked, night after night, after sex in a room on the eleventh floor of the Americana, about architecture and social class. He had definite notions of these as they appertained to his existence, which is to say he wanted to live in a house that had three fireplaces and a wild forest in the back. He thought it would be fun to pilot his own Cessna. He also talked about politics. He believed that the mechanisms of profit were natural ones, that in the affairs of men those with exceptional talent and who were fated to lead nations automatically rose to the tops of their classes by virtue of their gifts and what he called Nature's "allowances." He expected, she deduced, he would soon be such a person. She allowed him to buy her delicacies from Bloomingdale's and became exhausted listening to his conversation. She found that she was more and more a woman who looked forward to the touch of a man's finger in her vagina, a tiny and timely manipulation that could easily be arranged, and that there was very little else to say. So, one afternoon, when it was strongly raining, and after he had written a multiple-choice examination in History of Macroeconomic Revolutions 203, she said, "Look, let me pronounce an utterly preposterous ultimatum, just to be entertaining. Either (a) you should get it over with or (b) we should stop seeing one another." He lifted himself. "Over with? It?" "You should ask me," though she had had no training in theatre she cleared her throat rather theatrically, "to Marry You." She now told herself the fellow would put himself to sleep with hesitation, would indeed care about stepping on the dandelion under his foot more than spending a life with her. He was quite adorable, and there was something about the colour of his neck she had to admit she would miss if he chose (b). But, "Yes, yes, my God! Marry me!" he cried, dropping to a knee, looking up with the saddest blue eyes in all the world, "Yes, yes, my God! What could I have been thinking about all this time! Yes!" To seal his bargain, Marlowe had bought her roses, and sported her off to Massachusetts (a state where blood tests were not required); and to seal his, the Prince had bought Jillian Arturo Benedetti-Michelangeli playing Bach.

•

There is no limit to a desire for fireplaces. Now that he lived in a house with more than three, Marlowe craved more than six. It was a question of not, for a second, taking one's eye off the market, off, really, *any* market, and he exercised his vigilance by means of a computer connected to a satellite and a telephone line that never rested. If he became wealthy he also came to require Prozac. Some of its side effects made him hard to live with. His appetite was unpredictable, Cowrie found: if she bought red spring salmon he suddenly wanted beef. The door to his room came typically to be closed. He spoke, more and more, in arcane mathematical formulations to which she could in no way attach herself. He developed into a cipher. And he went over the books. "Marlowe, what the hell are you doing?" she proclaimed at the end of the month, because he was at the dining table with her purse contents spread in front of himself like pieces of a puzzle. The receipts he first uncrumpled and flattened, under a ruler made of coloured glass. Then, utilizing categories, he arranged them in a number of piles. Then he applied an adding machine and scribbled in a notebook, removing the notebook to his office upstairs and transcribing the contents to his computer. "Apple juice?" he queried. "Pantyhose?" "Cigarettes? I thought you had given up smoking! I want you to give up smoking, Cowrie, I'm serious. We don't need suicidal tendencies." She had an explanation that suited him for virtually everything. "Apple juice for when you insist on entertaining people who don't drink," she said. "Pantyhose for when I have to come in and serve them, looking kempt. Cigarettes for when I need to keep from losing my mind doing all this." "Give up smoking," he commanded. And he asked how many ounces of salmon she typically bought, and for how many people, and how many pounds of ground round, and how many potatoes. Cowrie was reading Anne Sexton and Louise Glück and examining the photographs of Julia Margaret Cameron and doing a clipping file of the *New York Times* Arts and Leisure just to keep herself from paying more attention to Marlowe than Marlowe's interrogation necessitated. "How much money, exactly, Cowrie, are we spending on piano lessons?"

•

Prince Andrei felt his young career was an orchid that would not be allowed to thrive. It was delicate, and also astonishing, and climatologically under threat. First, he had been born into entirely the wrong social class. Money was not, therefore, to be seen in all directions, and the leisure to play the music he valued had to be bought with the proceeds from too many lessons given far too frequently to students who lacked the ability to appreciate. Then, Jillian, who certainly professed to adore him, and whose sincerity was not to be impeached, had taken up the call, somewhat more courageously than he would have wished, of his pronouncer, probably in order to service through the agency of his success her own immodest needs. She told everyone what a handsome figure he made as a teacher; how demanding, how comprehensive; and with what glories his students were accoladed whenever they played; and how very taxing was his schedule, so that arrangements had to be made months in advance for being taught by him. All this contrived not only to raise his rates, of course, but to attenuate the time available to him for pure performance, and as his students multiplied, according to a law indiscernible to him, he bridled under the yoke of children who did not, he felt, merit in their art the refinement of his attention. Something, he came to feel, would snap. Nor was the grip of this feeling loosened by the monumental—some might have said, uncivilized—demands Jillian made upon his sex. Whether the point was that she wanted a baby (or the first of many babies); or whether pleasure alone drove her (because she was driven); he felt certain it was not musicianship that led her bizarre mid-afternoon choreographies (always between Felicity who still couldn't play Brahms and Virgil, the graduate student who thought his interpretations of Bach had been directed telepathically from the seventeenth century). But something was going to snap, he could tell in his bones, or, more to the point, in his marrow, because he had—you could say this if you could say nothing else—a sense of himself. Something would cave in. And one afternoon in May, as he sat near the Sheep Meadow upon a lawn strewn with dandelions in the sun, it did.

•

What happened was this: A gentleman he thought he recognized, a gentleman no longer young, strode toward him out of the shadow of an elm, in a grey and red kilt. This was not, in Prince Andrei's scheme of things, a graceful happening, nor was the gentleman a distinguished gentleman. He trudged, as if the hillock he had to mount was all the challenge of a heroic life, and his features were contorted into what could not, by someone who appreciated Debussy, be called a pleasing expression, and his cheeks—it became apparent as he neared and came into the sun—were strewn with the veins one associates with Malt. "You are the young man who lives next door to me," he nevertheless contrived to say, in rather a delicate voice, "On West 69th Street. Whose pianism entertains me morning and night. You are that young man." Each gave the other a sociable little smile, the younger smile colder than the older. "See here, I don't mind if I come to a point. I have something on offer. May I steal a moment? Name is Cardoch." Cardoch said music was his business, and his business was music. He went further. "I am not a believer in coincidence, but one must acknowledge when one's life is somehow struck. Know what I mean? Make a dollar, as it turns out, booking concerts. Work for Shaw. Big boys. The biggest. Been hunting for someone new, young, untried, lovable in Europe. Know what I mean? Always in the hunt, of course, but then, most of the time, not really hunting, 'f you get m' drift. Willing to find but not desperate to have. But now we are hunting most energetically, know what I mean? Energies most faithfully directed. And here are you! My neighbour. The Man Beyond the Wall! How alarming! But you do fill the bill, don't you. Have been listening to your Schubert and your Skriabine, your Bach and your Bartok. Beg your pardon. You do fill the bill most admirably." Prince Andrei was stunned. To give him credit, he was a gifted musician and a skilled performer. And he was just sufficiently distracted from the inner contours of his music to have a mind for so rank a thing as a career. He had a mind, and he thought interminably, and indeed he indulged himself with daydreams of receiving ovations in the Wigmore Hall. The colours of Cardoch's kilt were garish against his lily yellow skin. "You fill the bill, is what I'm saying, young man, and I intend, with your permission, to make you famous." Prince Andrei's first thought was, "Jillian will never let me go."

•

But Jillian was not to prove the problem, Jillian who had had her bags packed for some time. "We'll get out of this miserable flat," she said. "We'll be able to have a family." He didn't know about families. He hadn't worked out the connection between kids and cadenzas. Cadenzas, he knew, could be intriguing. But Jillian was aglow. Fame, however, would require concerts; and concerts would require tours; tours journeys, and journeys absences. But could his poor students be left behind for an extended time? He began with Virgil, who should by all rights have been thrilled, since he had but six months to finish his dissertation (upon "The Evolution of a Symbolic Language in Gerard Manley Hopkins' Correspondence with Beatrix Potter") and the absence of the piano teacher was planned for the selfsame six months. "But I am perplexed," he said sourly, "I am disappointed and saddened and perplexed. You have made a commitment to me. The piano is a source of the greatest relief and pleasure. Now that you are interrupting my studies, I will have to concentrate fully upon academic matters. This will place intolerable strain upon my mind. I think it likely I will have to give up the dissertation altogether. I will never get a job. My career in academia will be destroyed. I will no doubt end up committing suicide, or, at the very least, having to take out a bank loan." Felicity was worse. "This is awful," she sobbed uncontrollably, "This is simply awful! This is simply—" and she couldn't even say what else it simply was. He encouraged her, but she couldn't. He encouraged her to have a cup of tea but she could only run a finger around the rim of the cup. "My sister!" she suddenly said. Her hands were shaking. She tried to play a scale but tears fell upon the ivories. "My face!" Now she was gasping and he thought she would have an attack. Collecting her sheet music to go, she tore it. Outside it was pouring. Then a librarian, who was only beginning to play the two-part inventions, said, "Look, you obviously don't need the money," and made an exit worthy of the Moscow Art Theatre. A plump fellow who loved to play scales said, "I won't notice. Go ahead. I'll just sit and play scales while you're gone. When you come back, everything will be exactly the same. I won't notice at all." This was cheering. Prince Andrei had to look in his little gilded mirror for a moment, because he had the chilling sensation he didn't exist. A middle-aged fellow, who ran an antique shop, and whose fingers were rather stubby for playing the piano but who attacked Mozart with gusto, said, "I am thrilled for you. Absolutely thrilled, my dear fellow. This won't inconvenience me a tad. I'm off to Malaysia, then I'm off to Bangladesh, then I'm off to Costa Rica, then I'm off to California, so really, we'll both be off together and everything shall be peachy. Just go play your heart out." Cowrie and Marlowe didn't say anything, which Prince Andrei took to be the greatest support and the very greatest relief.

•

Prince Andrei was sold out in Amsterdam, Paris, Antwerp, Berlin, London and Vienna. No smash could have been sweeter. It was at about the time that he was studying his scores in his hotel room in Paris—a nice little room, with only one mouse, on the Rue Gît-le-Coeur—that Cowrie first thought to herself, "I should perhaps tell Marlowe about the piano lessons being suspended." She was very afraid of her husband not because he was violent, although he was—the petit mal alone engendered this—but because he was admirable. She thought him wonderful, superior, perfectly aware (as, in truth, he thought himself) and therefore she looked upon his judgment and reproach with the greatest temerity. Whatever he said to disesteem her would be right. And she had not—it was plain—in this matter of the music lessons been forthcoming. She had not been forthcoming because Marlowe was fastidious about nothing as much as money and the money she was spending—one could say squandering—was his. Why this should have bothered her was an interesting question at any rate, since Cowrie never thought twice about parting with Marlowe's money, but here, around the altar of the piano, the money had taken on a special gilt. Marlowe, in any event, knew nothing of what the lessons were really costing, and they were costing a pretty penny; and he had no suspicion that Cowrie's sensibilities had led her to pay for sessions in advance. He did not know, for instance, that Prince Andrei cut in Cowrie's eyes the pathetic figure of the starving young artist. He did not know that Prince Andrei cut this figure, or that Prince Andrei contrived to cut this figure (no more did Cowrie); and that Cowrie's heart was brought to pity by the picture of so talented and so magnificent a creature in such a desperate strait. That she thought of Jillian as "that poor, mousy little creature attached to him" Marlowe did not divine, nor did it occur to him to notice that Cowrie regarded Prince Andrei as strapped not only with bad fortune but with a helpless wife. So the Prince became Cowrie's charity, and she donated bravely, paying with perfectly inscribed cheques into his cool, moist palm, and receiving hastily scribbled receipts in a purple ink upon pieces of cereal carton. That was how it was.

And she had paid for six months in advance. And the lessons weren't happening. And Marlowe didn't know. To give him his due, he was a busy man, or as busy as a man can be whose two secretaries have trouble locating him on his two cell phones. He was busy sitting in parking-lots in the sunshine making cell phone calls to a partner in Rio de Janeiro, and then busy having café au lait, and then busy watching kids trying on roller blades and wondering if he was too old. But money rolled in, and so he was too busy to know about Prince Andrei, and in truth, Prince Andrei, drinking *his* café au lait in Paris, reading through various passages in his Rachmaninoff, was too busy to think about him. Would it be churlish to say that Jodi and Adam were tickled to lose the piano lessons for awhile? Jodi got her own telephone and made good use of it. Adam took up Warcraft.

•

But Adam, being eight, also put everything into speech. And the way he put it, at the dinner table, in the middle of a party Marlowe had invited Cowrie to throw for a gentleman named Estéban from Caracas (who possessed a great number of shares) was, "Prince Andrei went to Brussels Sprouts." There had been heavy and quite good Staffordshire china, with tender asparagus tips in vinaigrette, and real Sheffield silver, and a quite smooth Vouvray in Waterford, so that clinking had been the order of the day, and some scraping sounds, and polite conversation about the Empire State Building having been opened in 1931, and prodding of one child beneath the damask cloth by a second child and vice versa, but now all action stopped and there was silence. "What did you say honey?" said Marlowe, demonstrating with a smile how he loved his son. "What about Brussels Sprouts?" "Prince Andrei," said Adam with finality, pushing one asparagus far away with a spoon and using a finger to bring another to take its place. "Prince Andrei likes Brussels Sprouts? Why is he talking about Brussels Sprouts?" Cowrie put on the sparkling face and said, "Because he absolutely abhors them. All children absolutely abhor them." "Not in Caracas," said Estéban. "Big in Caracas. We cook them in vinegar." "Ooooo!" said Jodi, before being stared into submission, "doesn't...sound...very...." "Prince Andrei *went to* Brussels Sprouts," Adam announced. The smile on Marlowe's face now became ambiguous, and met the ambiguous smile on Cowrie's. She saw his pupils shrink, then shrink again as the knowledge he was having and the thoughts it was producing sapped his power to see. She saw him, in point of fact, go blind with realization. Estéban said, "A dinner from heaven!"

•

She was working every night from midnight until two in the morning on a book called *Orbs*. It was poems. One of them, "Lion Mouth," went like this:

> Stamens I would bequeath you
> But here instead I watch fishermen without choice
> And lick my half fig, spoiled by your
> Face in premonition.
> Then, flagrant with purpose,
> I swallow you as regret, penance
> For what I dreamed we were,
> Awake until morning.

She wrote it on a silent word processor and printed it silently on an inkjet printer that sat on the corner of her table next to a little vase of grape hyacinths. Beside her on the desktop were little photographs framed in silver: Marlowe, Marlowe and the kids, the kids, she and Marlowe, and, in a rectangle with roses at its corners, Everden Quayle. The picture of Everden Quayle had him shucking oysters into a pail next to a splash of rhododendron. He was the one she had written the poem about. In fact, all of the poems in *Orbs* were about Quayle, and she wondered whether Marlowe, if ever he read this book, would come to that conclusion. Marlowe didn't read literature, though; there was nothing to worry about. Marlowe read company reports. Quayle would read the book, and he would surmise, "She still loves me." What a beggar of questions he was, since she had never loved him, and she did not love him now. But she knew he would think—and she was entirely right about this—"She still loves me, and if I am sweet to her I can have her with a bottle of wine and a ribald story." There was, in the top drawer of the desk, but as yet unframed, a small colour photograph of Prince Andrei. It wasn't only him. He was in the right foreground holding a Gauloise. Far in the background, out of focus, at a table, was Jillian, and she was holding something fuzzy to the eye that might well have been a spotted cat. There was a look in Prince Andrei's eye that said, "I am beyond all this mundane reality," but the photograph had been taken on an afternoon a very long time ago when he was not at all beyond this mundane reality and she had whispered to him that she loved him and kissed his cheek and he had sighed into her ear the young male sigh of exquisite relief. How one's life, she thought, is composed of regrets and the precipitates of regret. Then she thought, "Women should be without men. Men are obstructions to women. A woman should be able to learn to exist on her own in life. In fact, there should be schools for women who want to learn what it is to live without men. Girls should be able to go to such schools. There should be a school for Jodi, where she can learn what life is without men. I love men but men will drive us crazy." She had heard, indeed, that there was such a place, the Charleston Academy, and it had as a motto, "She Goes Forward." In the morning she would go forward and fill out an application. Having made this decision, and as if a permission had been given in silence, she opened her drawer and took out the photograph of Prince Andrei, wiped it with a kleenex, substituted it for the picture of Everden Quayle in the silver frame with roses in its corners. She also wrote "Whimpers":

> In your universe, I am the snail
> Modest and patient and good to eat.
> Troubling to seek you
> Surrounded by noxious flies
> I hope you place yourself where I'm crawling.
> You are splendid, tall, and bright
> But the grander form is mine.

•

In the morning while he ate his oatmeal Marlowe explained the most sensible way to interpret the business with the piano teacher. "See, honey, he's robbing us. It's very simple.

He's taken money from you for lessons in advance, and then he goes out of the country, with that money, and spends it building his career. Nobody asked my permission. And I think he should be made to come back now and give those lessons. Or at least pay back the money, with interest." He prepared the oatmeal with butter in the centre and a neat ring of brown sugar around it and then a lake of cream in which all of this could be an island. And he sprinkled a little salt. "I mean, I don't think he has to come back *tonight*, I'm not uncivilized. I think he can make his plans and do it at the end of the week. But I think we should have the lessons." She didn't know where to begin, so she went to the heart of Prince Andrei and began there. "Marlowe, are you aware that would ruin his career?" Marlowe was aware, it was certain, because he began to flip through the NASDAQ quotes without looking up. She couldn't stop. "He has gone off to make something of himself, because he is a young man and in this society musical young men are not often given the opportunity to—" He looked at her with knife eyes. "I do not wish my son to lose his opportunity to learn about music at an impressionable age." She knew that her spirits had become horses, and that already they were stampeding, but she summoned from some force above the strength to hold herself from speaking. He flipped a page. She stared at her coffee, at the oval of her vision which changed proportions as she leaned forward or back and told herself, "Quiet, quiet, quiet." Then she said, with the greatest deliberateness, "Marlowe, I can't imagine how anyone would contact him to bring him back." He, at this, was aglow and pink. "Oh, that's quite easy, don't worry. I'll just prefer charges. He has defrauded me, after all. You were nothing in all this but my agent, it's not your fault. I am the principal contractor. It shouldn't take more than one or two quick calls, and the FBI or Interpol or somebody will take it after that." Somewhere in all of this she could feel the presence of a great evil, a great and saturating evil, not an evil that inhered in Marlowe but one you could sense swirling around him like a cloud of smoke, but all she could see were tiny problems adding up to nothing that had a shape. Somewhere in a shadow was something immeasurable, and in the centre of it, blackest and most alarming, Marlowe was protecting her.

•

Cowrie had taken herself once to a psychiatrist. Not on one occasion, but for a course of therapy at one time in her life. He had been a rather dominating, but on the whole a very bright, man. He did not have an office in the city. He was located in Sunday, Long Island. She did not like to drive, and in fact had learned to do it late in her life, but she took her car up the West Side Highway and got onto the Cross-Bronx Expressway and connected by way of the Throgs Neck Bridge and the Cross Island Parkway with the Long Island Expressway, that monument to the failure of civilization. Her appointment was for Mondays at half past noon. She found that if she left at 9:40 in the morning, after a yogurt and a cup of espresso at a place on 72nd Street, she could make it nicely by 12:15, encountering virtually no traffic. And at two in the afternoon, when she headed home, no other person was going into the city. Instead of driving with the radio on, she would talk to herself and work out poems. Dr. Savage, or Doc Savage as he preferred to be known, adored to read these; in other words, he read them eagerly; and often expressed ideas about the way the mind worked in language that would be natural for a poet. He taught her, for instance, to conceive of her neurosis as a metaphor. But the point was, and it was a sad point, he did little now, when she called him near midnight on a Tuesday to complain, to salve her in the matter of Marlowe and Prince Andrei. He made a bit of a speech, but he did little to salve her. He said: "You love your husband and you think you love this young musician. Or you think you love your husband and you love the musician. But either way, there's a difference between facts and thoughts, which is typical for a poet. Also, there's a difference between your experiences of these two men. And one of them is attempting to destroy the other. And you are convinced your husband doesn't know about the affair—" She interrupted to say her husband definitely didn't know, to stress that Marlowe's knowledge was confined to an arcane mathematics. "You are convinced, as I say, that he doesn't know. I'm taking the scientific view, which is to confine oneself happily to the data. And your husband believes you are feeling taken advantage of by the musician, so he has become your redeemer. It's all quite classic. Why don't you write a poem about it?" She said she had written a volume of poems. "Why don't you write a good poem? If you'd written one good poem you wouldn't need the volume. Why don't you sit down right now and write a good poem about what it feels like to be saved by somebody who's trying to kill your lover? Write the poem and fax it to me," he said. "Men like to think they are accomplishing things. Your husband is trying to make some sort of order out of what he feels is chaos. You told me once that he was an epileptic, didn't you? Epileptic males are very sensitive to disorder. Think of this musician as a mess that Marlowe is trying to clean up."

•

The next day in a panic—what she would have called a panic, what Doc would have called excitement—she drove out to Long Island and parked in his driveway. She stared into his yard, where under a cherry tree at a picnic table he saw his patients. There he was, with a plump woman who kept bobbing her head. Cowrie told herself, "Wait and he will see you." But instead she backed out, turned around, drove back into the city. When she got home she wrote:

> Hrothgar knew no such invective.
> My body is the world you cleave
> To shape. Barbarian, my blood
> Has been yours since breakfast.

She was not at all happy with it and felt that she would split if she couldn't scream but there was no-one to scream at. Then in the kitchen out of nowhere there was Marlowe. She opened her mouth. But he was sitting at the table, a plate of olives beside him untouched, having a seizure. This is what was happening: he had his hands spread on the table and he was flicking his fingers as if trying to shake something out of the tips of them; and he said he smelled chocolate, he said it over and over, but there was no chocolate in the kitchen because Jodi was allergic to chocolate; and he was breathing quickly, gasping for breath. She watched this calmly, but this was always the part one could watch this way. Now he turned and looked frightened. She took a step forward. He collapsed into a slump and then leaned forward and fell softly onto the floor. She came up and took his head onto her lap. His face was bluish, then distinctly blue. He had stopped breathing. She held her breath and prayed. To whom was she praying? She had never known the answer to this. She didn't believe in God but she was praying to Him. "Make him breathe! Make him breathe!" Marlowe started to breathe. Colour came back to his face. His arms and legs tensed and relaxed, tensed and relaxed, again and again. Now he was calming. Now he was still. After a few minutes his eyes opened and he sat up. "I was trying to figure out the yield for Braza Nickel," he said quietly. He climbed back to the table and took the newspaper and pored through it as if nothing had happened. She left and came back after twenty minutes. He had eaten all of the olives, and left the pits in a set of concentric circles.

•

Prince Andrei Bolkonsky came back from Vienna much earlier than planned and called her immediately. He seemed very unfriendly, curt, harsh of tone, and morose. Jillian had stayed in Europe. The cat kept trailing around his legs and he kicked it away. "Jodi," he said, "really has less talent for piano than one might have supposed. I think she should study something else, perhaps guitar. Buy her a guitar and leave her be. Adam must work much harder." Adam was given arpeggios in B-flat, which were a torture for his little hands. Saliva came out of the corners of his mouth, in fact, as he tried to play them with both hands together. Afterwards, while the children sat out in the garden, Prince Andrei made two cups of tea. She knew with her heart pounding this would be the epitome of the evil; that he would confront her; that he would sneer at her smallness in not supporting his career. He would say, "Your filthy husband has ruined me, and all because you, because you cannot tolerate to put forward the money for six months of lessons, which is nothing to you and everything to me. My career is gone, my marriage is a ruin, my life is over. You can content yourself with knowing you have produced this, with your tool of a husband. And I will never trouble your pristine happiness again." He would say this while she drank his tea, the ultimate impossibility; and in his usual way he would offer a slice of some blueberry cake he could ill afford; and he would sit smoking his Gauloise and looking distractedly out into the Madame Lemoine lilacs at the back of the garden. He would say, "I loved you!" and it was true the long stretches of afternoon with him while Marlowe was away on business trips were all the evidence she needed, his hot neck, his unending urgency. If the evil made her sink, if it made her plummet, she would now be given the sense of bottomlessness. And he would touch her. And he would want her again. And she him. So that they would make plans to meet. But she would be nothing more than a shell of what she had been. And he would either fail to notice or take her in her emptiness as worth more than such a pathetic case of a woman could be. Prince Andrei sat down without his cigarette and did look outside for a moment before clearing his throat and finding her eyes. She prayed he would be kind. But in a voice far smaller and shakier than she could recognize, "I have a confession to make," he said. "I don't know what came over me, but I did not play very well." She didn't know how to make response to this, because it was far too crafty. He was showing the very greatest gallantry by giving her a way out, saying a graceful goodbye. Given the power game Marlowe had initiated, who could have played particularly well? And this boy—he was scarcely more than that—had no training at all for jousts with Marlowes. She was thinking of how to tell him she was sorry without at the same time seeming worthless. But he went on as if he were on a completely different page of the score: "My Rachmaninoff was just plain weak," he said, "In fact I've never felt so alienated from it, so out to lunch." "Your Rachmaninoff? Your what?" And suddenly she knew Marlowe wasn't what he was talking about at all. "The chops were there," he said, "but musically it was like an empty shell. And that's what the critics said, which is only right. That was in Paris. And also in London. Truly, it wasn't good. Maybe I just don't have it." She wanted to reach forward and seize him but the children were looking in. "I am perhaps a pianist and perhaps not. I perhaps will be a pianist some day. But for now, I will teach. It is a very great disappointment." The cake he had bought was not blueberry but hazelnut and it was exquisite, with an icing that melted in the mouth. She had two squares of it. He had two, too, and began to smile a little. "It is not so serious, because I am still young," he said, "and teaching, if you want to know the truth, is my life." Still, the thought clung to her that all of this was a story: Marlowe had pressed his charges and the police had brought him back. He had paid Marlowe the money. He was living in defeat. But what she preferred was to imagine that the music he had not found yet was still buried in him, waiting to be born; and that she, perhaps, would be the one to help him deliver it. "You know, your husband very sweetly sent me flowers," he suddenly said. "What!" "In Vienna, yesterday. A truly gigantic bouquet, it took two bellboys to carry it. The card said—I will certainly never forget it—

    Stephen from Marlowe,
        May you light the world.
           In the warmest of friendship.

It is what I will remember of Europe more than anything else."

Honeymoon

The age of honeymoons was gone; she had decided that before agreeing to a wedding. Honeymoons had been replaced by guaranteed travel miles. They made vows in a gazebo studded with baby's breath. "You Can't Always Get What You Want" was performed by a trio of flautists. Afterward they had a few friends for secular Valpolicella, packed knapsacks with little stars-and-stripes sewn on the flaps, flew off for a month in Italy. Over Labrador Peter allowed her to baptize him Pietro; and he called her Elisabeta. Better: Beta. At the airport he had purchased a little marbled notebook in which to make Ruskinian drawings from rocky promontories, but now, during Grieg's Concerto in A minor, from a steward in nylon trousers he bought a pocket computer translator that taught him *"sessuale," "provocativo," "fiorista," "lugubre,"* and *"quello appartiene a me."* But there was no "pickled," and no "herring" and so he began to panic. He stood up and snapped open the overhead compartment, fished out the notebook, pencilled his name on the flyleaf, and also the date in Roman numerals, MCMXCIII. She drained a glass of Brut at the steward's insistence, and went the colour of cooked lobster—*"arragosta bollita"*—because she was not, and had never hoped to be, a "drinker" (*un'ubbriaca*). Indeed, she had no vices for which one traded in cash. Pietro used the lavatory quite a lot, climbing over her with his gangly legs and muttering, *"Scusa. Scusa."* The leather patch on his jeans almost brushed her nose. It was perhaps the first time she had noticed the modesty of his bladder. The second movie was *sex, lies, and videotape*—*La Sessualità, i Menzogne, il Videoscrivente*. She found that she was a little offended, or perhaps bored—*annoiata*—by certain passages one did not wish to speak about enough to identify; but instead of watching she read in *Cosmopolitan* a masterpiece called "What He Wants in Bed" and was tickled at the description of positions she could not bear to see pictured. *Titillata*. The horoscopes were on page 28. Hers said, "Look for a tall, dark stranger bringing olives."

•

Faraway in Siena, they prepared flowers, banners, grandstands, and ambulances for the Contrade. Around the Piazze del Campo shields were lashed up on balconies: the magenta and green Drago, the Leocorno in peach, blue and white; the green and gold rhinoceros; the giraffe upon red and white; the white goose upon emerald. Whistling boys cleaned out the fountain of joy, but it was all very serious, there was no mirth. Tourists paced out patterns of vortices, photographing architecture. A tanker full of water drove slowly around the half moon, spraying the bricks violently while two old men shouted and swept. Arturo Benigni, the postmaster, rode by on his bicycle, cursing the wet road, struggling and huffing on the uphill parts. The smell of frying bacon mixed with the smell of fried rapini. Massimo del Corti the supervisor of *carabinieri* sat and smoked, his uniform jacket folded neatly at his feet. He might well have been thinking to himself, about that great race, the Palio, the smell of which was eager in the air, "This year it will be difficult, *faticoso*, because so many people hate the Chiocchiola and they have arranged it. So profound is the feeling against the Chiocchiola. There will be violence." The caravans were already pulling into town with straw. It was going to be miserably hot. The blood, yes, would boil.

•

Pietro, extremely tall, and dark, was sleeping beside her as the plane descended into Rome. He snored lightly and she realized that she adored his snoring. A balding man across the aisle was using a laptop frenetically, steaming up his granny glasses. They landed in a kind of yellow fog. "I love you," she said, either a little tentative or a little weary. They walked out into the raucous terminal. "I love you, I love you, I love you." He raced to get the bags and then corrected her: "*Io ti voglio bene.*" He said they had two hours to get to the Stazione Termini and catch the train to Siena. She bought *fumetti*, *Coloromantica* and *Medicea*, and *bigne* and *brioche* for the ride. The train rattled and stank faintly of Grappa. The countryside was burnt, rolling, covered with grotesque trees. Fields were purple, then lime green, then ruddy brown and studded with brazen groping *olivi*. "I love you," she said and corrected herself, *"Io ti voglio bene."* He fell asleep on her shoulder and snored beautifully. "Pietro, Pietro...." This woke him. "Yes? *Si si?*" It was true there were feelings that could not be put into words, because now she was flooding over with one, because he was part of her and yet she felt not the weight of him. Indeed, his voice, the timbre of his voice, was different than it had ever been before, *"Si? Si?,"* and she didn't know him. She put her hand on his thigh and he shifted some and slept again, soft against her but also a boulder against which she could feel the earth. The conductor, taking the tickets, winked at her and said, "Is beautiful, is very beautiful! You come from state of Alabama?" His face was by Piero della Francesca. Screwed under yellowing plastic into the bulkhead of the compartment there was a faded colour reproduction, and it showed Siena by twilight, the Palazzo Pubblico, with a man standing on the Torre del Mangia as if to throw himself off. Or was it a gargoyle? Or was it a shadow? In Italy, she thought, the sculpture looked human, and the humans looked like sculptures.

•

Siena inspired Pietro with an immediate desire to flee. Perhaps it was the fever of the Contrade in the air, the smell of straw, of horses. Perhaps it was Beta's nervousness, because on learning there was no river she had become distraught. "Where will I see the reflection of churches?" He learned that nearby, in the fortress town of Volterra, there was also no river but one could camp. He bought matching sleeping bags and acquired a map at a shop hardly big enough to hold him next to an antiquary with brown Pulcinello plates in his vitrine. She watched him pencilling a route and suddenly, once again, he seemed like a stranger, all quirky movements and unfamiliar perspectives, and she felt lost; but then he was familiar again. *"Io ti voglio bene,"* she said. He went to pee and changed his clothes. He wore cotton, from bottom to top, but she adorned herself with metals. Her belt was silver, her neck bore a chain of platinum. Her wrists were banded in gold plating and even her jeans were stitched over with sequins that simulated burning mail. They went up to Volterra by a bus that was overheated. Outside it was fiercely hot. They soaked a handkerchief in Pellegrino and held it in front of the open window. Dimly, and with as much desire as contemplation, she had made a plan for her life with him: now, in Volterra, she would become impregnated. She had always wanted, secretly, to mount him in a glade of Tuscan ferns, to ride him and to win a race. There was nothing unreasonable about this, if it did smack of deliberation; by careful agreement they had been enjoying a thoroughgoing, but disciplined, intimacy, yet with the proviso that a licence would deliver them to freedom; and now they were licensed; and now it was her desire to entice the explosion from his daunting control. He went to pee again. The green condom packs he'd insisted on bringing to Italy she deftly lifted from his knapsack and stowed in one of the outside zipper compartments of her own, inside a box of tampons where he would never think to probe. They walked into the sunshine and moved slowly, half-consciously, through streets as slim as *linguine*. Her metal jangled. In a niche between two buildings, she wanted him, and she imagined that in this heat she would provoke him to a kind of seizure of delight. "Pietro?" "What? *Che cosa?*" He was lost, apparently. He was turning every which way. The alleys had become darker, less catty, dank with vinegar, cold. Peter felt himself to be a prisoner in Volterra. The walls of the place, which were labyrinthine, were fat with demand: "Show us your power." The passivity of America would never be comprehended here, one had to stand up, lift the eyes, take action upon the world in the permissive heat. He felt out of place, confounded and terrified by vistas from tapestries. They came to a basilica in a tiny piazza where a man stood smoking and leaning against a fountain, watching Beta carefully. He was dark, tall. He had a green bottle: olive oil? "America!" he smiled. "My name, Cavaradossi. You have need for *cicerone?*" They shook hands a little stiffly. The man told them a legend of two lovers trapped in a cavern beneath the town. He offered cigarettes. Beta pulled back into the shadow of Pietro. Cavaradossi said he was a *carabiniere* but now he was off duty visiting his mother. He said his mother was demanding. There had been old age and there had been senility but now there was second childhood, and every day something new was demanded. She asked every day for a dog. He could not bring her a dog, as she couldn't care for anything. He brought her a picture of a dog. They looked at the radiance of the sunlight on him, and at the worn yellow stones in the buildings behind, and the vast cupola of pallid sky. Pietro said he had to pee. Cavaradossi pointed to the church. Pietro squinted, pulling back. "There, yes, yes. Behind. In the passageway. Fear nothing. Nature is everywhere. *La natura è dappertutto.*" But instead they said goodbye and wandered back to the gates of the town. There, in shadows, he pissed against the wall and she stepped forward to watch carefully with caught breath while holding his arm. Instead of camping out, they decided to take a room. The hotel was the Albergo San Lino. There were blue and yellow awnings that appealed to her. The *padrone* was called Brunelleschi. He smoked a cigarillo, watched television, "Cagney e Lacy." Pietro knew what she wanted from him, by the way she put her head on his shoulder, which was her signal, which was one of the central steps in her dance, but the fact of her wanting it made him afraid. Now, of course, she had paperwork to back her up. He felt they were tumbling into a kind of Piranesi garden, all density and darkness and ineluctability. Late in the afternoon there was a breeze that nudged the curtains. She had placed herself vulnerable and unclothed on the bed, which he thought was too soft. "I keep thinking babies, overpopulation, deforestation," said he. Her underwear, tossed on the pillow, provoked him. She sat up, staring. She seemed, by a pout, to say, "You are a child. You are incapable." She touched his leg. She lay back again and turned her head to the side. He had a lithe dancer's body, but he never danced; he made riddles, prevarications. She admitted to a sudden passionate craving for lettuce. "Open your legs," he whispered. She prayed but he did not answer her prayer, he fell back and stared at the ceiling as if for messages.

•

"The Black Death came three times to Siena," he said. "The third time, in 1348, almost all of the artists died." He went to shower. The soap was flavoured with almond. It was still possible to return to Siena in time for the Palio, and they decided that was the thing to do. He asked himself if girls in general were more highly sexed than boys, or whether it was just Beta. "Do you think we'll get a room?" she asked, but he had already arranged for one, using a telephone number provided by his father. The bus ride was bumpy. He realized he'd always thought sex was something boys invented and foisted on girls, so her hunger was disconcerting not only for his appetite but also for his philosophy. He wondered if she was disappointed in him. He was surprised that here, in Tuscany, he should feel very little desire. The fields were ruddy brown and full of *olivi*, praying desperate trees, and the fields were lime green and then purple. Siena was humid, the air was pink. They had lunch at a place called Al Forno and he drank three glasses of Gavi. This loosened him. He looked at her breasts in the rosy sun. He thought that perhaps, because he would not lie with her, this was not a marriage. Her father, a major figure in a major firm, would arrange for a divorce when they got home if she asked him to. She was reading the *Coloromantica* which had a story about a young man being seduced by two women on a yacht. The photographs were explicit. In one frame, which he could see clearly but upside-down through his Gavi balloon, the boy had a look of terror on his face. "Nothing particular, you know," she said, "has to happen on a honeymoon. We can just have a wonderful time. There is plenty of opportunity later." This meant, of course, "You are a disappointment." *Uno disappunto*. In his notebook he began to sketch an elevation of the fountain and she said, pointing to one of the pictures of the boy in her magazine, "What's *incapace*? One of the girls is telling the other that's what he is."

•

There were two old men sitting at an adjacent table. One, silent, took sips of Cinzano with lemon, and the other was lecturing. "Siena's a lovely town. Sensible little town. But I don't know why anybody would come here. The Palio is one thing, but everybody has plenty to do in life without seeing the Palio. I mean, a horse race is always a horse race. Siena's an instructive town. Lovely hills, don't you think? But what's a lovely hill for?" The drinker didn't say anything so the other continued. "The hills are lovely, but you have to get a good place to see them from. The tower's a good place." He took the opportunity of pointing, although his friend wasn't interested and looked away. He pointed up into the sun. "You know about Mangiaguadagni?" The friend did not know. "You don't know about Mangiaguadagni? There was a bell-ringer once named Mangiaguadagni. Went crazy. Why do you think they call it the Torre del Mangia! Half the people in Siena are related to him. Half the people in Siena are probably crazy." From somewhere off in the distance came the sound of a scratchy recording of Lisia Albanese singing "*O mio babbino caro*." The lecturer looked up and closed his eyes. "You hear this song? This is the only thing in *Gianni Schicchi*. Other than this it's an elaborate nothing. An envelope. But this is very nice. Makes me wish I had a daughter instead of a cat." The drinker called for another Cinzano. The waiter growled putting it down, so that Pietro, listening carefully in a kind of dream, thought it was all being written by Hemingway. "This is a good real town. This is a good place to eat ham." Pietro, meanwhile, tried to seem brave and masculine while the goddess looked him up and down and determined how he would spend the rest of his life. He decided that her breasts were two apples, and that if only he had two apples it would be nice to pose her nude in sunlight cupping them in her hands, if only he could draw.

•

The Palio could be seen beautifully from the rooms he had obtained. There were damask curtains to take pleasure in drawing back, high as mountains, and walnut floors one could see one's face in. Pietro became enchanted with his face. Il Duca di Montalcino had once lived here. The balcony reached away from sad gargoyles. The Piazza del Campo was all banners and shuffling throngs. It was infernally hot. There'd been sun early in the morning to burn off the mist, and there'd been flies, great fat golden ones, but now the sun was behind clouds. The horses were pressing their riders as they paraded in shiny many-coloured silks and in the head-pieces of the *contrade*: rhinoceros, dragon, lion, urchin, turtle. "Look at those animals!" said Pietro, a little blankly. They had brought ham sandwiches and some Orvieto. The crowd was now somehow out of control, out of form, and Beta was pressing close to Pietro's warmth. The movement of the crowd was the nauseating movement of a vortex. Kids were dangling from columns and posts all round the square, swatting at banners. Some kids with snails painted on their shirts were climbing up directly below, trying to get the treasured banner of the Chiocchiola, a team no-one had ever rooted for until this year, when it had suddenly become the talk of the town, and one boy cursed "Pippoli!" and spat and the second boy just spat. The race was delayed by something, and the crowd started to shift and shout more raucously, and the kids were now tossing paper bullets up and one hit Beta in the arm. The sun came out and banged off the trumpets during the hideous fanfares, and then hid again. Two kids near the banner were fighting one another off, clinging to the balcony frame with one arm each. One had a white shirt, black tresses; the other had no shirt and his hair was painted green. The horses were straining. "Look at those animals!" A great cheer went up because the race was on. Then Pietro thought he heard someone below say, "*Coltello!*," a word he did not know.

•

During the Palio, it is the custom to talk of love. Suitors find amorous phrases for teasing their lovers' ears into blushes. Secrets are whispered. "I want you forever," Pietro whispered to Beta. She took a moment, and then, "I want you," she whispered back. The horse wearing the colours of the Chiocchiola—tomato red and tomato yellow—was challenged immediately by the horse of the Civetta—burgundy and black—and people underneath them were yelling, "Pippoli! You bastard!" The horse of the Vipera—red and green stripes on a sunflower yellow ground—and soon after the horse of the Istrice—silver grey and black—gave one another a run for it, and were pressing, and actually touched, and then these two horses were sandwiched near the Fonte Gaia. The crowd went mad. The boys underneath Beta had the Chiocchiola banner now and were giggling as they stared up at her breasts. The boy with dark curls had magnificent green eyes, and a little moisture was on his mouth as the eyes locked on the points of her nipples beneath her silks. Now they dropped back to the street and started running with the banner and people went up in screams, surrounding and devouring them. "Beta!—" said Pietro, but it was too late, because more boys were climbing up walls to seize more banners, boys were climbing up this wall under the neighbouring balcony where the Civetta banner flew, and the horses were whining. This Palio belonged to the Chiocchiola, which was why everybody wanted their banner, and why everybody was yelling at Pippoli, the Chiocchiola jockey, who certainly wasn't pressing enough. The Chiocchiola had put something in the horses' feed, that was for sure. Caffeine on the carrots. But now Pippoli's horse was down and families with ribbons were screaming here and there as if the world had ended. "*Diavolo!*" they were shouting. "*Fischiato!*" Peter grabbed her arm and drew her inside. They closed, then barred, the windows. Great smashing explosions of voice filled the Piazza, and now screams. "What!" he said; "Oh my God!" He listened but the sounds weren't repeated. The crowd was certainly stampeding. "*Coltello* means knife!" he said in a shock. He sat with her wrapped into an embrace, and they ate the ham sandwiches and sipped the wine. The wine was warming. "What were those screams?" she asked. He wanted to be out of Italy. "Are they going to finish the race?" The boy's green eyes swam over her memory, and the way he had gasped with a hunger that had no shape.

•

The radio said the Palio has been a catastrophe. One jockey had been shot and was close to death. Another had been attacked by a crowd. Pietro called for room service, for *cappuccini*. The waiter seemed drained of colour. "There are good Palios and bad Palios," he said. "This was a bad Palio. Some of the horses have been killed." Pietro tried to prevent her, but Beta wanted to go to the balcony to see. The square was strewn with shirts, pieces of banners, horse blood. At sunset men came with sawdust, and the police directed traffic. The smell of urine and horses was in the air. Two men passing below were talking and it was from them Pietro and Beta heard a young man had also been killed, right here, below this balcony, clutching the banner of the Chiocchiola, which was not his clan.

•

Pietro went down to the street, found a *carabiniere* who would tell him about it. This man was tall, very tall; and dark; and was named Del Corti. "One of the families in the Chiocchiola," he said, "which is the *contrada* of the snails, one of the leading families, is the Tezzufi. And it seems perhaps the elder son, Teo, was climbing here with his friend Gambolo, trying to save the banner. They were right up under this balcony you can see." He pointed up into the pink sky and Pietro recognized where Beta had been standing in his arms. "But when they came down some strangers from outside attacked the two of them and one called them Civetta, which is a most bad thing to do," said del Corti, "and he was killed. It's simple, and pathetic." Beta said nothing but held onto Pietro, and del Corti stared hard into her face with his brown eyes. "This is not a violent country," he went on. "We are passionate. We do not control our passion, which is our shame but not our fault. And therefore to be in the Palio down here is not, perhaps, so secure as to be watching it from up there." From what seemed like a balcony he was looking down into Beta's face, smiling, and she felt the strangest tingling, as if the proximity of death were nothing but a drug to quicken the speed of the race of her blood.

•

"Something occurs to me about you," she said; "You are the epitome of civilization." It was very late. She'd had a few Glenfiddichs to straighten the bends. Chilled, he had put on a dressing gown over his flannels and button-down, with a tie still loose about his neck. He had a brandy with ice, and he was seated at the credenza scrawling in peacock ink into his notebook. "You are Edwardian." When he looked up at her he was somehow innocent. He had very long eyelashes. She wondered what bizarre fantasies he harboured, but he was not harbouring any fantasies and about this he felt ashamed. The world was matter of fact for him. But—and now for the first time he was learning this about Beta—she had a hunger that allied her with beasts. In the middle of the night, while he slept, she went beneath the covers and found him with her mouth. More with technique than with passion she attacked him, until it was possible with a persistent hand to bring potency without disturbing sleep. His breathing was a meticulous cue. She kissed his belly, his chest, his neck. She sat and rode into the darkness. He was frenzied without waking. In the heat of the war she retreated into sleep.

•

The rooftops of Siena were brown, apricot brown, in the twilight. "I'm in love with Siena," said Beta, "It's changing my life. Let me tell you, in all my life I've never stopped wanting before, but now I've stopped wanting." For Pietro Siena meant a position on a map. Buy tickets to Italy, proceed to Siena, spend two weeks, leave, proceed to Rome. Make your way home, establish your career, become someone else, make use of your power of enchantment. That night, in the centre of the roadway of her life, she did once again what she had done the night before. This time she felt the structure of his dam give way under the concentrated ray of her intent. The walls caved, the river came through into the valley. She had learned from his computer to say, "*Il fiume*," the river, because it was the one thing she wanted, and Siena could not provide it. "*Il fiume magnifico.*" And then, at breakfast, at the Ristorante Bardonello, she took his hand. "I am the mother of your child." He was jotting on a napkin train times between Rome and Paris. She bought a scarf which was the colour of the rooftops of Siena, and which was laced through with golden metallic thread, and wore it over her hair.

•

On the plane to Paris he told her how they should invest their money and she wrote it all down, nodding. At Orly they really had to race to get a cab that would have them in Roissy with time for a sandwich before the New York plane. There was a news kiosk and one of the French papers had a long report about the Palio. He had to go at it slowly but it yielded. There was the history of the *contrade* of Siena, the mouse *contrada*, the snail *contrada*, the woodgrouse *contrada*, the falcon *contrada*, and so on. And then it reported what had not been said in Italy: that a man his age—not a youth—had been killed, his throat cut from ear to ear, during the very climax of the race, on the sidewalk directly under the balconies of the Albergo di Bellino, and that the killer had been caught and identified as a member of a youth gang. A photo showed the *carabiniere* dragging at a boy with curly locks and the banner of the Chiocchiola over his shoulders. "The Albergo di Bellino—but that's where we—" choked Beta. He kept reading. It was apparently a revenge killing, perpetrated in response to a killing the year before, which itself was thought by knowledgeable insiders to have been occasioned by a killing the year before that. "My God, a ritual!" she said. She knew, too, that the passion she had felt, and that she had thought to be born in the mystery of animals and dust, had been part of a great, and bloody, cycle. Italy had been a panorama, all heat, all murder. And not just Italy, Europe. The heat flowed like lava over a map. Spain, France. Paris. Terror, suddenly, filled her brimful; Italy, France, this airport all terrified her; and her own sex terrified her; and the life she carried within terrified her more than either. Now it was announced that the New York plane would be late. She felt she had to escape at once or she would be strangled here. She turned to Peter and prayed that he would rescue her. But he was no longer, stunningly, in flight. He was content to sit reading the cryptic paper, to run his hands up and down his corduroys, and he said now he desired to return to Siena and walk around the square. She thought he must be joking. He wanted to buy a house, and see if he could join the *contrada* of the dragon. He wanted to sport colours and ride a steed. The dead man had left no family behind. Beta did not buy magazines for the plane but settled instead with E. M. Forster's *A Passage to India*, a book that could be trusted swiftly to put her to sleep. She slept all the way home and was happy for any American stimulus that might assist her to forget her honeymoon, like the Sunday *New York Times* in the hands of a stewardess and *Sleepless in Seattle* flickering on the little screen. When they got home she took a very long shower. The scarf from Siena she folded into a brown envelope for the Salvation Army.

Koi

Into the house that had everything, on the day after the hurricane, Ettie Savage brought a koi. It was a dapper little thing, with a face all splotched purple and silver and a brow anointed with rust. She called it, perhaps without the deference to the Orient it deserved, Josephine. And she gave it a buddy, a plump blue fantail which came swiftly if not automatically to own the name of Napoléon; in the fabulous aquarium she arranged for them with Ludwigia and Anacharis he lolled back and forth with an especially precocious fillip of the tail. Napoléon had mammoth, omniscient eyes. And he kept opening his mouth, in a kind of imitation, Ettie thought, of Bojangles Robinson. Josephine was as demure as a fish could be, and hid behind the greens and then behind the little magenta castle and then behind Napoléon's pendulous gut. Ettie had done everything the instruction book told her to do, since—although she'd admit to knowing horses and dogs and even, upon full moons, cats—she'd never been possessed of a fish. She had filled the tank with breath suspended, and with two thermometers, and had waited days for the bubbles to disappear, and had repositioned the castle, which had three turrets, at least twenty times; and when she introduced the fish she put on a Beethoven sonata; and she erected, from *Studies on Hysteria* by Breuer and Freud and two volumes of Hughlings-Jackson and the styrofoam plate of a nectarine pie from the Farmer's Market (and following a drawing of an ancient Japanese *kado* in an encyclopedia) a lean-to to cut some of the afternoon sun. But in this paradisiacal shade Napoléon and Josephine wouldn't eat, wouldn't do anything but huddle near the bottom and stare pathetically at her. Doc came down wheezing exactly at 30 minutes after four, dropped a typewriter ribbon in the garbage, took a peek at the new residents. "Precarious business," he said. He dropped a piece of celery top in and it floated upon the surface in the pattern of an infinity sign.

•

"A thing about fish:" said Doc. "About fish psychology:" He

was old now—it looked as if words were failing him—but he had been vigorous; and in his vigour he pursued inquiry as to the integrity of people's minds; more than a psychiatrist, he was a mentalist; and also he fed a lot of birds, and he did paintings, and he sculpted out of tree trunks some, and cooked a very good bouillabaisse. He cooked an award-winning bouillabaisse, or it would have been if there had been awards given for bouillabaisse in the Incorporated Village of Sunday but Sunday was a community without awards, and he knew a thing or two about folk music. Renaissance man. Renaissance man from Texas, incongruous, and he couldn't rope a steer, didn't even like eating steer, but he knew wine. He made a quite stupendous bouillabaisse, was smart enough to know you didn't serve bouillabaisse with Bordeaux. And he knew about headaches, he was putting words to paper about that, he'd long been putting words to paper, he'd done three, maybe four, chapters, maybe four and a half: chapter a year. "Fish metaphysics: that little fish you're watching, that Japanese fish, is intelligent. I mean not: 'is endowed with the capacity for intelligence' but: 'is smart.' Quite the little—" He breathed. He breathed again. The emphysema wasn't doing a thing for him. He breathed twice again. "Quite the little activist. But the blue one, there. The blue one's—" He looked away in disgust, not, Ettie hoped, with the fact that she had bought fish, "The blue one's—" he coughed, "migranous." Here was a new one, a migranous fish, and she actually put her cigarette to the side and her coffee cup down and lifted her eyebrows demonstratively. "Look at the way he moves, see," he wheezed and wheezed again, and quickly for a second, with a smile, she saw the man she had married, "Look—a little this way, a little that way. Migraneurs do that, kind of continuously renegotiate space." He grimaced, "Migraneurs're confused. Lose the sense of direction. Comes from a basic conflict between the way they conceive of the world," he waited for a cough that didn't come, "and the way the world is." He made a circle with his hand. "Basic unresolvable conflict. They've got bad fit. That fish has got bad fit. Look at him." Ettie looked at the fantail, who was hovering and twisting and hovering and sadly looking. There was something undecided and cloudy about his bearing. If he'd been a person you'd have said he could use a bowl of good soup. "Probably doesn't feel pain," Doc said. "Probably feels loneliness. Related to agoraphobia. What would you call it, okeanophobia?" And the koi was cuddling against the fantail now, rubbing against his belly, but the fantail looked lost, as if he could use a nice glass of Bordeaux. "God, looking at these fish makes me want some of your bouillabaisse," Ettie said, but she quickly went to tasting smoke again, because if wishes were horses beggars would ride.

•

Trudy Kay, who had been invited for dinner, showed up with two Azuma bags and a migraine. "I'll tell you one thing: you don't know what it is out there!" she said. "It's supernatural." She had blue lips. Her eyes kept looking around and she was flashing her teeth, as if to say, "Do you get it? Do you get it? You don't get it, do you." "Dear Trudy," Ettie began in her lecturing voice, "We have been having a major storm. When you have a major storm you—" "*You've* been having! *You've* been having!" barked Trudy Kay, "You never go anywhere! You never get out of the house! *I* have been out of the house! My God, have I been out of the house! You should see what it is! Do you want me to tell you? I'll tell you." And now she had the wonderment that comes with confronting miracles. "Half the trees are down, *in the whole town*! *Half*! Do you know what I'm saying? Do you know what that means out here? These trees are 600 years old! Trees all over the road. Branches. Telephone wires. Mailboxes. Telephone booths. The flags at the golf course!" "Hmph!" breathed Doc; "Mumph!" But Trudy Kay didn't wait for him to restore himself: "You don't believe me, I knew you wouldn't believe me. You never go anywhere. But it's truly incredible. I find it truly incredible! I went out to get a flashlight, I couldn't find one anywhere! A flashlight! Pfffft! I could have been looking for uranium! Finally, at the drug store of all places—" She took a flashlight from the first Azuma bag and put it next to the red and black and grey flashlights Doc and Ettie had already stood up on the sideboard. "I've been here almost 40 years, I've never seen anything like it. I was frightened out of my mind. I'm telling you, I was positively in a state of primitive, you could say mesozoic, panic. Police cars. Broken windows. You wouldn't believe the broken windows! Dick Winterfield will make a killing on new windows! The plumbers will make a killing, they're all going to be millionaires. If they aren't millionaires already! I've got trees down all around the house, all around! You want to know how many trees I've got down? I've got enough trees down to open a paper mill. Who's this?" She had been looking into Ettie's chrysalis green eyes and then past Ettie's eyes over Ettie's shoulder and her eyes had fallen upon Ettie's fish. "What's this, an aquarium! Look at that! Look at the blue gravel, that's really something. Hello, fishies!" She bent down and flashed her teeth again. "Hello, fishy fishy! They don't do anything! Look at that, they're like politicians, they don't do anything at all!" Napoléon and Josephine were still suspended side by side, moored to the glass. "You think possibly they're lemons? They don't look too with-it to me. You have to admit it's not much of a life. I mean, what kind of experience can you have in a little cube? They look as if they might be stupid. They don't respond." "Hrmph!" Doc coughed again. "I'd do a thing or two with that space, of course, Ettie, if it were me. I'd redecorate. I'd maybe make the floor red, I think you can get red gravel, and I'd put in the left corner a castle without turrets, something more Romanesque. The one you've got is English in style, with the turrets and the parapets, and it's cute, but these fish aren't going anywhere, they don't need Anglo-Saxon, they need Roman. A sense of history. Don't you think so, fishy? See—they don't respond! They have bad *feng shui* in there." Trudy stood up and gave a great sniff of pleasure, because the macaroni and cheese was coming out of the oven. From the second Azuma bag she presented to Doc a library copy of Ogden and Richards's *The Meaning of Meaning* and a little plastic tub of chocolate mousse. He opened the book and saw that someone had scrawled on the half-title page, "For Xavier: Expectation is the mother of disappointment." "What's that?" Trudy said. "Somebody wrote something? I need my other glasses." It took some time for one pair of eyeglasses to be exchanged for a slightly heavier pair of eyeglasses, the bridge of which was covered over with plastic tape; she stood as high as Doc's elbow as she took a peek. "Is that profound? Sometimes I can't tell anymore. Probably some writer donated this book, Norman Mailer, Joe Heller, they write things like that, don't they? Why doesn't he say the father of disappointment? Lemon mousse was sold out. Everything was sold out except what I brought. What did I bring, chocolate? That little fish doesn't look happy to me. And the big blue one," she pulled back her ears and squinted while she thought, "The big blue one is a basket case. I've got trees down it will take weeks to clean up. Maybe they'll turn to coal."

•

"Tell me about your headache," Doc said to Trudy Kay after dinner, because she'd said to him, "Why don't you ever ask me tell you about my headaches?" Ettie had a cigarette and sat back. "Tell me with precision." He had a yellow legal pad and a black felt pen poised in his fingers. Trudy Kay spent a couple of minutes working with a cigarette pack and not succeeding, let Ettie help her in the end. "The world is coming to an end. I feel locked in. Like one of those fish. How's that?" With a great deal of effort she turned around and looked at Napoléon glaring forward and Josephine blinking. "Yes," she said to their sucking faces, "You know. You do know. You understand. And the world feels as if it's collapsing around me. The pain is right at the centre of the top of my brain. Little dots. I feel totally apathetic. Even Jim Lehrer doesn't phase me. All I want to do is watch reruns of 'I Love Lucy.'" "Cold hands?" said Doc, inhaling and inscribing. "Cold feet? Coldness anywhere?" "No. Should I have cold feet? I never do anything the way it's supposed to be done, I'm a maverick. I do get visions of chaos. And I want to be a ballerina, isn't that preposterous?" She was looking around the dining-room through eyeglasses that drooped upon her nose. Catalogues and knitting and medical texts and pieces of the *New York Times* were everywhere in awkward ganglia. A jigsaw puzzle of Manet's "Odalisque" was a quarter done. Suddenly Trudy spun around again and stared at the fish. "That fat one," she said. "I feel prescient. I feel prophetic. That fat one is up to something."

•

Trudy Kay had been married to the poet D.D. Kay, married loyally for 55 years. Having published three significant volumes with City Lights, he had died and left her alone with her thoughts. She had always been the girl with thoughts. And nobody could fool her. When she sold real estate it was snap, crackle, and pop. She'd sit at her desk and the phone would ring. Somebody would ask for a certain kind of house. Two hours later she'd meet them, watch carefully as they had a cup of coffee and a piece of pie at Eddie's, and take them to exactly what they wanted, seven million three hundred thousand later. She never got a customer wrong, the quiet cashmere sweaters in their Bentleys, the Kelly bags in their Maseratis. She never misread a blink. And although they all thought they knew what they wanted, she knew what they didn't know, and what you don't know is always the real truth. Now she stared at Napoléon and Josephine wondering what kind of house they would be in the market for. Every twitch, every flicker of the tail, every glazed-over petulant stare, every sneer of the lip. "That fat one," she said again, watching Napoléon glimmering around, and you could hear the click-click-click of Ettie's knitting needles and the scratching of Doc's pen. "That fat one is an event about to take place. Reminds me of...him," and she was scanning the room and fixing on the spot at the other end of the dining table where Doc sang, "Chew chew chew" to catch his breath and stared at her while he searched for a word.

•

At the close of twilight with the hurricane gone, Ettie went out to check on the rose campion. Here and there, stooping, she was ruthless with a weed. Twigs and branches hadn't taken the place by force, since the tall pines had succeeded in blocking the wind. She stood with her hands on her hips saying, "Well!" to the spread of the garden, went far into one of the corners, where the little gate opened to the horse path. Looking back she could see the roses all correct, if a little bruised, in their beds, the myrtle-strewn lawn blue but clean, the buddleia ready even at this hour to become beclouded with butterflies, and in the distance Doc and Trudy Kay jawing in the yellow cube of the dining-room. What, she wondered, are men and women constantly talking to one another about? What are they trying to accomplish? Now the waning light was slowly turning the green grass to grey, and a lone firefly was announcing a firefly parade, and somewhere in the distance a kid called to another kid to hurry. Life seemed to be sharp and fragrant, even too fragrant, and inexplicable.

•

Doc didn't wait long after Trudy Kay had gone to make a pronouncement. "Not migraine. What she has is disaffection. She might have plain headache. Lots of people have headache. But not migraine. The world isn't going the way she wants it to go. She has a significant amount of want." Ettie had half the dishes done. "Isn't that what you say migraine is, though, dear? Lack of fit?" When he was working on a book, and migraine for Doc was nothing if not a book of books, he paced like a panther, dragging his big dark cat feet with a mug of tea in his hand and a felt pen behind his ear, and he was pacing now. "It's one thing for the world not to be what you want it to be," he said softly, rather lyrically, "and something else for the world to be what you can't understand. I'm gonna drive out and take a look at those trees." The Rover coughed awake. The darkness had cascaded like a curtain at a finale. The roads were poorly marked at the best of times—they were roads on which some of the great minds of the twentieth century had careened to death—and now branches thick as kine were posed at all angles around every curve. Thoughts would come to Doc out of nowhere. Now came this: "It's one thing to identify yourself with a tradition. It's another thing for a tradition to identify itself with you." Then he thought, "Whyever did I have that thought?" But no third thought followed to answer. He took the road slowly, with his high beams on, staring up once in a while at the indigo cup of the sky stuck with rhinestone stars. Once in a while he took a sip from the mask of a portable respirator that was nestled on the passenger seat. "Chew." With the window open he could smell the salt of the sea and the occasional sting of pine. The pond in town, long and thin with a slight elbow, bordered an ancient graveyard. Most of the trees had been spared there. One or two great elms were split down the middle, and one great branch fell across the tranquil water shining bottle green in the street light. But at the head of the pond, where the graveyard opened, two ancient willows had stood long married, silent, comprehending what passed before them upon the grass, upon the roads. One of them was still reaching upward, exaggerating its proudness. The other had been hit not far from where it broke the ground. In one great burden it had come down, the partner seeming not to notice, and the branches were intact upon the grass, and one of the branches lightly dipped into the dark water. Doc pulled over a little awkwardly. He had an impulse to approach one of these trees, something told him it had to be one, not both, but he could not direct himself either to the living or the dead. "Life is a hazardous business," he muttered to himself, and he passed his gaze back and forth between the two old trees but he was thinking—he could not stop thinking—of Ettie and himself. He went slowly back and took some more oxygen and drove off in the direction of the foggy beach road. A cold cone of lamplight fell into the space between the standing and the fallen willow.

•

Ettie was as white as porcelain when he came in. She seized him by the sleeve, something she had never done. "Now dear—I think maybe you should have some oxygen." As if trapped in a foxhole he gaped all round, reaching out in a dream darkness to block an alien horde. "What? What?" It was obvious she was trying to catch her breath, that he had walked in upon a disaster. Alabaster white, she leaned back against the sideboard and made clicking sounds with her tongue. "It's Josephine, dear. She's gone." The words almost gagged her but she said them clearly. For his part, it took Doc some time to run through the long list of names he possessed—friends, dogs, patients, children—so that it was not at all swiftly that he calculated a Josephine. But then he caught the image of her, swimming and then approaching and staring from up close. Staring with huge glaucous eyes. "Utterly impossible," he put on his scientific voice. "Beyond physics." Ettie was in her bathrobe, a loose Japanese thing that exaggerated all of her movements somehow. She was shaking. Her pewter hair that she always wore tightly wrapped was all down to her waist and brushed shiny so that she had become sculptural—he saw suddenly that her clay-coloured lips were beautiful. She was saying, "I've looked and looked, believe me. I've looked in the filter holder—see, under the cap it's a kind of tube affair, but she isn't in there—and in the vegetation, and inside the castle, and behind Napoléon. She isn't to be found." This was surely, he was now concluding, the most preposterous of preposterosities, that a fish could travel, that a fish could go on the road. "Fish don't go. Isn't anywhere for fish to go." There wasn't anything but to make a rigorous examination. He put on his glasses, with the little black band that hung at the nape of his neck, and bent over to come very close to the aquarium glass. Napoléon was motionless behind the two remaining strands of Echinodorus bleheri, with the filtration bubbles streaming past him. There was no other fish, no image of a fish at all. The thought came, "There never was a Josephine. She was all in my imagination." And also, after a moment, "She is only hiding. She is skilful and she is playing Oriental games." And the tactical assessment, "One of the cats came and fished her out with a paw. At this moment she's underneath the sofa, flipping in the dust." All of these were ridiculous, of course. Josephine was in the tank where she should have been. She was in the tank where she always had been. Ettie was having some kind of hallucination. So he sat and calmly looked from each side of the tank, and from the top; and, to cover every base, he made himself bend down in front of the sofa; Josephine was truly nowhere. He waited 30 minutes, gasping, "Chew, chew," staring in a trance—as Napoléon circled and hung—at the cube of beautiful light in which she should have shown herself. Then, with a straight simple little voice that had a knife edge, softly, she plainly enough said, "Napoléon." The chill of the accusation passed somehow into Doc's spine, so that he shivered. Napoléon had still not turned but was waiting, forbearing, like a beast in the jungle. He was not facing them. The digestive system was making regular movements. The eyes were bulging and retreating. The word "monster" came to Doc's lips. The blue mouth opened once, hideously, and closed. "You think Napoléon has eaten her?" But Doc was already concluding Napoléon had certainly eaten her, that she had been taken whole, sucked into that hideous blue mouth, and that now he could even see the outline of her, vaguely printed upon the scintillating blue flank. He thought, too, he could see, as if here, now, in front of his eyes, Josephine being drawn into Napoléon tail-first, Napoléon slowly incorporating Josephine, his eyes almost popping out with the strain of turning her into paste. Yet it was true the world held only solitary Napoléon, swollen blue Napoléon in the greens, a fish becalmed. "I did read on fish," Ettie said flatly. "If this one isn't a fantail it's a veil tail, in which case, cannibalism. The poor sweet koi. It's terrifying." Napoléon chose the moment to move. He made a slow circuit of the tank, very calculating and bloated. "He's a goner," she said and Napoléon stopped swimming as if he had heard her. Doc saw, in a flash, upon Josephine's face as she disappeared into this fish, a ridiculous mask of hope.

•

He sat up half the night with his legal pad and Debussy's "Poissons d'or" cycling on the stereo. It was a problem of trying to establish in a clear sentence the relation between disjunctive language and the fragmentation of the visual field. The felt pen, with its luxurious fluidity, wasn't a help. In the stark fluorescent cube Napoléon kept his position, gagging silently, his greedy eyes swimming in his head. Doc closed his eyes and thought of Japanese mysteries: cherry blossoms like fields of snow; great stone-lined pools filled with massive koi darting in and out of shadows; wooden temples surrounded by stone gardens. He went to the aquarium and confronted the fish man to man. It fixed him with popping, unsatisfied eyes. "Take you down to the beach and throw you in," Doc said to the empty room, "Take you back to the fish store, you can eat the whole tank and sink like a stone." Ettie sat up in darkness thinking of cannibals and cannibalism, fantails and veil tails, how she really did do her reading but one could never read enough, thinking of libraries full of books one didn't have the time to read, thinking it was hopeless. The hurricane, the desecrated trees, the beach winds whipping and screaming, hopeless, all hopeless, the children with their insoluble problems, a hopeless world of fish eating fish. Doc skipped on to Trudy Kay. Trudy Kay was too self-absorbed for migraine, of course. Migraine came to those who have devoted themselves to the world, for whom the world was of so many parts they could not possibly be brought together into a single whole; for whom the sea of the world could become unnavigable. He leaned over as his eyes began to sting with overuse; put one, two, three, four, five pieces into the border of Manet's "Odalisque," and one final piece into her fan.

•

Ettie came down at daybreak to make tea. Outside the light was stretched in thin creamy lines over the widows' walks. This part of the world had been settled in 1630, and virtually nothing had changed. The room was green with morning light. Napoléon and Josephine were swimming in long loops, attending, it seemed desperately, breakfast: dark innocence; pied inscrutability. She saw before she knew, so that for minutes she was staring without a thought in her head. Then, "Where on earth—?" came like an explosion; "How ever—?" But the telephone made an entry. It was Trudy Kay. "I need some boys to clear my trees," came the voice, bubbly but all business, "Probably two boys. I thought you have those neighbours and they have boys. The lawyer. Maybe he'd loan me his boys. I'd pay $5 an hour. To each of them. And I had another thought for the migraine book, if one of you wants to jot it down. Whenever people tell me no, that's when I get it. Yesterday I was at the IGA to get a quart of milk and I asked the girl if she could make change for a hundred and she said not without going to the bank, and that's when I got the migraine. Maybe one of you can make sense of that." The tea Ettie made was Lapsang Souchong, beach beige once the milk was in. She put it on a little oak tray, something Doc had made years and years ago from a trunk he'd found in the forest. She treated herself to a butter cookie. On the patio, she was thrilled to see, the finches that had vanished before the hurricane were back in business again. In perfect silence, next, she offered a teacup to Doc, who was watching the goldfinches hop and chatter through the great window, a smile of certainty shining on his face.

The Cereal Hour

Ettie had three children and married them off in three Junes, June after June after June, at the house where the birds would not stop feeding in the garden. For the weddings, in what became a ritual, Doc gussied up the garden with cedar chips and prodigious plantings of late primula. Owen, who'd come out once a month, came out specially and lugged the cedar chips on his tanned young back. There were always dogs as well, a companionable array of dogs. Because it gave Ettie sadness to see her children grown and leaving, her dogs were always being joined by more dogs, and she nursed her dogs when they were pups as if they were children but at the time when these dogs were grown she acquired new dogs that were pups so she could continue to nurse dogs as if they were children. Through all of this, Doc smoked his cigarillos and catalogued his book and filled the bird feeders in the garden and taught the dogs philosophy. Example: "Language isn't the same as thought, Wilt. Lot of people make the mistake of assuming humans think on a pretty sophisticated level, because they can form complex sentences. But you're a pretty sophisticated thinker in your own right, aren't you, Wilt?" Wilt was the Pomeranian. They were little dogs all, and Ettie's procedure (in the Parisian style) was to let them hop up on her, spend their days doing underneath her chin what it is that resembles a grin—where the side teeth pop out over the lip like fangs and the eyes become kindled—and never, it must be admitted, did they become very well housebroken (they did not become housebroken at all), and she made little cooing, little singing, sounds of approval to them nevertheless, "Ohhh, well! Ohhhhh, well, Miffie! Ohhhhh, well, Snappers! Wilt, Wilt, Wilt, Wilt, Wilt!" as she wiped up after them. She spent her time receiving cheques and paying cheques at the dining-room table when she wasn't phoning Trudy Kay or Ophelia Goldman or knitting or reading catalogues or seeing to the dogs. She went out and planted around an old teak garden bench a puddle of violets with the reassuring thought, "Violets are young."

•

In May, from California, by plane and rental car, for their annual visit, came Babs and Collyer. Said Collyer, with his alien brightness, "There are so many interesting people out here: writers, painters, actors, thinkers. Every time I come I could write a book." And Babs looked up at the sky in the vicinity of Manorville. "There's a little rose colour in the sky here. I've never seen that anywhere else. When I was in second grade I used to go to the beach and paint that. Sometimes I'd stay until the stars came out." And she thought, but didn't say, "Now, of course, it's all strangers." Collyer drove quickly, because he knew Babs was eager to see her friend Juniper again, to be sitting alone with Juniper and talking about the present and the past. He was pulled over by a State Trooper for doing 80, and later Ettie, who was informed of this by Juniper (along with the fact that Juniper had decided they would put off Mother's Day until July) reminded him the speed limit is there for a reason. "Very like a mother," he told himself. "Not a mother but very like." Of Collyer and Babs, Ettie and Doc said to one another, over hot milk, when all of the children had gone to their beds, "Not our children, but very like our children." There existed, after all, air and clouds; the beach; the sea; the dune grass; the rabbits; the hawks; the children. Blood, moment, light, movement, a knapsack, bare feet, seashells, sailboats. All children were everyone's children.

•

Doc was smoking a cigarillo but because of the emphysema he laid the thing down once in a while and applied an oxygen mask to his face. He had six grey-green oxygen tanks—one in his bedroom, one in the dining-room, one in each of the two cars, a portable one he could sling over his shoulder, and one in a corner of the garage. Everyone else at the table waited for him: Ettie fussing with a piece of pink yarn and the dogs grinning up at her in worship; and the kids—Tommy the eldest, a scowler, Juniper the youngest, an optimist, Pamela Anne the one in between, who did needlepoint very very carefully, very very carefully, and Babs who wasn't in the family biologically but was in the family in every other way—

smiling and being polite while Doc breathed. Ellen the maid was running dishwater. She was also in the family, and had been for 40 years. Weariness had taken her over, in fact she was bent over holding onto the edge of the sink, because she had had trouble with one of her boys, police trouble, and she was moving slowly because one of her pelvic bones had taken a hairline fracture. In the living-room were the rest, and it was a crew—Tommy's Alison, who had a tendency to look away and not speak when spoken to, especially to look away from Juniper, with her little Maggie bouncing in a bright red corduroy jumper on one knee; and Pamela Anne's woolly Gareth, scanning through a hang-gliding magazine, whistling at pictures of the action near Alfriston, in England; and Juniper's Harley, his jeans and shirt covered with organic material from the farm, his mind racing with goat prices, his eyes flickering with Tom Brokaw who flickered on the screen before his eyes, still and always young. Juniper's little Charlie did Lego on the floor between his father's feet, occasionally banging a red piece into a yellow one with a yelp. Doc finished breathing, put his apparatus to one side, turned to Collyer who in the kitchen was removing the vestiges of the fluke from the pan in which fluke had been fried for decades. "You say you're doing *what* out there?...He's doin' something in California." Collyer told him dissertation. "Dissertation, mmph! Dissertation on what?" Collyer told him benzyl oxidation. "Hmph!" Doc took the apparatus and did some more breathing, and while he breathed he attempted to cough up phlegm but the procedure was very difficult. "They'll find me dead on the floor," he whispered when he was finished, "Well, life's a hazardous business. Benzyl oxidation...? Yes yes. You mean, *outside* the normal conventions of pressure and temperature. You mean, *intensive* oxidation." "Yes, *intensive*, absolutely," Collyer was overwhelmed; "Yes, yes, very." "Honey—" Doc's eyes were not as bright as they once had been but he was letting them twinkle at Babs, "Babs, your actual name isn't Babs, is it? Babs is a contraction. Your real name is Barbara." He had known Barbara since she and Juniper had been four, so he knew Barbara wasn't really Babs, and he also knew he wasn't to call

Babs Barbara, but he had that twinkle in his eye. She told him for the thousandth time that yes, her name was Barbara, actually. "And,...do you have a middle name?" She reminded him she had grown up in this house. She said, "Eve." He gasped a little for air. "Barbara Eve?" She told him yes, Barbara Eve. "And you're doing a thesis, too?...Everybody's doing a thesis." She was, yes, doing a thesis too, on Dorothy Richardson. "Well well, Dorothy Richardson," he said, "Well well." He looked with calm cool blue eyes at Juniper, who wasn't doing a dissertation on anything. He stood there giving all his concentration to taking another breath. "Then, Barbara Eve—how 'bout you gittin' up and fetchin' me a glass of warm milk?" Ettie had put the yarn down and was letting the yelping dogs out but she laughed a little at him and said, in her chirrupy voice, "You in a William Faulkner novel again, Walter? Walter's very good at adopting and relinquishing that drawl." Harley was fussing with little Charlie, moving his yellow and his red and his blue Lego around and getting him angry, and he was making faces at Tommy's Alison, curious, unintelligible faces, but she was only staring at empty space. "Shall I make coffee, Miz'?" said Ellen, trying to establish her balance. "Yes yes!" the Doc said with flare, and then he needed to breathe again, and the three kids were looking at one another with fettucine still on their lips, and Collyer was smiling so very warmly it was a mystery, and a moment soon came when Doc had finished his breathing and the particular tiny actions of each one of them had come to a hiatus—Barbara Eve was pushing the milk spout back into the milk container—and it was the kind of moment in a gathering, precisely, when an occurrence occurs. Juniper moved her spoon a quarter of an inch further away from her dish of chocolate ice-cream, which sat next to Tommy's vanilla Swiss almond and Babs's plain vanilla and Doc's double fudge almond and Ettie's strawberry and Pamela Anne's strawberry; and said across the table, but loudly enough so that everyone could hear, "Welllll—I suppose I should let everybody know that I'm pregnant." Doc looked up, and he regarded his apparatus as if maybe it should be applied to his face, but he didn't move to apply it.

"What? *Now?* You are *now?*" Ettie was plum laughing. "Wow!" said Tommy, red as cognac at sunset, "Wow! Wow!" The dishwater was loudly running. No-one at all heard Pamela Anne whisper, "So am I. So am I very, very, very."

•

The school had once been a farm but now it was renovated and avant-garde. Babs and Juniper painted it and lay all afternoon in their fifteenth year in the adjacent cornfield looking up at the sky. One day they bared their souls to Rachel, the English teacher, who had been the person responsible for exposing them to T.S. Eliot. "I," Juniper had been adamant, "will never marry. I don't believe in marriage. I can see well enough from my parents what marriage brings. I'm going to be alone, and I don't need to be smothered with children. No husband, no children, no taxations." And to prove this she had taken some women's magazines and composed a little scrapbook of all the pictures of women nursing their children, cooking for their husbands, cleaning up the house. She had titled the scrapbook BULLSHIT and had given it, for Christmas, to Rachel, with an epigraph by T.S. Eliot:

O dark dark dark
They all go into the dark;

which had been responsible for bringing Rachel to a convulsion. As Juniper had rejected marriage, Babs had rejected education, saying, "And I'm not going to college. I'm not reading any more books. I don't care about my academic record. To hell with academic records. To hell with reading." Rachel, to give her a little credit, on the day of their graduation had taken them aside and made a prediction: "This is where you'll be in fifteen years. Juniper will be married, and she will be cleaning her house and making dinner for her husband and taking care of their little children. And Babs will be getting a Ph.D." "Dear Rachel," Babs now thought to herself, although she said, not without irony, staring at pregnant Juniper, "Extraordinary!" "What?" replied Doc, "What's extraordinary?...Thinks something is extraordinary. What, my Juniper? Not extraordinary at all"—for he had truly read her mind. "My Juniper is very far from extraordinary. She's natural. Juniper's had a very hard time of it, you know. Charlie is a real attention-getter and Maxwell, with his learning problem, needs her constantly, and she's a wonderful mother. Really she is. She gives both of them a really enormous amount of support, and at the same time she's very helpful to Harley which is difficult in itself because he's so busy with the farm and his schedule is so unpredictable. But she's really an ideal mother, and you can tell, by the way Charlie and Maxwell behave with her, that her tone and her approach are just right. I don't think, in other words, that man could ask for a better estate." Then Babs watched him draw the oxygen apparatus closer and put the mouthpiece over his nose and lips and she observed the bubbling in the humidifier and the variegated birds feeding on the patio outside the window. He was wearing a bright red viyella shirt, and when he finished his breathing she heard that he made repetitive sounds into the air, "Chew...chew...chew," which corresponded exactly to the sounds made on the branch of the spruce tree by the proud cardinal.

•

A marathon Raisin Bran toss was on, between little Maxwell, little Charlie, very little Maggie and big Gareth, although little Maxwell was cheating with a big box of Cheerios. Gareth was virtually moulded over, he was a maquette of himself all stretched on the floor, the Raisin Bran coating his face and the Cheerios dropping off from the Raisin Bran at all angles, but Pamela Anne, peering over a Smith and Hawken catalogue, was ebullient with disapprobation. "Really! How profoundly out of place! I should have thought, Gareth, dear, you'd see yourself above such business!" Juniper thought she would split if she didn't whisper to Babs, "*Dear* Gareth hasn't been off his leash in years," a comment Pamela Anne, spying a trio of pearwood pencil boxes, couldn't tell herself she hadn't heard.

•

"I've known all along she wanted more than two," Ettie said, lighting up. The cigarette was something she waved and stared at, but not something she much brought to her mouth. "It's just—well, that it's not exactly clear whether—well, it's never been really clear whether—Harley—is a long-term investment." Doc looked askance at her: "See, there you go inserting yourself again." She sat up and turned away and enunciated—but while staring hard at something or other on the tablecloth—"I'm not doing that at all. I am simply aware that there have been problems. Perhaps irresolvable problems." He lit up, too, and smoked a great deal, and then breathed and said, "Just...withdraw." "Well, now, really," there was a protest in her voice, but only a very little, and modest, protest, "I'm not sure I see what you're getting at, at all, here," and since it was at moments like this that one took most comfort from one's knitting she stood up, not without difficulty, because of that left knee which had been getting worse and worse from June to June to June, and brought her knitting to sit with and give her comfort. "I'm saying," said Doc, "I'm saying...," and he waited so that she would be able to taste and relish every syllable of it, "This is her cereal hour." A face crept onto the surface of Ettie's head. "Her *what?*" "Cereal, from Ceres. Goddess of fertility. A woman goes through a period when reproduction is on her mind." Ettie smiled a little to herself at that one. "Reproduction—is that what you call this? Well—" "Look," he was as definitive as a judge on this, and this was certainly nothing if not a courtroom, "Look. There *is* a body of knowledge in medicine. And I *am* a doctor. You sometimes forget that. I am a doctor who is privy to a rather well-developed body of medical knowledge. She is going through her cereal time. He's a capable father, he can make arrangements to provide. She's happy." Ettie didn't know whether or not this was a moment to speak, but she did have the direct and reliable sense that it might be interesting to know whether men also had a cereal hour; and also the direct and reliable information that Harley's provision was hardly substantial, nor what a reasonable person could call a good investment. And she knew—although there was no need to say—a thing or two about money. And there had been—she did open her mouth and say—there had distinctly been, problems. "What in the hell sort of *problems?*" said Doc, "What in the damned hell sort?" But she had gone three stitches too far without changing wool.

-

Babs had to wonder about Doc and Ettie whether they had always been like this, the way they were, the way they discernibly were. They talked but they didn't connect, that was a certainty, and they danced in a brilliant choreography—if at a slow pace—without colliding ever, without disturbing the air molecules around each other. Had Doc and Ettie ever been cozy, as she was with Collyer, had they been snugglers and jokers? She and Collyer were snugglers and they were jokers, watchers and wigglers. They knew how to sit and look at a Modigliani. An aria from Mascagni or Puccini or Debussy was always afloat around them. But Doc and Ettie had no music, there was never music, and there was never a mention of Modigliani. Had they been young, but suddenly one afternoon decided it was time for serious business? Had Ettie left Doc to finger his manuscripts and quiz his patients, had she retreated into her sweaters and her catalogues, her children's lives, the nightly news, pruning the roses? Had they made an agreement in writing, signed it in blood?

-

The room in which Doc Savage worked was a small one: he liked, for inspiration, to keep it a mess. It had once been Juniper and Pamela Anne's room, and they had slept there in beds covered with yellow and blue spreads. On Juniper's bed his book was squatting in the form of a metropolis of index cards. Around and upon Pamela Anne's was a vast display: there were coffee mugs with dried milk and tongue depressors for stirring—hundreds of them. There was a stainless steel bowl that had held cat food, where a plump roach had drowned in what had been fresh beef gravy. There were copies of *The Nation*, very old copies. There were four pairs of scissors and a pile of half a dozen plexiglas picture frames, all empty. There was household oil. There was a thermometer and a boxed set of Trollope's Palliser novels in paperback. There were multi-coloured plastic tubs containing Doc's indexes in five incarnations. The walls were covered with cork boards on which coloured tacks had been spread. There were some Agatha Christie paperbacks on a bookshelf and a jar of pencils, mostly not sharp, and a jar of Vaseline, and a space heater on the floor. Peeping from beneath one of the bedspreads were three packs of cigarillos. There was a mirror. There was an Elvis Presley recording in a foxed and faded jacket. There was a box for a Polaroid SX-70 Alpha camera without a camera in it but with the instruction booklet. Doc paced around this room, brought himself coffee, wheeled in his oxygen, smoked a cigarillo. Once in a while he settled himself to indexing, but he indexed rarely. He turned ideas over and over in his head, or he turned notions, which would become ideas when they had matured or aggregated with one another. Doc could be a precise man with language and he thought it was important to distinguish one from the other, an idea and a notion. He frequently said so to visitors, who might settle themselves in the house and then perk up with an *idea* for something or other. "*Notion*, really, is what you mean. *Idea*'s more complicated than a notion. *Notion*'s kind of elementary, kind of natural, uncomposed, rather the building block *out of which* ideas are made." Doc was sitting on the bed one morning with the blue spread, the bed that had been Pamela Anne's bed, when the telephone rang in the downstairs room. There was an extension he could pick up, and pick up silently if quickly, and quickly he picked it up. Juniper. She began: "—leaving."...*Who am I leaving?*, he thought, and he coughed hard. *What are you telling me, Juniper?* But then he realized Juniper wasn't talking to him, because Ettie was on, saying, "Uh huh, uh huh." Juniper wasn't talking to him, and it wasn't he that was leaving. So who was leaving? Who was leaving whom? "I have tried to hold it together, Mom. Tried everything. We've seen a marriage counsellor." Doc went red and hot. *Goddamn it to hell, what fuckin' marriage counsellor?* "He's seeing someone else. It's been going on for—" "Ohhhh," moaned Ettie, "Ohhh, yesss." But Juniper didn't want to hear Ettie moan. "She's—get this, Mom—eighteen. He says he just wants to be friends with her and there are moments when I don't know if I should believe him. I just wish you could *know* these things. You can't know. You can't know." Shoot his kneecaps off, Doc said to himself. One kneecap, then the other kneecap. But then, moving the camera of his thought away from Harley's kneecaps, bleeding, shattered, he looked at Harley's face, a young face, white with agony with his kneecaps off, and reconfigured his mind: Harley was just a boy trying to get his problems straightened out, being rushed into responsibility. Harley was like a sapling, needed time to make leaves. And what was that, he wondered with precision, a notion or an idea? And as long as the boy was a good husband in general, and a decent enough farmer, well—? Women sometimes demand too much. Juniper was certainly, if ever there was one, a demanding woman. Yes yes. He and Harley would just have to have a little talk some time, just come to an understanding. Not that Harley had ever seemed to have a lot to talk about. But he was a good listener. That boy was one of the best damn listeners Doc had ever seen. Juniper would just have to learn to recognize a man for his strengths. Doc Savage smiled to himself as, having settled all this, he put the phone down noiselessly. He therefore failed to catch Ettie issuing some therapy. "Juniper sweetheart, you can come anytime and live back here with Daddy and me."

•

What Juniper had been planning that the old man hadn't heard, or at least what she had been thinking about planning—because for Juniper the thought was always immeasurably far from the act—was that she would leave it all behind, Harley, the house, the animals, the chil—. On the children she had to stop cold and see that separation was completely impossible. She stopped very cold. But the one who decided to move in the end was Harley, all the way to northern Washington, cold northern Washington, under the volcano, as it were, because for some reason the eighteen-year-old—whose name (Harley had been struck with awe by this, and Juniper still had a hard time not bursting) was Replete—had a yen to go where Jack Nicholson had gone in *Five Easy Pieces*; to go there and, as Jack had done rather sensitively, play the piano, although, of course, she had never touched a keyboard in her life. But then she changed her mind and said, as the very young will, "Big Sur, Big Sur, Big Sur!" Harley, at any rate, vanished into the mist. And, more or less at the same time (and from the same airport), Babs and

Collyer were flying back to Palo Alto, back to thesis-and-veggieburgerland, so Juniper drove over to spend the afternoon with Babs at Doc and Ettie's—Doc and Ettie's was where Babs and Collyer always stayed, of course—to have her hour, which was the hour, to be honest, she lived for, when it was possible to go back in time to the forest of dearly cherished mysteries that was youth. Babs had been certain that eventually Juniper would want to actually talk about Harley, proceed from phrases to complete sentences, that Juniper might explain what on earth it had been that Harley did to light her up, but instead Juniper talked at length about having children. Or, not even that. She talked about the intricacies of daily routine, the tiny invisible things that always turned into mountains. Charlie sleeping with his sheet stuffed into his mouth. Maxwell asking for pudding. While she went on, Charlie cried softly, even politely, for something to do: one of these days, she said, this behaviour would drive her crazy. Maxwell always liked to eat off Juniper's plate, which Babs found charming but Juniper kept saying she wished he'd stop. And the reason she had him in his green outfit was because he slept better in the green one than in the blue one, but she couldn't explain this but she was wondering about it, and wondering, really, *why* she couldn't explain it, because you'd think a thing like that would be something you could explain, I mean, sleeping better in green than in blue. And she told of his different ways of crying, depending on what he wanted, his sob, his mope, his rant, his trauma, his incantation. Charlie walked around to Babs and let her play with his hair. The fancy Burgundian stew Collyer had whipped up did not, for some reason, appeal to anybody but Collyer, who was eating it with French bread virtually stale. Juniper, while she talked, ate potato chips. "He doesn't know the difference yet between Harley's voice and other men's voices on the telephone," Juniper was talking about Maxwell again, "but in person it's different. Harley can do imitations, he can imitate Jimmy Stewart for instance, but Maxwell always knows it's him. That's one thing Harley does perfectly—Jimmy Stewart." The kids took naps. "I have trouble," Juniper said, "realizing Maxwell's not a baby anymore.

I keep thinking he's two, it's like I've only learned how to go a certain distance and I just keep circling around and going back again and again. I certainly keep wishing he were a baby, that's true, because they're so easy to take care of, they just seem to float wherever you go like a delicious living bubble. And then they start taking...shape." To illustrate, she opened a book of pictures of African animals and giggled at the baby hyenas that came on the page after the depressing pictures of the elephants' graveyard.

•

With Maxwell on her lap Juniper talked about how babies fall asleep, and also come awake, more easily than adults seem to do, and she was bouncing him up and down, and Charlie came near her with his careful lapis eyes upon the baby. But she wasn't watching Charlie and moved when he moved. His hand grazed the baby's soft head. "Charlie! Don't you hit your brother! Don't you dare hit your brother! You say I'm sorry Max! You say I love you Max! We love our little brother! We don't hit our little brother!" Babs called him and put her arms around him and knew that he had meant only to move himself close to Juniper, to put his golden head against Juniper, and that there was no way to tell Juniper this at all. And then Babs knew in a darkness that time had changed Juniper, and time had changed her as well. They had emerged from the forest into the light. She couldn't tell Juniper anything.

•

But as with everything in life, what Babs felt was more precise than it seemed, even to a precise mind. More precisely, Babs no longer wanted to be here for this Savage time. She had wanted it once, certainly enough, the special, brilliant warmth and the envelopment, and had booked the flight with a spark of genuine enthusiasm. And it was true that in her talks, her long talks, with Juniper, which as often as not had in late years come to be situated on the telephone, she could still, after more than twenty years, sail happily. But now to visit Sunday was lamely to discover oneself in a position, an awkward, if not less comfortable, position within the—what could you call it but—fracas of Savage life.

Opinions, for one thing, would be legion there, to such a degree that one could not contemplate for lack of perspective, could not discern for the sheer rush of inchoate thought, and opinions would be unorganized; controversies would be spontaneous. More: analysis would confront every molehill, so that life in this company, in this perduring conversation, in this tank of thought, was utterly textual, was like reading dozens of footnotes, footnotes to footnotes, and arguing like a lawyer. Difficulties—this was the feature that both captivated and stunned her—would grow up in every corner, upon every consideration, so that one would inevitably wonder, only days into an excursion there, how the Savages survived, indeed, how Sunday itself survived, when she was not there to funnel the eager and scandalous talk, the gratuitous anxieties about one another's plans for the future—the future!...plans for even a cup of tea!—and their lively wonderment. Why could Pamela Anne not agree to just show up for the beach picnic even though she didn't have the right kind of bathing suit, for example, because, after all, lots of people don't worry about what they wear to the beach? Or even more perplexing, why couldn't everybody—this was Juniper's plaint—why couldn't everybody just tolerate the fact that Pamela Anne didn't show up at the beach picnic, instead of making a federal case about it, since nobody really likes beach picnics so very much anyway? Why, in short, were people so strange and inexplicable? Yet this was precisely the kind of song that Babs, having heard it, could not get out of her mind, the virus that felled her, since the strangeness of people was their charm in the end, and certainly the fact of nature, and there was hardly reason to be continually wondering about it. The fact, taken alone, that every morning each of the family had to know where the other ten were, and where the other ten were going to be, and why the other ten were going to be there; or that Byzantine shuttling arrangements had to be concatenated whereby couplings and triplings and quadruplings could be made for one or another local hike—to buy a scarf, to get vitamins, to pick up film, to return a book to the Free Library; or that all of these recipes were at each moment subject to wholesale revision; or that no-one knew until the event how many bodies to expect at dinner, which Collyer would as likely as not be cooking, although he, too, was supposed to be on holiday, drove her to nothing but caffeine; and doses of it; so that within a day and a half she was electric with sensibility. She came positively to crave California. To be able to sit through an afternoon saying to oneself, in a warm swimming-pool, "There is nothing I must do!" To look up at the coconut palms and think, "No strange behaviour to explain, no persistent riddle to unravel." To be able routinely to inhale jojoba. To eat freshly brewed yoghurt. To think about ecology instead of mothering, to think about *anything* instead of mothering, because here in Sunday she had thought, or at least had spoken, of very little else, as if mothering were life; as if she knew anything worth telling about mothering; but also as if mothering had to be explored, talked about, revealed, inspected, as if mothering were a Mystery. She knew that if ever she were a mother, it would happen and she would devote herself to it, simply and carefully. But it would not be necessary to make of mothering a project, a circus of complication and involvement in which multitudes had to participate and opinions and philosophies had to dominate. "Yes yes yes!" Doc came in, mumbling of who knew what, "Hazardous business." He was meandering around the room as she was making this little estimation to herself, and the emphysema was making him rather bark. "Yes yes! Clams for dinner! Get me some clams, make a chowder! You like chowder, Barbara Eve? You ever eat my clam chowder? Best clam chowder in the East. Maybe anywhere. Maybe instead you want lobster? You want lobster, just say so!" She didn't say so, but she did want lobster. Collyer, who was reading the paper, was lascivious in the face of lobster, but he said only, "Adolfo Celi died. He was the bad guy in *Thunderball*, or was it *You Only Live Twice*?" which sent Doc off coughing. You didn't, Barbara Eve knew with a pang, live twice; and it wasn't that she wanted to be in California, either, because California was a motion and she wanted a fixity. She wanted to go live on a Japanese island and dive for pearls. And Collyer wanted to live on a Swedish island with a wooden bowlful of pears beside his bed, just like in *The Passion of Anna*. Or was it *The Touch*? Green small pears, a polished pine bowl. She wanted to sit on a misty beach laid with fat stones and meditate. But here, here and now, Savages were always making—then analyzing—crisis: a stew of crisis: a garden. Everything had to have a theory. Doc shuffled back with a piece of manuscript dangling from his hand and saw Barbara Eve, who truthfully looked as if not a word were passing through her head, and said, "At six o'clock it's going to rain. Now, I don't generally believe the forecast, and the forecast said chance of rain, so I think we'll have rain for sure. Bad rain. I can smell it. And that will be the end of our beautiful summer. Do you believe in forecast? Probability is always 50-50." The next morning it didn't rain but Tommy and Alison had another fight, this one cold as ice, and drove off back to Connecticut in a cloud of dust. "He could have that carburetor looked at," Gareth said very mildly, and Pamela Anne looked up, bright as an owl, and said, "Ummmm."

•

It looked like rain for weeks but still it didn't rain. Doc finally drove out and came back with a hundred pounds of thistle seed, Niger seed, and put it in string-woven pouches for the gold finches and the gold finches came with purple finches and with grackles and with a female pheasant who pranced with grace. He breathed in his machine and turned it off and walked around among the great pine trees. "Chew...chew...chew." Ettie was watching him through the big window. "Get that book finished!" she whispered, with her cigarette smoke curling urgently in a vortex and her coffee cooling. On her face it seemed she was gazing into an abyss.

•

The end of summer. Since Pamela Anne and Gareth, in Paris, were exhausting themselves preparing for their baby, the arrival of whom had now been made quite public, Doc and Ettie, to give them some comfort, took the Concorde; and Babs flew out from California again, to live at the big house. Everything had been put away: the magazines, the coffee mugs, the thick files of notes, the packets of pineapple hard candy; the mail, the bulging tomatoes; the knitting; the telephone messages on long paper strips like encephalograms; the six grades of pruning shears. She watered the jades and the jasmines and the jacarandas and fed the dogs and put seed for the birds and cut the grass around the pear tree, the cherry tree, the bird bath. She called California and told Collyer how quiet it was, that he should tighten the gears on her mountain bike. The great house, because nobody was fluttering in it, and though it was bright, felt desolate. Barbara Eve sat down for the weekend and read through Doc's book on jokes and mental processes, the pages of which were a palimpsest for his annotations. (What would he do, publish the old thing over again, restlessly, in completely new form? And what of the new manuscript, or could you call it a manuscript, or what could you call it?) Carefully, in all of the many rooms she did not plan to use, she laid white dropsheets over the furniture; and the lambent sun turned them pink, and golden, and later mauve, and covered them with a dumbshow of shadow that was different every day. The place was like an estate made vacant, as at the end of *The Cherry Orchard*, and she remembered how at once, on the morning of the flight, everyone had been here in a turbulence of intention; and how there had been tears; and Juniper had gone off with the children in one car, and Harley in a second, and Tommy and Alison with Maggie in a third, once again as if they had been having a fight, and Ettie's old crony Trudy Kay had in neighbourliness brought an apple cake that didn't get eaten and had driven off, finally, in a fourth car and in a fourth direction to sell some beach property for just short of five million dollars. Then Doc and Ettie had taken seats at the great table and had looked at one another resolutely, as if marking the end of a century. And they had nodded. And Doc had gone out, rather in a flash, with his oxygen on wheels and his great tweed coat, and Ettie had turned around once or twice in the kitchen before following him. Babs had heard her call, from outside, "Goodbye to all!" And the sound had rung in the air and slowly died, and the car drove off, and there was silence, and a bird called, and there was silence. After what seemed an endless moment, perhaps half an hour, there was a sound at the door and in walked a young man with a knapsack, eating an orange. "I'm Owen," said he, "Where's everybody?" He looked Babs up and down, smiled a little, inhaled the silence. She told him, and he said oh, this was his weekend to come out and help but that was all right, he'd just go back into the city again. "There are plenty of beds, you can certainly stay the night," Babs said, but after drinking a cup of tea with her and filling up all the bird feeders, methodically, one after another, he just picked up his sack and headed for the station. It was Friday, he said, and everybody would be coming out so nobody would be going back to town and the train ride would be quite pleasant. Babs took herself down to Sunday main beach, when the afternoon was about done, the eastern sky foreboding, the waves trumpeting onto the wide hard sand and throwing blankets of yellow foam. Gulls swooped and strutted, seemed to mock her. Some of the sand had been turned up by the trucks the fishermen drove early in the morning. She breathed the stinging salt air and threw her head back to get a better taste of the wind. The soles of her feet knew every step of the beach closely. When she had been young, when everything in the world had been different, this had been an empty beach. Nobody came here and trampled the dune grass. Now things had changed. You had to keep your eyes open. You closed into yourself. It had become almost dark. She thought she saw a couple riding bikes in the dunes about half a mile ahead, but it might have been birds. In front of her, a yard off, she found a pristine sand dollar. Its ivory white face was etched with petals; on a thin chain it would be wonderful around Collyer's dark neck. She kept walking holding it in the palm of her hand. She came to the bikes now, tangled upon one another on a pathway that cut the dune, and saw beyond them the nest of legs, and could hear the girl recklessly laughing. She turned into her own cold footsteps. When she came back, Ettie's daffodil garden was barely luminous against the pewter sky. A pair of indigo buntings was in the cherry tree, one brown and one as blue as the sea. They too would mate and there would be chicks before winter came.

PART 2

Sand

On the Lido sand was copious, but one was not enchanted with the sand. The sand called to mind—albeit dilute—the stench of Venice. One did not wish stenches with one's sand. One wished purity, one wished an apotheosis of texture, one wished for one's childhood. The pain of this was inextinguishable, unbounded, a form of lust. Olga wished for her childhood, now and frequently, flicking her toes in the impudent sand. This was not sand for filtering through hourglasses, nor holy sand. The sand said, "Empire. Antiquity"—with quite a pronunciation—which was all very good but brutal and dry, and she wanted something more than that, the ocean that came slowly rolling and toward which one could cha-cha. What were power and time, after all, in the absence of delight? What was anything? She gazed. There was the Principessa, ensconced upon the sand, everything and all of royalty here and forever. She had been dipping with Oleg and was now a croquette, all evenly dusted and brown, and frowning: "Daddy, Daddy, Daddy, Daddy!" A distant little police siren. He placed her on his shoulders. "Daddy, Daddy, Daddy, Daddy, Daddy!" His shoulders were very high up, and Olga thought the lass would be a goner, she even pictured the kid stuck in the sand like an ostrich, the legs kicking for a moment, and she wondered why she had ever married a man who was interchangeable with a giraffe. You could walk him to the zoo and pen him in with some nice edible trees and bring the giraffe to Venice. The sun was merciless. Oleg's shoulders were burnt crimson so that the Principessa left white marks on them as she bounced. "Walk her by the waterline," said Olga and he complied, with a little shuffle, and then she said, "Bounce her up and down some more, she's having a transcendental experience," and he complied again. "Bounce her up and down! Bounce her up and down! There she is! There's the Queen of the Adriatic!" He was marvellously compliant as she sang, he was trained. "The kid," she thought, was a goner. "Why did I marry a man like this?" The sand was hot where he bounced and it burned his feet and he started making faces. He smiled the broad egregious smile of the lonely. The Principessa was still breast feeding when she should have been ready for martinis. Now she had the misfortune to look down, see how far away land was. She cried hideously and Olga took her to a breast, but not without a comment: "I will take this child to my breast. But I will be suckled to death by this child." The child went immediately to sleep. "Put a towel around me, for God's sake," said Olga, "Put a towel around me, these are private breasts." Oleg led her into the cabana where there were towels and cool sand. The sand was cool and utopian where Olga sat, under a stream of red and yellow sunlight, but there were tiny obsessive insects in the damp cool sand. She wished to be in the air far, far from insects. "I do love Venice," said she, "but I hate Venice. I loathe Venice. I wish Venice would sink. I pray every night, I say, 'Dear God, sink Venice.' Venice is like a womb from which I can never escape." Oleg, who had indeed paid for Venice, was saddened, and he said, quite sadly, "This afternoon I will get you a nice cup of cappuccino, with some nice cake, and I will make arrangements to take us away. Where would you like to go? We still have two days." He went into the water while she thought. It was warm and alternately grey and turquoise, and he threw himself around like a boy, thinking primarily in nouns: "Cupola. Stripes. Clams." "I have to admit," Olga said to him as he came out grinning, "I have never seen you make such a fool of yourself as you do in Venice. What we will do is, hit London. I can have a decent cup of tea. A decent cup of tea, Oleg, is worth more than one can say. We can do theatre. Sidewalk buffoons will alleviate my overwhelming sadness. We'll take the Principessa to the Tower, and show her the room where heads rolled." The Principessa slept, dreaming of bears emerging from a forest where a man was singing at a piano, "La la la, ho ho ho, won't you come with me?"

•

Why was she sad? Olga had not, in this life, received; but she lived with the idea that every other person was subject to receptions. As far as she could see it, life for other people was a continuous stream of merits, and they were unceasing beneficiaries; compliments, bank drafts, adoration, blini at the Russian Tea Room. Olga suspected there was no limit to the adoration other people received, or to the caviar that came with their blini. She received scant adoration; and no caviar; although she was allergic to caviar and once in a while Oleg did say, "You are a most wonderful wife. I will not be slapping you with a lawsuit." But where, indeed, was the big reward, *el premio grande*? Where was the stretch limousine? Even now, it is true, while she sat alone on her Venetian bed—her too-ample Venetian bed draped with white Venetian linen—thinking about her unfortunate position in life, and about sheets she was not at the moment buying on a platinum Amex card at Bloomingdale's, and monogrammed silver mint salvers she was not buying at Tiffany, and lunch she was not eating at the Bergamasque East, all the sacrifices she had made so that she could be here in Venice merely thinking about them, tall pink Oleg was outside in the street, being accosted by an amicable Berliner in a T-shirt the colour of goldenrod who exclaimed, "Mein Gott, but you are Chimmy Schtewart! You are the doppelgänger of Chimmy Schtewart!" Oleg was always Someone, while she was never anyone. A horsefly looked more like Jimmy Stewart. She certainly didn't want to be told she looked like anyone, that wasn't it, but she did want, at the very least, to be served from platters, international platters. Crêpes from Taillevent. Little beefy cakes from Simpsons on the Strand. Torte from Sachers. Why should these necessities of life be withdrawn from her, and so interminably? Oleg was not only prosperous but also generous, and this smote her. He had time for everyone while she felt she would be pressed to death by unfulfilment. And how could he have time for everyone unless he were stealing time—this had to be said—from her? How? The world had Oleg around its finger and she had—what did she have, in fact? It felt as if she had...spiderwebs. She was a butterfly caught in a spider's web. The spider would make a meal of her. She, meanwhile, needed a meal. She needed many meals, lined up in a gastronomic parade. About this hunger Doc Savage, a meritorious psychiatrist if ever there was, had been outspoken to the point of rudeness, emphasizing that there was something unresolved in her relation with her father. She paid him the rather exorbitant sum he charged for his sessions—that is, she commanded Oleg to pay him—and told herself psychiatry was a load of claptrap and that Doc was an insidious provocateur for sending her bills. "You wanted to devour your father, but you didn't dare. It's basic mythology." Doc noticed she never paid him attention and thought that proved he wasn't charging enough. But Doc didn't matter here in Venice near the cold grey sand. He was in her mind, also trapped in the spiderweb, and no-one would find him.

•

It is impossible to know how, in the airplane that was taking them from Venice, the decision came to be prompted. Even Olga did not see with clarity in her own mind the patterns that configured it. But when they had climbed at rather a steep angle for rather a long time, producing in her a sense of nausea unequalled by the many other senses of nausea she could recollect having experienced, the many senses which made up the mosaic of nauseations which was her life; and when they had turned toward London; she thought suddenly that she had to have good sand, perfect sand, that she had been denied it—that it had evaded her—all of her life. "I have an appetite for sand," she said out of nowhere, and Oleg, who in his snores had been rowing a gondola on the Canale del Brenta, turned to her. The little reading lights were on, casting pristine pyramids of illumination onto his lap where the Principessa was asleep. "In November," he snored quietly, "We can go to Puerto Vallarta," meaning, "I am given to understand you would like to be on a beach somewhere soon." She smiled toleration. It was a penance to have such a husband, but what had been her sin? She felt squashed, and also a little giddy, and suddenly realized that she was going to throw up. She made an exit to that space that pretends to be a room, and put her hands in soapy water in the basin. When she came back she spoke with a great deal more reserve, and the kind of smoothness one hears from chief magistrates. "November is tomorrow. I don't need sand *domani*, hypothetically, proactively. It might be nice to have it in November, but I need it now. My need is coterminous with my experience. I need it today. Get me sand." The Principessa gave a little snort and an eye popped open. "Daddy, Daddy!" "Daddy's going to get us sand," Olga said, settling back into sleep. Oleg waited a full ten minutes and then took his life in his hands and nudged her exactly at the point where the aircraft was passing over Dusseldorf. "There's no sand of the kind you want in England," said he, "They have grit. We'd probably have to go back to Venice. It's a pity I didn't know when we were still there, at the Lido, sitting on the sand, that you wanted sand." She fixed him with a Medusa gaze. "You actually awakened me, you actually elbowed me awake, in order to tell me that? And I have an incipient migraine. Airplanes always give me migraine, you know this, Oleg. That was migranation with intent. Furthermore, this airplane is disgusting. It's a wonder I didn't get a migraine just looking at it. The Principessa gives me migraine when she says, 'Daddy, Daddy.' It's too much. And as for Venice, it's history. How can you put Venice on the table at a time like this?" He let her fall asleep again, and waited for the Principessa to fall asleep as well, before he struggled under the Principessa's snoring form and drew out his chequebook, opened it on the little drop table, examined the beautiful little numbers in the pristine little pyramid of white light.

•

Life was bullish on possibilities but bearish on guarantees. The only possibility with a guarantee was the Côte d'Azur, and this meant turning around at Heathrow and paying three and a half times what it would have cost to fly there directly from Venice. They had been many times to Venice but never to the Riviera, so he chose Nice. There was, according to Schwartz at the office, a wonderful, if exorbitant, hotel and, also according to Schwartz, decent ice-cream and, according to Schwartz's secretary Alda, palm trees. The Principessa was in love with palm trees, especially if it could be claimed they were full of monkeys; and what child, he thought, holds a father to a claim? They landed at night, and the air was intoxicating and flowery, and the sound of lapping waters filled the taxi that took them to the hotel. "Monkeys!" cried the Principessa a little desperately. The air was full of orange blossom, and mimosa, and lavender. "Monkeys!!!" The hotel had a coffee shop where you could get ice-cream sundaes at eleven o'clock at night. It was Eden. However, when the sun came up in the morning it became apparent that there were neither monkeys in the palm trees nor sand at the beach. "No-sand-at-the-beach?" said Olga, "What can this mean? Are we in Hell? Can this be a hoax? Can this be a practical joke, Oleg, that you are playing on me while I succumb to migraine? The one sandless beach on earth? You are pushing me to the edge." Oleg was himself confounded that on something meritorious of being named a beach sand might not be supplied, but he was able to draw into a packet the reasoning powers of his mind. "It can mean pebbles," he said, gazing at the sea of pebbles that led down to the Baie des Anges. The waters were jewel bright, and the empty palm trees were swishing all along the Quai des Anglais, but it meant pebbles from the road to the waterline, big fat hot pebbles, and as well most of the bathers were topless. "Topless!" said Olga. "Topless, mein Gott in Himmel!" Was she gasping or developing asthma? "I cannot go topless when I have migraine. I have breasts. I am self-conscious. I will implode." They tried the beach at any rate, because one goes to beaches, but the Principessa was uncomfortable lying on the pebbles—so that Olga kept saying, "Brilliant, Oleg! Brilliant plan! Brilliant recreational management!!!" The Principessa became more alienating by making a castle out of pebbles for a spider. Olga said if you couldn't produce sand with a chequebook you could certainly do it with your mouth. She was possessed of a very little French, whereas Oleg had only a very little Italian, so she took matters into her own hands, said to the concièrge, with her sunglasses upon her nose, "*Mon* husband...*a fait un erreur. Mon* husband...*pense que je désire la Riviera, mais je désire...je désire....*" The French people could be quite impossible The beast was just staring at her, as if she were lunatic, and she couldn't drag up the word for sand to save her life. She looked it up in that pathetic little thing Oleg had bought in an orgasm of stupidity at Heathrow, that had been published originally in 1954 and been reprinted a hundred times and still didn't have the French word for migraine. There it was, at any rate. *"Je désire le sablé." "Ahhhh!"* the man stood back in his tuxedo and made a quite wonderful smile, *"C'est que vous cherchez des sablés!"* It was only a matter of two blocks, he said—or she understood—and then she would be happy. *"Tout droit, tout droit, tout droit,* and you will be perfectly satisfied." They certainly went to the right, and to the right, and to the right, and to the right, and came right back to the hotel, where a woman scrubbing the marble in the lobby said, *"Oui, oui, tout droit!"* "I don't think *'tout droit'* means to the right," Oleg whispered, but what did he know. It meant straight ahead, of course, and they found out after circling around to the hotel two more times and running into a fat little man from Niagara Falls who had a better dictionary and also a street map. The place, apparently, was called Nièpce. Odd, but it wasn't near the water, it was on a street in old Nice full of stores. "Follow me, Oleg. My mind has been boggled. Sand." It was very hot and the sun was high. He had the Principessa on his shoulders and she was crying, "Daddy, Daddy, Daddy! I want monkeys! I want monkeys NOW!" When they had walked two blocks Oleg was convinced Olga was Hannibal and he was an elephant. He thought to himself, "We're going to find sand. We're going to find sand." Then there was the sign: NIÈPCE, right ahead, yellow and green. Sand! But Nièpce was a bakery. Inside there was a beautiful little display of sugared shortbreads marked "Sablés." Olga realized she abominated the French, a nation of torturers. "Oleg," she said, very sweetly, "Can't you do anything right?"

•

The sands were in Cannes, only a few miles off. They rented a car. There were palm trees on the beach. Oleg looked up and could have sworn he saw a monkey, a great orange gorilla kind of monkey, and the Principessa made him take her up and down the beach so they could scan each and every tree. Most of the bathers spoke Arabic and had skin the colour of topaz. The waters were clear, and there were sailboats, and someone somewhere used an organ to play enchanting songs like "I Love Paris." "Oooo-la-la," said Olga, because this was the epitome of epitomes and she loved the French, the French were all heroes. Or at least the most cultured people on earth. She had picked up from a charcuterie called La Sonnambule some cold poached salmon and some *macedoine* of vegetables and some herring and some fried potatoes, some leeks vinaigrette, some *salade de riz sauvage*, some beets mixed with blood oranges. She sat up now and examined the sand by letting some of it rain through her fingers coated with PABA. It was thin sand, it was white, it was silky. Gourmet sand. It glowed. There were no flecks of detritus. It did not exert a gravitational force upon the bottom part of her stomach. She was in love. She touched it with her toetips. It was Cannes sand. Sean Connery had stepped in it barefoot. Brigitte Bardot. Montgomery Clift. She dipped it upon her thighs, coolly. It was aristocratic sand. She sniffed it. That great emptiness came into her, the ultimate emptiness. What lovely emptiness! The Principessa was now lapping in the waves with her father, high up on his shoulders and screaming with joy. Olga realized what had to be done with this sand.

•

"We must bag this sand," she said. "This sand mussen in baggen goen." He didn't understand but he acted, which was the great fact about Oleg, his modernism. He didn't fathom but he created motion. He took the Principessa, because Olga could not bear "Why can't I go in the water anymore, why can't I go in the water anymore?" and walked off the beach for bags. "Also get sandwiches," she said, because one couldn't possibly delve into charcuterie without putting it in context. She hoped he wouldn't do a screw up, as he so very often did, because this was France, home of the tongue. And she hoped as well that he would forego his stupidity long enough to see that they needed drinks. He came back dry. "You wouldn't go back again, I know. It would be reproachable of me to ask you to, even though I am probably dying of thirst, and I understand completely that in this heat you wouldn't conceivably have a motive of your own." She gave a perfect sigh of surrender. He went back for drinks, carrying the Principessa again, because the Principessa had said, "I want drinks! I want drinks!" The sun threatened to melt the beautiful sand. Now he returned, victorious if flagging. "What are the bags for, by the way?" because it couldn't have been serious, what she'd said about the sand, and one hadn't bought anything else that would need stuffing into bags on this fleeting little voyage to paradise. "I have to bring back this sand. It is a formal requirement." To give the poor man credit, he didn't even begin to fathom. "Work with me," she cajoled. They worked together. She directed and he scooped, and soon bags were full, bag after bag, and if a little piece of seaweed dropped in, she made him stop and go fishing for it with tweezers. There were now four nice hefty bags and he had them under his arms while the Principessa, on his shoulders, hung on underneath his chin. He trudged slowly up the beach to the car with the Principessa holding on and the four bags of sand grown heavier with every step.

•

The sand came back quietly to New York. Oleg had the bags in his suitcases, among his dirty shirts. He had one suitcase, pure lead, in each hand, and the Principessa poised on his shoulders, down the torturous jetway, down one grey corridor after another, and in the long pathetic line at Customs. The room was a cavern, with flags and neon lights and echoes from other planets. Olga had the beach umbrella, which she bore with steely hauteur like a Roman centurion holding his pilum, and now and then the Principessa leaned down to swat it. "One more time and I will arrange for them to keep you here until you are 71 years old." Her throat was dry. She had a regal migraine. Migraines can bring flashes of wisdom, and having one she saw now that the sand was—or might be said to harbour—biological material, and they were illegally importing it. They would be causal agents in a plague, no doubt. They would be imprisoned until Venice sank. They would be drawn and quartered. Their scalps would be hacked open with machetes and boiling oil would be drizzled onto their brains. The inspector, of all possible inspectors Oleg could have chosen in his ineffable sagacity, was an overweight high-school sophomore with a moustache—awful sign—and stubby little fingers. She thought if he hadn't been human he would have been a warthog. He rubbed the outsides of the passports before opening them, and when he opened them he squinted. "Coming from?" he snipped. "Lie," she whispered, "Lie, in the name of all that is holy!" Oleg said England, which was very close to the truth, both geographically and historically, of course, so close that she couldn't figure out why he lied. "How long away?" She had a coughing fit while he revealed another truth, causing her two ear drums to be sucked into an embrace behind her nose. "Purpose your visit?" "Do not say anything at all about the beach," she prayed, as he said, "Beach." With his wet beige eyes the warthog looked into her eyes and through her head. England? For a beach? He had a computer and he went to play with it. He played for a very long time. While he was playing, the Principessa found a perfect moment to say, "I want to play with the SAND!!" Now, smiling malevolently, the warthog finished with his computer and scanned the Principessa. "I want to play with the SAND!" she tried again, just to make sure there was no syllable he could have missed. He stared at Olga again with his warthog eyes and then opened his warthog mouth. Olga felt herself sliding down into quicksand in the African jungle in a 1936 Tarzan movie. But now, suddenly, the warthog was waving them through, bags untouched, his mouth still open to swallow the stale, recycled air. It was inconceivable and therefore she couldn't conceive it, so she looked at Oleg as he smiled and nodded politely—he had the most disgusting ability to muster politeness under the gun—and at that moment, grandly, sinuously, explosively, it happened. She had been holding it in although it had been pressing with force; and now she could hold it in no longer, so out it came, rather like a liquid: "Thank you, thank you, thank you, thank you, thank you, I have such a migraine, thank you, I will drop dead, thank you thank you. Thank you for not holding us up and going through our bags." He held up a warthog finger on the word "bags," the Finger of Second Thought; the Finger of Protection and Prudential Security. Oleg froze, became in fact something like the carcass of a petrified mastodon. Olga felt the quicksand reach her nostrils. The warthog leaned close. He ate into her eyes as Doc Savage always did. What are you hiding? What are you hiding? She smelled the miasm that was his Aqua Velva. His untutored beast lips parted. "Excedrin," he said, and tapped his temple with the Finger of Hippocrates. "As per instructions on the bottle. Lots of water." When they were home and Oleg had put the Principessa to bed and made tea with honey and orange peel, she said, "One is rather good at smuggling, you know. One should do it professionally."

•

And now the sand came home to Pelham Manor, to a winding street with huge old houses that looked like castles in an enchanted forest. Before bringing up the sensitive problem of where the sand was to go in this particular castle, Oleg sat down and asked himself if there were any obvious answers, because she was forever complaining about his refusal to think. He could think of none. So, "Where," he said, timidly but to the point, and hoping to include absolutely no inkling of tone or attitude, "did you want me to put the sand?" He had brought up a little tray of egg sandwiches and *café au lait* and sat with it on the side of her bed. It was dark and his voice was velveteen and strange. "The what?" she lifted off her sleeping mask and grimaced. "The what?" Migraine drove some people to frenzies of regret and others to intensities of calculation, but with Olga it had the mercy of producing, behind the eyes, a vacuum. She became a robot waiting to be programmed. "What sand?" He reminded her he had carried sand from France on her instructions. Heavy sand. Sand that was the antithesis of stinky Venetian sand. With trouble, and groaning, she sat up. It was still in his valise, he said, obstructing his unpacking. She gave him a wet look. "Throw it in the sandbox? I don't know...put it in the garden?" He laughed nervously. Did she want him to just mix it in with the dirt and the weeds and whatever else, just make it disappear? "I..." he tried. People have buttons, or at least Olga had buttons, and this one syllable seemed to push them, one and all. This one syllable produced the end of the world. "Here's what you do, Oleg," she had climbed back into uniform and taken up her cudgel, "You take it, with the Principessa's little green shovel, and you shovel it into her sandbox. Whether you mix it with the other sand in her sandbox, in any proportion whatsoever, or just leave it sit by itself in a corner of her sandbox, is moot. Do you grasp what I am saying to you? Moot." He took the bags of sand out of his suitcase and lugged them downstairs. Here was a good hundred and fifty pounds of sand, at least. Delicious French sand; although the truth is, sand that looks delicious in France looks a little less delicious in Pelham. "What is the point of bringing sand from Cannes and dumping it in an American sandbox," he asked himself, "so that it will disappear into the dominating presence of the American sandbox universe, all those sandboxes in all those castles in all those enchanted forests?" He knew Olga must have a very good reason, one that would confound his philosophy. "Olga," he tried again. "Olga?" He was making a little tattoo on her door with his fingertips, keeping his voice low, almost funereal. He approached the bed. "You know, Olga, in the sandbox we really don't need any more sand. I mean, not really. Our sand levels are good. Not falling. I do keep an eye on our sand levels. Perhaps instead, the next time we go out to Sunday, I could just put it on the beach." "Einstein," said she, "there is no point in bringing sand from a French beach to an American beach." There was such a majesty to her logic, it was unimpeachable. Indeed there was no point, no point at all, and seeing that, he knew he had come to his wits' end. But he had to say *something*, make some kind of a noise, to distinguish himself, at least in his own mind, from the furniture: "Maybe, the tub in the guest bathroom. We could redecorate the whole room to make it look like the Lido. You could sit in there with espresso and read the Italian papers on Saturday night." She stood up in the darkness and went to look at the guest bathroom, fixed him with her calculator eyes. "The wallpaper we'd have to import from Venice," she said, "Nothing else will do. Here, they don't have wallpaper. And the faucets have to be gold, real gold. You'll have to make money. We can't have plated faucets." He took libel cases—tedious but lucrative. He took, too, a consultancy out in Sunday, an exceptionally fat one, Wednesdays, from morning until night. The wallpaper and the golden faucets soon materialized, and for moon effects, recessed lighting. From an antiquarian on Madison Avenue she picked up a few Italian novels published by Mondadori and piled them on top of the toilet to give the effect. Olga also had a reason for driving out to Sunday. She rented a nanny and booked hours with Doc Savage, hours for naked truth. "What I want to know is, am I crazy bringing sand back from Cannes? I insisted, I demanded. I couldn't imagine surviving unless I had that sand. What's crazy about bringing sand back from Cannes to throw in my kid's sandbox." The guest bathroom looked like a vista on the Lido at twilight, meanwhile, and the bathtub was filled with the cool perfect sand. "I have to have speakers in here. I have to be hearing Vivaldi," she said. He arranged candles, he arranged Vivaldi (with a CD player hidden behind the towel rack). "Do you think I'm seriously crazy," she asked Doc Savage, "making my guest bathroom into the Lido? Or just unconventional?" She told Oleg she had decided it was in fact a very mature move, providential, prudent, because now that the guest bathroom had become the Lido, there would be no reason to fly every summer to Venice. "Think of all the liras we will save, in our submarine bank account that has reached bottom." She spent a lot of time in the sand, trying to figure why for her hungers there could not be found satisfactions. It was very comfortable sand. On such sand one might encounter the spirit of Lawrence of Arabia.

•

Psychiatric privilege keeps the names of patients from one another, if patients themselves do not, and Doc Savage was pristine about psychiatric privilege, one could even say monkish, so it was the case that Olga never knew Oleg had no fat consultation in Sunday, but on Wednesdays every week was visiting Doc Savage instead. "Is my wife just unconventional turning our guest bathroom into the Lido, or is she crazy? More important, am I crazy putting up with her?" He told all about bagging the sand, carrying it in his suitcases across the ocean, a hundred and fifty pounds of sand smooth as cashmere. Doc Savage loved to walk while he listened, so he led Oleg down to the beach and they strode along the sand. It was sumptuous, innocent sand, covered in places with driftwood. They sat at the edge of the dune. No-one else was there for miles, they had the sand to themselves. "A neurosis is like a pearl, if you think about it," Doc said, pointing to Oleg's head. "You get a grain of sand in there, and it irritates, and you form a kind of excrescence as a way of diminishing the irritation. There are some neuroses that are quite magnificent. 'Course, not every grain of sand is troublesome. What irritates one man will tickle another." He had a smile both amicable and interrogative; and it was partly the handsomeness of that smile that made him a collector of psychiatric fees while other people were merely payers. "Maybe you got a neurosis here, maybe you got entertainment." Oleg found this exceptionally helpful—as indeed it was—and when Olga next said she had a migraine and needed immediately to fly to Venice he sat back and smiled to himself in the pleasure of appraisal. It was as if a source of light had been positioned in the heavens. When she started to shriek, "If you do not pick up that telephone and make reservations forthwith, I will sue. Already I am experiencing paralysis," he just took off his clothes and, putting on Crosby, Stills and Nash doing "Judy Blue Eyes," sat himself in the guest bathtub until the sand came up to his navel. Cool, perfect, gourmet sand. Sand for princes. Medici sand. "Oleg, divorce is only the beginning. I will file criminal charges." Now, the Principessa was apparently crying for pudding and Olga was banging on the door to say that pudding was beyond her capability. But Oleg was staring up at the moon. The moon on the ceiling, mauve and beatific, seemed to cast a balm of light on the stretches of perfect sand. She was still banging on the door. He realized this was the first moment in a very long time he had the feeling he would survive. The purple sand was a planet, his planet, and the planet was at peace. When he brushed off and dressed and came out, he found her serving the pudding nicely in the dining-room, and they kissed the kiss of civilization.

A Matter of Definition

It was a palatial room, gilded at the cornices. She lay in her agony like a Chatterton, and the coverlet was rumpled around her as around an odalisque. The windows had been shut firmly against the breezes of incipient spring which blew an odour of muscari and peat around the capacious lawn. Light came lazily upon the framed Fragonard, and upon the Daumiers like sentinels flanking the fireplace, and upon her not very attractive feet. A clock ticked somewhere, but we could not find it in the room, and the Persian carpet was strewn with books from the university library about Teilhard de Chardin, Pascal, Delacroix, Corneille, Leconte de Lisle. A man sat on the end of her bed, or rather a mature boy, and he fiddled with a cigarette but did not light it and finally put it back in his coat pocket and mustered a smile. "I should be on my way, Cowrie dear," he said, seeming in his tone to be concluding a long conversation but seeming by his look to have avoided conversation entirely, "but I wanted to see you with my own eyes. You'll be quite fine, won't you. You'll be good and fruitful. Or we'll just have someone in and put you down." She made some kind of wounded animal sound and clasped her face. He got up and adjusted the position of a rather luminous glass of milk he had put on the bedside table and looked away from her. "My fondness remains with you," he said, "here, even under that coverlet," and he walked out with a care to making no sound with his rubber soles on her polished hardwood floor that stretched for miles, past Vlaminck and Derain, down the corridor. She turned herself on the bed with great difficulty, grabbed at her nightgown, and opened wide her eyes in a whisper. "What a very great shit you can be." One of the cats, the snow princess, had come in to listen to her. The purring was torture.

•

Marlowe could become very legalistic when he'd been drinking, and now he did just that, straightening himself into a kind of surveyor's rod and wiping from the corners of his eyes, with a monogrammed handkerchief, tears that could not be explained. "Cowrie, I think we should talk about extra-marital affairs," he opened, not, apparently—given the way he raised his hands to protect his face—expecting the best. "I think a certain philosophical position needs to be taken, and we should lay matters open upon the table, so to speak. Not have anything up our sleeves. Not because I want to push you, but because you are, in the end, my wife—it's a matter of definition—and I should hope you would be as frank with me as possible." She had no idea what he was talking about, but she had always been willing to share frankness with Marlowe, especially over coffee. She busied herself with the espresso maker. He liked a slice of lemon balanced on his demitasse and she arranged it by giving a strident little snip with her yellow-handled kitchen shears. He had placed himself at the kitchen table, in the warm glow of the hanging lamp and adjacent a Boston fern, and he spoke in a low, almost choking, voice. "Not that I believe you would have an affair, Cowrie, or that I would, but for the sake of the children, because they have to be the first thing we think about, for their sake, an arrangement should be made, if ever we do. That's what I mean: if ever we do." She was quite struck, really, but nothing showed. "If ever we do?" Very like a lawyer—more like a lawyer than a lawyer—he cleared his throat and repeated himself calmly. "If ever we do, because it's that kind of world. One thinks, *ever*. I think we'd both be outraged. I know I would be outraged. And I presume you would. And I think the children should be protected if and when we divorced." Her hand closed on the handle of the espresso maker, which had begun to whistle hideously. "If and when?" She managed to navigate to the table. "It's just, Cowrie, that you're a complicated woman, you know I've always thought this, and you want much more out of life than a conventional guy like me can provide. So inevitably one of these days you'll find someone else and we will have to settle terms in the end. I don't like having to think about things like that when the pressure's on, so this is the perfect time. We're calm. We're feeling buoyant." She wasn't feeling buoyant. She watched him stand, move to the cutting board, slice a tomato into quarters, put them on a plate, bring them back and feed himself squarely without in the process collapsing onto the pile of bath towels she should have been laundering. He was a kind of monster, no question, but what kind? There's the rub. "If we have a divorce," she said methodically, forcing herself not at all to smile, but gamely, because she was a gamer who would condescend to play his games and this was indubitably a game, a game he thought he would win, "I want the house, the children, one of the cars, and 50% of everything you earn. And your sperm in a sperm bank." He didn't know whether this was funny or not, so he opened the paper and read the stock prices.

●

"My God!" said Olga, covering her lips. They had been walking for over an hour, along the East River, and had come to a bench on the embankment whence peanuts could gently be dropped to gulls. The water that came lapping was sunny, putrid. "My God!" Cowrie merely looked at her, the lips curled down in a wry comment. "My very sweet God!" If Olga hadn't lost the innocence of 1969, which was a particular and a holy innocence, she had discarded it. "Let me understand this. He sat you down and had a formal reckoning. He spelled out to you what action he would take if you had an— if you—" She could not say it. She looked around and dropped peanuts and her face lit up with what might have seemed to a stranger like merriment; and the language wouldn't come. "He actually uttered the word 'divorce' and he said he understood there was some possibility this would happen?" Cowrie could no longer prevent herself from laughing outright, and as she did so the laugh exacerbated so that the gulls took refuge in the air. A shabby barge was towed past by a green tug. "And you have told him nothing about Everden Quayle? He knows nothing? He suspects nothing?" Cowrie's eyes were stunned open, a woodsnipe's over the guns, and the mouth was frozen in mirth, and the head was comfortably nodding. "I have left no clues. He has no knowledge. Everden and I meet in the afternoon, during a seminar hour for which we are both scheduled. Marlowe corners Everden when Everden comes to dinner and feeds him the best bourbon money can buy, and they talk about the stock market, and Everden gives Marlowe poetry to read. His own poetry." It was Olga's turn to drop a jaw. Quayle wrote mediocre poetry, but he was committed utterly to the belief that his poetry had a place. He pontificated about it. Olga, who was herself a divorce lawyer but not a lawyer who would take her friends as clients, and who knew that Cowrie also wrote poetry, poetry, indeed, that *did* have a place, had heard him do so, and had clapped her hand over her mouth. If Cowrie would not claim place, if she would not see herself as one who could and should, still Everden claimed place brutally, so that she was afraid of him. And he winked at her—telegraphically. She had seen him drinking with Marlowe in a bar made to look like a British pub and he had seen her seeing, and had given a very provocative wink. "And what's young Mr. Quayle like, in the way of being *like* things?" Olga asked a little impertinently, but by this time Cowrie was incapacitated by a laughter that was far from genuine; and could bring herself to say only, "Monolithic." If Everden had entrusted her with his monolith she, unbeknownst to him, had written many poems about it. There were enough for a book.

•

"What has your friend Olga said to my friend Everden?" Marlowe said, as he was chopping celery and finishing a cognac with the baseball scores open beside him and Bach's Goldberg Variations on the radio. "She has very much put him off. He keeps yaddering on about women. Women this, women that. What women, you and Olga? What other women could it be? And what about women? What has Olga gone and done to him?" The cream sauce was all but thick, so Cowrie could neglect it carefully. "Done? Everden doesn't *do*." There was absolutely no point entering a debate with Cowrie, she would bring in epistemology, and there was no point discussing Everden since Everden was openly neurotic, and either way Cowrie would defend herself in his face, Marlowe knew that. He kept chopping, as if it were religion. And as if she were watching him, following his every movement, at the very last chop Cowrie let go the bomb. "Marlowe, Olga and I had a long talk yesterday afternoon and the conclusion we came to was: that this extra-marital business you insisted on talking about the other night, this extra-marital business, and Mr. Everden Quayle, at least in your mind, are inextricably connected. You are plotting something about me. You are plotting together. He is showing you where you can run off. Sorry, but I don't know any other way of saying it." This was inaccurate. She knew plenty of other ways of saying it, but she didn't know a clearer way of putting it, or a more polite, and so she leaned back against the counter and rested a little, the timid rest of the worker with phrases who has found the phrase. In her rest she firmly shut her eyes, and so the way he lost colour and got blue in the lips totally escaped her. Then it was the doorbell and the sacrificial goat had arrived to dine.

•

"One couldn't possibly be gladder Cowrie waited to go to graduate school," Everden said, taking his napkin, folding it into a crane, "because otherwise she'd have gone years ago and one would never have had the pleasure of taking a class with her. She's quite magical in a class. And one is positively enriched by association with people older, like the two of you. You are used to all this, breaking down the age barriers, I know, because in the sixties that is what everybody did: I mean, everybody rather *touched* everybody. But for my generation things are not that way. So I grow, every moment I am with either of you, and I just thought I should say it. I mean, short of being together in school, I don't know how people like us meet. Because I am young enough to be—" He did a little mathematics and made his crane lie down and die. "A younger sibling, certainly. I am young enough in relation to you. I spend half my time, in fact, wondering about all the secret legacies of the sixties you haven't brought out of the closet yet. Sensitivity. Lust. Capacity." Marlowe very capably played waiter, wrapping the Sauvignon de Touraine in a napkin like the one Everden had now interred on his lap. "Marriage, of course," came the decoration upon the cake, "was a foreign object, no, I mean back then? You didn't talk about it, you didn't do it, you just combined and connected, like so many amoebae. Oooooo. I must have been hardly older than five." Cowrie mentally undressed him and saw that he had the chest of a five year old still, little pink nipples like a girl's. She remembered that he had said all his pleasures came through the lips—that he liked to taste her (and she certainly knew that) and that he liked to give her lectures—and now she wondered if sitting behind the rack of lamb with mint and roasted new potatoes and creamed celery he was lipping still. "What did you think when first you met me?" he was saying, and she thought, "I imagined a redwood tree, thick and old, in a dark forest, and how nothing you could do or say on this earth would cause it to take the slightest notice." Marlowe had made some exquisite slices of the meat and was passing them. "I thought, ambitious little fart," he said, with a gracious smile.

•

"He guessed at the dinner table," Everden said, as he bent to let his trousers onto the floor. She had already removed everything that was going to be removed and was positioned on the angular little desk. The carrel was impossible for studying, all angles, and for privacy she had taped—against every rule—"Primavera" by Botticelli over the window. He took a moment while his muscle finished standing, his arms folded behind his head, to examine the faded colours, and flipped, "In posters you *do* have taste, if in little else." Then they set to work, making one of those poses only graduate students can imagine since they are conditioned completely by the shape of the curious little place only graduate students can inhabit. All the light is fluorescent, dynamic, objective, and you cannot destroy it. Bookshelves are situated cleverly to attack the heads; legs must dangle hopelessly into a space inadequate even for solo activity. The floor is cold. Everden was afraid to make noises as he moved himself into her, because through the partition was a prudish Armenian studying phasers through the night, a fellow who complained, indeed, if one sneezed too much. But he did say, once again, rising to his occasion, "At the table he guessed for certain." She was not able to derive pleasure talking about Marlowe as Quayle worked. When he stopped she sighed and announced, "Marlowe believes that I have approached my menopause and that sex is quite beyond me." "A male knows," said Everden, "when another male is aroused, and I sat through dessert with a penis as big as your table leg. Clean me with your lips." Later, on the telephone, to Olga, she said, "I don't think I believe it's true a male knows when another male is aroused. Do you believe it? Everden's paranoid." And Olga responded, "Being paranoid, I have trouble calling people paranoid. It's like asking a fish if he thinks the fish swimming around him are wet. Further, I have such a migraine the thought of male knowledge of anything pushes me over the limit. I am over the limit. I am lost. But what a sordid little novella has been made, sweet Cowrie, of your life." Olga had actually sliced part of a cucumber for her eyes, as she talked, and was now using the other part in a way that would have made Sweet Cowrie rather jealous.

•

Gerald, said Everden Quayle, didn't really deserve Gudrun, and Rupert did not really deserve Ursula. It was a question not of sexes but of temperaments, as indeed is the case with everything. "Someone should sue you, that would shut you up," was the comment Olga made, "Bend over and perhaps I will sue you." He did bend over, and for half an hour she sued him from behind in a way he had never been sued before. He gasped with the novelty of it, and she thought, "This is what young men are for, a sentimental education." Wind was gusting along the curved pathway between beds of hosta and allium, the speckled hosta and the giant allium one sees only in the enchanted forest of Pelham Manor. He had found her having coffee with Cowrie and had agreed to escort her in the direction of Madison and 69th in order to have the opportunity of discovering whether she was an ally. Now, in the castle to which graduate students did not usually have access, she proved what a skillful ally she was. "Gerald," he provoked, "deserves no-one." "Let me tell you," said she, using her mouth to make him gasp again, "I read D. H. Lawrence 27 years ago. You weren't imagined yet. If D. H. Lawrence were alive today, he'd be totally unknown. The moral world has eclipsed him. His kind of sexual danger has become banal. Consider," and now she moved her mouth a little so that he would understand the meaning of the word "Consider," and he did consider, "Consider...your own case." She hardly knew whether to go on with this, but blindly she went on as he came to a standstill for a moment and pretended to admire her eucalyptus leaves in the tall glass vase. "You are a member of a generation that takes what it wants. I know Cowrie has observed this to me, and I have in the past agreed with her. She finds you—by which I mean the aggregation of you—both tantalizing and fearsome. For instance, in your sexuality you lack a sense of form." He waked again for a moment, and caught his breath. "We have observed the way you allow yourself to be defined by situations. And the question of desert has come up, somewhat in the sense that you have just now posed it. We have wondered...." Since he was no longer writhing it occurred to her she might back off, might indeed go have a long figgy shower and if she were lucky he'd get dressed and leave. But he simply turned over, faced her with the goods, and filled in the equation: "Whether or not Cowrie is deserved by me. That is what you mean, isn't it? Whether or not a runt might attach himself to a queen. Yes? Are you going to tell Marlowe? Are you going to serve me up on a platter?" Olga, who had no particular regard for Marlowe, said as much, in one percussive four-letter word; and would give Marlowe no unsolicited gifts, and said that, too; and didn't know what she thought of Quayle, precisely, although he was certainly fun to eat, but said, "Cowrie enjoys your company. You make her feel, a little, young. You're an entertainment. A delicacy. Smorgasbord." It was not what he wanted, needed, to hear. He didn't want to be a toy, he wanted to be a presence. He said so. "But you *are* a presence *and* a toy, my dear, and that's why it is so much better. Better buttery batter." And with that she sucked him dry. Now she was apparently turning her mind to other things because she began muttering to herself and feeding the parakeets. "Shall I bring you out to dinner some time," whispered he, "and we can go on discussing *Women in Love*?" She stared past him, as if he didn't exist.

•

Cambridge was batting against Oxford on the 32-inch

screen. Marlowe was sipping a tepid Guinness. Cowrie was muttering, "I wish I had grass that looked like that." And then: "I've thought that even if you did have a lover I wouldn't care, Marlowe. You're set in your ways, you'd come back. And I'd have you under my finger, so I could live with that. Whoever it was wouldn't give you well-roundedness, which is the only thing on earth you're addicted to. The wholesome completeness of glorious, rotund family life. She wouldn't give that, and if she gave a fresh body it would only mean a little less wear on mine. We don't care about sex. I don't think you do, at least. Your sex is cricket. I have writing to do. I want to do my writing. You can go ahead and have an affair and instead of divorcing you I'll just sit back on the throne and rule." He asked her if she'd like a Guinness as well and she said yes, she couldn't think of anything she'd rather have, so he went and opened another two and poured them gingerly into glasses that had been chilled, taken from a large collection of glasses in this state of grace. If he could be glued to the game again she could be glued to him. His eyes? She came closer, edging on the carpet, and saw the shine in his eyes. If he was crying it would mean he loved her. If he was crying he would never be with anyone, ever, and he was hers in fact exactly as in her imagination. It wasn't tears, however, it was the test match reflected from the television in tiny puddles that fidgeted in light.

•

Her mouth was curiously square as she gazed at him, and he did not flinch. Her eyes were scolding. "I have come to the realization that you are changed," went her voice. "Once we had so many things in common, we even hunted together for sights of rare birds, and we shared cigarettes furtively in shared guilt. We adored Rossellini. I can still remember that after we first saw *Voyage en Italie* you became so excited, you went all red and your voice was strained, and you said, 'That is how we should live life!' I told you about books I was reading and you told me, and we read to one another in bed at night. I remember you read to me Iris Murdoch and I read to you Verlaine from that little book I got at the library sale.

Je fais souvent ce rêve étrange et pénétrant
D'une femme inconnue, et que j'aime, et qui m'aime,
Et qui n'est, chaque fois, ni tout à fait la même
Ni tout à fait une autre, et m'aime et me comprend.

What did I pay for that book, 25¢? Well. It doesn't matter. Nothing matters. You have changed. All you want now is to make money, and I cannot talk to you about anything. Except for the children there is no reason for us to be living with one another. I certainly don't feel I understand you. And you aren't even interested in whether or not you understand me. You wonder about Everden, I know you do. You can't bring yourself to stop wondering what Everden is intending with me, and the simple fact is, we can sit on a park bench and have a civil conversation. He wants to hear what I am thinking about and I find that I want to hear about him. It's not that I *like* Everden—God knows he's hard enough to like, or to imagine liking—but he fascinates, and he allows himself to be fascinated, and he isn't counting the dollars on a kind of time clock the way you are. I hope you make your millions, but I worry about what you'll say when you've done it. I don't believe it will make you happy to be rich, but I think you will smugly look down on the rest of us and convince yourself that you have achieved something we are incapable of. Of course, in a way we are. We are incapable, Everden and I, of submitting ourselves to the idea of becoming fabulously rich. We are swarmed over by words. As you once were, Marlowe. As you once were. The names of birds and of flowers and animals and poets all captivated you, but now you think only of winning and losing and who's ahead and who's behind. And to stay ahead, if that is where you really are, you have become so penurious! That the house decoration, which was rather important to me, should have been on a room-by-room budget is one idiocy. But that the children should be denied toys! That I should be reduced to hanging, in my hallways, framed reproductions, as if you wish to procure the impressions that high culture merits without spending the money for high culture. I mean, really! Posters in gilded frames! So that is why I have retreated. Posters in frames is the reason I seem to be in a vase. And you may have the feeling I am not quite conscious of you. You exist for me as a memory trace. A blip. The tail of a blip that is evanescent. When I eat dinner with you the man at the table is a cold stranger. The Marlowe I married, my marijuana Marlowe, my *artiste*, my adventurer, my philosopher, is a cloud." The sun had virtually gone so that the light upon her cheeks was ruby and dark and her eyes were barely visible. The mirror, she now saw, looking from her face within the surface to the surface that had netted her face, needed cleaning. There! Something important one could devote a life to. One could tidy bookshelves, and refresh the water in the roses, and bake pies. The mirror wanted fresh gilding as well, Marlowe had to have everything that could be gilded, gilded. Marlowe, behind her back upon the sofa covered in William Morris, was still flicking through the market listings. She was relieved to have laryngitis, because now it turned out her long silent gaze had made him tranquil. To have actually said all this! Heavens, no! He looked up and smiled gently and she spoke, in the smallest and driest of voices. "I'm going to offer you a glass of wine." Marlowe said that would be perfection, because British Gas had just gone from 59 5/8 to 60 1/2.

•

The *wunderkind* was upon the bed, yawning, nude, desirous. He was covered over, in fact, with pockets of baby flesh, but there was lasciviousness in his eyes. He had had coffee and it made him critical. "What I find gruesome about your house is that instead of art on the walls there are tepid posters," he said, and turned over to offer a view of his sloping, tanned back, the result of reading the Marquis de Sade on the beach in Aruba. "What I find untenable is the pretense to tastefulness. What I find morbid is the stiffness in all of the floral bouquets, as if one wanted spring but wanted also to save money. There, you see—I am not happy. Is there anything more important than happiness? If so, we can't name it, can we? Listen, I'm an awfully astute detective, don't you think, teasing out the Olga letters? You must give me credit. I told you she was dangerous. Come, have your shower and lie upon my legs." Olga, who was a letter-writer, and who became florid when she entered the personality that wrote her letters, had written many letters, letters that had contained plain intimations. Intimations only, but belief could easily follow. There would have been enough in the letters to arouse the imps of doubt, to produce discomfort and even a little displeasure. And if by the handwriting Everden had caught the envelopes, by lamplight he had taken the liberty of screening them for précis; so that a quite careful Bowdlerization could find its way into the air. "Indeed," said he, with his fingers intentfully upon his pubis, "I have missed my calling." The snapping sound of the shower stimulated him. He had placed pillows underneath the small of his back and was half in a trance when the shower stopped. He closed his eyes so the approaching footsteps would be magnified, isolated. He was picturing himself being joined in a cuff of flesh as he said, "I'm the quintessential sleuth, wouldn't you say, Watson?" Marlowe, lowering himself methodically into position, answered in the Cockney he had long since polished over, "You're the quin'essence of everything, I do believe, dear Mr. 'Olmes." Outside was the quintessence of winter, snow on everything, ice palaces. Stars were emerging everywhere in the chilly periwinkle sky.

Death in Venice

"Venice" became the operative word. Four days, maybe five. Olga would shapeshift. Beatitude would emerge in beads on Olga's chin, she would sing, "Mia Venezia! My Venice! My Venice!" Of course everything depended on Alicia the Wangler, centre of the universe. Regally—with a $150 box of Godivas, she would have to be brought into the picture. Phone for a courier, he told himself, thinking about chocolates with candied violet, because violet would send a signal, opening mentally a mental golden box and biting into a mental mocha praline. Or he could phone L.A., for that matter, and have Sees send out a huge box of bear claws by Fedex overnight. Two boxes, why place limits? He moved his finger toward the telephone, which itself had begun to seem edible. Even more pressing was Signora Arcangela. A fax would have to fly to her. "*Signora, Signora, la bellissima Signora.*" He made a silent little prayer that the pain in his ribs would go away. It was like a dozen pin pricks, and then like a sheet of tin slicing him in two. You think about the idea of pain and then you believe you feel it, then you know you feel it, but do you actually feel it? Instead of thinking about pain, he thought about Olga, frowning under her mop of carrot red hair, in bed with her cup of tepid herbal tea. "I'm at the bottom of the well," she had said, "I'm empty. I'm a dried leaf the wind throws around. The children don't tickle me, New York doesn't tickle me, *fettucine alla putanesca* at Babbu don't tickle me, nothing tickles me. I cannot be tickled. I have tried to tickle myself. Tickling is history. Everything is history. Do something, Oleg, or you will be history." She had been reading Toynbee for some arcane reason; she knew about history. Olga, he told himself, will experience true happiness, Olga will be tickled. And it was true that Olga became a sort of fish whenever they went to Venice, sleek, glistening, spiritual, a creature of depths and beautiful silences. Oleg, for his part, felt he was becoming something of a jellyfish. Or that he had become something of a jellyfish. Certainly inside him there was a jellyfish, here, there, and everywhere, without shape, without purpose, floating sadly in tepidness, waiting sadly, being seen through. The pain moved to his bowels and then back to his chest, playing ping-pong with itself across his diaphragm. Olga, yes, would be textbook. Olga would bounce. The children could stay with Mrs. Plate, who was a charmer with puddings. And Olga always brightened when she dollied away from the children, she began to whistle "Blue Skies" just as if with her own two hands she had created the universe. Yet it was Oleg, in truth, who had originally found the *penzione*, dug it out of the ashes, tenderly brushed its surface, put it on the map, although certainly one made a point of never having a map of Venice, never having a view. To Oleg, at any rate, at least mentally, Venice belonged—the mental Venice—and the Signora was therefore entirely his Signora, so he proceeded to send a two-liner asking for the normal room, addressing it, as per normal, "Mama," it meaning nothing to him at this moment that neither he nor the Signora were Italian, that the Signora was not and never had been his mother, that his mother, indeed, had always made a sour face when she heard the word "Italy." Although perhaps it could be said the Signora *was*. The way she smiled at him certainly always made his throat close off. Now the pain had become a rabbit and was trying to hide itself behind his lowest rib, but suddenly, just as he thought that by pressing on his belly in a certain way he could seize it by the ears, it transmogrified into an amoeba, stretching and pulling, and then made up its mind that it was a worm. The worm started near his left armpit and ended somewhere around his liver. On his CD player he started up Hoagy Carmichael doing "Skylark." He stood up and strode around the cognac-coloured thick pile carpet all good lawyers have in offices on Park Avenue. Good carpet that could be counted on to do the trick. On the East Side, good carpet was as close as one came to Venice. Should he not perhaps—now, at this instant—call the Wangler and put neck on block, or should he first consume an Americano, get zippy, get positive? One word from her could be instant death. Death of Venice. She could be, as Olga loved to say, a "monstrous rapacious bitch-hag capitalist." He kept reaching out the finger to the phone, twiddling the finger, smelling fried liver with onions as you can get it only in Venice, or as he had certainly once got it very much within the precincts of Venice if not quite in the heart of Venice, if not quite where Venice began. Should not the courage of the downtrodden be inspired by a vision of glory? A question something like this question swam into his mental pool, transformed itself into the pain worm, entered the finger and made it stretch to the telephone. The Wangler answered on the third ring, her sinuses inflamed.

•

"*Imposseebeelay*. Absolutely not, nothing, no single seat on any flight going to any city within a thousand kilometres of Venice. Not your Venice. Not my Venice. Nobody's Venice." Since Oleg was standing, and was half as tall as a tree, he saw the floor recede beneath him to infinity—Jimmy Stewart in *Vertigo*. The pain now materialized into an object shaped like Venice, one that settled into a corner of his stomach and deposited roots. "Venice California I can do you," she said, with no wit and with far too much cheer. "It's great there if you're in the mood. They have a Grand Canal. I've seen pictures on the Internet. It's quite lovely, with flowers and little bridges. And you can eat noodles. Venice New York has no canals, you could do that. They have mountains nearby. I think there's also a Venice Georgia and it's probably terrific—want me to find out what they have?" Olga would implode. Olga would fall into the filthiest part of some horrid inner lagoon. "*That* Venice, *the* Venice, the Venice to end Venices," the Wangler couldn't stop, "you gotta *shtup*." The click her telephone made was like the switch being closed on the electric chair. *Shtup* Venice didn't sound promising to Oleg. Olga's lagoon green eyes would narrow into slits.

•

Oleg and Olga had once been innocent—everyone, even they, had trouble imagining this. On their first trip to Venice it had rained. They had planned two days and it had rained every moment. They had arranged seventeen days in Europe, nine cities, Eurailpass, sleep on the train, half a day for the Louvre, skip England, try to do Barcelona, absolutely find Prague, hit Rome, Florence, Turin, and Venice, then Berlin.

Or perhaps Berlin first. Was it important to do Germany before Italy or Italy before Germany? Oleg had never been to Europe, Olga had been twice. Olga had done Venice, Oleg had dreamed of doing Venice, and really, when all was said and done, that was the enormity and the entirety of the difference between them, there, then, always, everywhere. But it had rained in Venice, and the canals had been silver and brown, they had eaten fresh sardines, they had drunk Montepulciano, the sex had been not only intense but adventurous, which is to say a flirtation with the criminal, sufficiently so that he, at least, had never forgotten a twinge or a gesture of it. They had eaten a lot of figs, fig jam, fig pie, fig pastries. Venice had been sardines and figs. The streets had stunk erotically. Olga had said to him, "As long as we come back to this place whenever I want, there will be life." Years had passed. Years and years and years and years and years.

•

The phone rang, *Dooz dooz dooz*, a frenetic little monkey sound. The desktop and the orange case file of Zimbalist v. Cohen were shifting a thousand feet below him, breaking into fragments. He was going to crash, his fragments were going to burn up in the atmosphere, he would be nothing. The pain had gone up to his head, was flying around like a pixie from hell. He felt certain he would be dying, if not today, if not this week, then soon, very soon, somehow in Venice. "It's me," said the Wangler, still sniffling. "Okay, okay, okay, okay, but *only* for you. *Two* seats. Not more. You have to leave tonight. Four days, not five. It's only available in first class—you don't care, you're made of money. I got you lobster dinners and bulkhead." Olga threw panties into the Vuitton like there was no tomorrow, naked as an eggplant and singing under her breath, "Bulkhead, bulkhead, cha cha cha." Olga no longer had the body of a twenty-year-old. But what was a twenty-year-old compared to Venice?

•

"I would consume this lobster," she had terrific enunciation when she set her mind to it, enunciation from the Royal Academy of Dramatic Arts, where she had never been a student, "if I were not mortally allergic...to things with claws, if eating this thing with claws...did not pose for me...a distinct threat of quick and hideous...death by strangulation in which...all the muscles...of my neck...contracted simultaneously and...caused my windpipe...to close off." To the thing upon her plate she announced, "I love you, but you will cause my windpipe to go out of business. It's you or my windpipe. You must be replaced." She tapped its carapace, all nice and ruby coloured now that it had been rewarmed a few times by the chief steward, with her plastic spoon, which was the limit of the security-correct cutlery. Her plastic *first-class* spoon, which was pink with tiny green flamingoes upon the handle—a spoon for eating a thing with claws that would put you under. "Do you not imagine, Oleg, that it might be possible for you, besotted as you are by this thing with claws, this thing with claws that your...monstrous rapacious bitch-hag capitalist co-conspirator...is using to snuff me, to extend yourself in any way at all...to save my life? Could you move one little muscle...to prevent me from dying? Even looking at it is starting up my response. I can feel my response. It's behind my nipples. I am getting the full histamine onslaught. I am getting the big H. Reach up, ring the bell, ask one of these pudgy robots to take this poisonous monster away from my...sight. In fact, I can't see it—my eyes are swelling. My eyes are cantaloupes, Oleg. I can't see!" Was she in delirium? She sounded, in fact, a little preorgasmic. "My gums are starting to bleed, I can taste it. I am bleeding from this lobster! I am going to exsanguinate, right here at 40,000 feet. There will be blood all over everybody, all the Mr. Clean in the universe won't fix this airplane, Oleg." In a moment he asked if her vision was normal again. "Of course I can see, what do you think I am, psychotic? This airplane needs a decorator. You would think one of these quasi-Nazi usherettes would lift a finger...for someone who is...paralyzed by...the very thought of things with...claws. This particular thing with claws, by the way, is a terrorist." The worm was still in Oleg's finger, making it itch and stretch. He slid Olga's tray onto his own table and watched—with the worm now crawling out of his finger and up his arm and across his chest and up his esophagus—as she sipped some water and started breathing again, breathing and hissing, "I'll string this airline up by its *cojones* on a Seagal v. Haffner doubled up by a Woo v. Wang." He tried to work out an easy formula for calculating how many Euros were in a dollar (because such mathematical dances had driven him crazy since seventh grade); the hotel was going to be 390 Euros, with bath, Mama having fallen through the cracks in the floor in fact, *dissoluta, scomparsa, perdita*, but the ever-obliging Wangler having wangled the Palazzo della Fumari Bianchi just off the Canal Grande on the Campo San Aponal. He knew he would collapse long before she would. He was well on the way to collapsing. Soon. Very soon. This was not going to be a trip to Venice like other trips to Venice. The past was only prologue. He felt the worm becoming a bird, a bird with a beak, although a little bird, but not a nice little bird, and it was nibbling away the nerves attached to the muscles that held his bones in place the way one ate a chicken. "Or maybe," Olga was droning, "it wasn't Woo v. Wang, it was that Portuguese couple—Oliveira v. Oliveiros?" She didn't think of herself as being on the airplane while she was saying all this, of course, Olga was almost never on an airplane except for the little moment with the oxygen mask. Only the visible sheath of her was on the airplane, her carapace, as if she were the lobster. Yes, that was it. *She* was the lobster: "They are asking me to eat myself." "What?" said Oleg. She wasn't there. She was in Venice, strolling outside Il Parcomento, where she would buy silk. She would buy, in fact, green silk, very dark green silk, the colour of turtles, and she would have it made into something. You bought silk and you had it made into something, you had it made into pajamas. She would make sheets. Sheets and matching pajamas, so that she could vanish, a green thought in a green shade. She would vanish and he would search for her but she would be safe in the cocoon of her invisible silk, watching, looking through him at vases full of lilies against persimmon-coloured walls. A pinkish cloud past the tip of the wing turned into a bowl of soup that had croutons bobbing around in it, tomato soup, and then there was an island with little people in feather hats. There were camels and priests running around in circles, and voices demanding Water, Truth, Pistachios, and somebody was calling out, "Lambozini." She awoke to a start and looked out the window to find that they were not above the clouds but on the ground. People were squeezing down the aisle. Oleg was snoring, headphones in his ears, his long fat fingers twitching, his face a little sallow. She realized, in an utterly Lilliputian way, that there was no way to crawl over the Giant, you would need to hook him up to a crane and have him hoisted. Outside on the tarmac was something smaller, a beautiful boy in a natty green jacket walking here, walking there, waving his arms in what looked like flagman's signals near the belt where the bags were shuffling off. His eyes were huge, he was nothing if not a Donatello, he looked up and caught her glance and smiled a dangerous smile.

•

You looked for Venice always, but especially when you were in Venice—Venice was the ideal spot for looking for Venice, not that you'd succeed. That was why you'd come back to Venice, why you had come back to Venice for 25 years. You looked for it, you tried to drink it in. All your love of Venice was a drop in the bucket. She couldn't see Venice, it was all fog. The fog was silky, you could have made pajamas out of it. There was no Venice, just a kind of pink moisture in the nostrils. A handful of people wandering around grumbling, "*Vaporetti. Vaporetti.*" The hotel wasn't exactly in the Jewish quarter and wasn't exactly near the Rialto, which implied a thousand *lire* a night one way or the other, except it wasn't *lire* anymore it was Euros, so how many Euros? She imagined a purse full of Euros and didn't bother to count them. Nobody talked about *lire* anymore, but she had heard people saying, "A thousand *lire* one way or the other." It didn't matter. You didn't count Euros when you were searching for Venice. She was starving—there was a foothold! She could have eaten— well, at least a fresh little salad. They would do room service in this hotel, an exceedingly fresh little salad, perhaps with Pecorino and oranges. It was one of those treasure spots where the food is brought up by cute boys in little green jackets, who don't speak two words of English but who look at you with hunger. "Get me a boy in a little green jacket," Olga said, "with linguine. Get me a linguine boy." There was a bedside radio, on which an orchestra played overtures by Rossini, one after the other: *La Cenerentola. Il Barbiere di Siviglia. La Gazza Ladra.* Oleg couldn't help remembering Bugs Bunny running around stropping a razor. He got up and went to the window. Mist, mist, mist. Not even a pigeon on the window sill. He looked at his watch, thinking that any moment Olga would say they had come all the way to Venice to lie around naked in a hotel room. Now she actually did open her mouth, to prove that great minds think alike: "Naked in a hotel room in invisible Venice for four days. I would take a shower if there was a shower. This is no shower"—she pointed at something dark and moist and square in a corner behind what might have been a toilet—"I think I will sue the Doge. Surely if you cannot even see Venice, they should have closed the airport. Why didn't they close the airport, Oleg, since they have closed Venice?" She went to the window, to see if she would see any other actionable offence, since it's always wise to make a package, but what she did there was whisper religiously: "O my God, look! He's there! My linguine boy! My God, where have I seen him before?" Oleg crept up behind her and stood as if his body were her body, yet not touching, because he had long ago convinced himself she withdrew from his touch. He felt the pain, somewhere between his armpit and his groin. A boy was in the street outside, eighteen, nineteen, slender, in sandals which would be cold for December, his hair curly and black, his hands waving around. He marched this way and that way, gesticulating. How beautiful he was, a Donatello, but Olga only said, "Are we crazy, Oleg, for coming to Venice again? Why do we do this? What is it that we want here? Has our life become such a formula even our getaways get us nowhere? When are you going to answer one of my questions?"

•

They had closed the airport, in fact, for three and a half days. But it was Christmas, the season when any living tourist is a gift from heaven, and so they reopened the airport, and one plane landed from New York, and then immediately they closed the airport again. Since Oleg had fallen asleep in the smaller bedroom, the one with the bidet and the mirror in this bizarre little suite that had two bedrooms and two doors, and since his snoring was outmatching the Overture to *La Gazza Ladra*, Olga went into the other bedroom, what Italians would have called the huge bedroom, the bedroom as big as a closet, and sat on the bed. She thought she would throw on something loose and fuchsia and stroll out to a gondola manned by a skinny gondoliere with cheeks like plums and eyes disappearing into the low-lying fog. Indeed, she saw herself leave the hotel, step into the gondola, nibble from a little bag of almonds. On the gondoliere's feet were frayed black slippers, and on the tops of his feet were scars, as if someone had tried to nail him to something. Maybe he was 30, she doubted it. She suddenly imagined his organ was elephantine. He rowed her for an hour, all the way along the Canale di Cannaregio and back, and she heard herself say, "Life doesn't get any better when you get old." The gondoliere muttered something under his breath, something a little bitter, and when she said, abstractedly, "*Che? Che?*" he leaned forward so that she could see his face, a beautiful face with enormous almond eyes, and repeated himself, "*La vita non è facile quando hai vente cinque anni.*" Now she took a sniff of what might well have been Bal à Versailles dumped into the canal, or else dead catfish, because there was fishiness but also flowers, and a diesel smell, and then roasted pork, and there was mushy newspaper, and pieces of straw bobbed like pick-up sticks. "Venice," she said to herself, "is a man." She saw a winter rose, blue-white. "*La porto qualche posto speziale,*" she was quite sure he suddenly murmured. It was unnecessary to care what he was saying, there were a thousand like him, each would be replaced by another and then in the end they would all be replaced, it was only important to stare at the mist now hovering a couple of feet over the water, to dream, to stare and wait, to wait and dream. It was unnecessary to attend to what he was saying. "*Ho un bel corpo,*" he was almost singing now, or was it a pelican? It was true he had a beautiful body, he had the very most beautiful body, but what could one do with it in a gondola when the water was making lapping sounds that reminded one of one's husband sitting in a bathtub? The gondoliere's melody came quietly, she knew she had heard it a long time ago on one of her father's records that he played on Sundays, Puccini, *La Fanciulla del West.* "*Possiamo fare l'amore che non dimenticai. Lei vuole?*" The water made lapping sounds against the gondola. The water made lapping sounds. "*Lei vuole?*" he said more forcefully. "*Si,*" she thought she heard herself say, but she meant, I want the past, I want a world without a future. "Take me to the Museo Civico." He turned the gondola and sang again, this time from the gut, a song she had never heard, something monotonous, and his voice got lost in the fog, which was lifting, and she drifted off. He's going to take me somewhere else, she told herself. And he rowed, but not to the Museo Civico. He entered the Canal Grande and then went off and twisted and turned, and after what might have been a decade found the Rio dei Mendicanti. He wasn't singing anymore. She didn't know whether this was a time for fear. "Where are you taking me?" He said, "Shh." On the right was San Lazzaro di Mendicanti and beside it was a small building with *altane.* "Yes, yes, you come," he whispered, tying the gondola. "Yes, yes, you come here with me." Yes, yes, she wanted the future to disappear.

•

Oleg stood up and took stock, his head rather near the ceiling. He felt that today was the day he was going to die. It was one of those definitive feelings, like when you know that if you walk into a room you'll see someone you know, or like the feeling that it will snow before twilight. Something in his ribs, something in his knees, something in the back of his neck—the three sacred places. She had gone for a walk, no doubt, since the connecting door was closed and she never closed the doors to bedrooms. She had gone to buy a dress. Perhaps if he went over to the Campo Menin he could get some nice carnations for her, three or four bundles, dark red, and find something to use as a vase. She loved flowers. Or a bottle of Amaretto, her favourite. Maybe both. They could dine at Fosca, a meal for the books. He knew he wouldn't be alive for breakfast, not that there was anything to say about breakfast in Venice. To Venice you don't go for breakfast. But gamberoni and tagliarini and lemon tart, a good Gavi, nice and chilled and mysterious: that was nothing to complain about. He'd die with the taste of Gavi on his lips. He'd take her for a gondola ride by moonlight, because the fog had to vanish, there would have to be a moon. He remembered one moon that was sitting upon the lagoon like a beach ball before he had turned 40; no, before he had turned 30. The past was what he thought about as he quickly showered in that slovenly Venetian fashion, the water salty and tepid, the shampoo categorically not lathering, and dressed in a plain white shirt. He was aware that maybe it was heartburn, but also maybe it was death. He didn't want to seem like an American, he wanted to belong to Venice. Walking out of the hotel he was the tallest person he could see. She had gone to buy a dress to celebrate being in Venice. And that made sense—how long had they been coming here? Twenty-six, no, 27 years. No, 26 years. He was flooded with the taste of liver with onions. They had made a ritual of hopping over to Venice, retreating, sidestepping, backhanding their way to Venice, and he had always felt ready and alive. She took such dense notes, and he never took notes at all, just as in school where she'd had all As and he had been an improviser. A hundred times at least they had been here, she had a whole shelf of notebooks. But the place was part of his body. He went over the Ponte di Rialto and into the Campo San Bartolomeo (and felt the pain shift from his gall bladder to his liver). Lots of bars, tables on the street, people with drinks sitting and gazing around, Venetians every one. He stepped over the dirty stream of the Rio della Fava and kept walking, through alleys he had known a hundred times yet did not recognize. Step. Pause. Step step. Pause. He wanted desperately to sit. A long time ago he would have arranged to take her to Murano and bought her glass; now they had vases and figurines coming out of the walls. Maybe he'd buy her a beautiful, heavy book, something with hand-marbled endpapers and old parchment and a blind-stamped binding. He'd write something suitably final in it. There were innumerable cats, stepping out of doorways, racing ahead of him on the cobbles, stopping, turning around, stepping toward his legs menacingly, retreating, running ahead of him, stopping. He smelled fried rapini. He remembered a bitter fight they had had at the Santa Maria della Salute in '86, after which they had dined at Fosca and had gone in a gondola under the moon and it had been wonderful. A red moon. Then the Principessa had been born. And Olga had retreated for a month to Florida, and he had done the bottles, the bathing, the changing, the pacing. He wanted to sit. Truly, there was something —somewhere between his kidneys, in that unspecifiable zone where things happen. He had moved well over a number of hillocks, where vague doubts are abandoned for clear uncertainties, but today he was almost 50, there was no uncertainty—something was going to happen. Something was lingering. Near the Calle del Paradiso there was a tiny café, he could see the pea green sign, the tables. He wanted to sit forever, or to fly like a bird and escape all this. *Due Alberi* the place was called, a name that suggested nothing and that was therefore a perfect sign.

•

She thought a lawsuit was definitely in order. He calls her at three o'clock in the afternoon when she's doing her pilates, for Christ's sake, and says maybe they can do a few days at the Signora's. He should know addiction to Venice makes one tender. There's nothing to do about addiction to Venice— except feed it and hope one dies happy. How can he think they'll get the *penzione* on half a day's notice—has he no brain at all? The Signora is never open in December. She's never been open in December. Why would she be open in December when she goes to Bermuda? Why would she want to cater to New Yorkers in December when New Yorkers, especially tall New Yorkers who need special bath towels, don't remember to bring her presents from Bloomingdale's? And now he's sleeping like a beast, totally useless, in a hotel room where the dog shouldn't have to sleep but the fucking travel agent gets a cut. And now she's going to be raped by a man who doesn't speak a word of English, so she won't even understand a word he says when he probably strangles her with her own necklace. He's walking up the dark stairs ahead of her, humming. Why is she following? She knows why. She wants to see him with his pants off, that's why. He's unlocking a door. He holds his hand out to show her the way and makes clicking sounds with his teeth. His name must be Marco, she tells herself, they're all named Marco. Marco Polo, no doubt. He's already putting a kettle on the stove. This stove, this apartment, this entire building is a grime pit, someone should replace this building. Venice altogether could use some replacing, some of the canals could do with Lysol. There's a radio, which he turns on to some woman singing *amore* this, *amore* that. Everything is *amore*, and it gives her heat in her palms and makes her think of a penis, some gigantic penis, not Oleg's. She walks into the kitchen and puts her hand on his shoulder, asking herself "WHAT on earth are you DOING?", yet it isn't like putting a hand on a shoulder, it's like watching a movie of someone putting a hand on a shoulder, she actually sees the hand go up into the air like some kind of mechanical claw and fly across space toward the shoulder, actually witnesses the fingers of the hand open up and grasp the shoulder and pull off the shirt and then relax as if the power's been turned off, and she also sees the muscle of the shoulder go tense and then relax and get gooseflesh. He turns. Somehow he has become naked. Has she become naked, too? She can't tell, she can't see her own body. Their faces come together. He tastes like a cinnamon bun. Bizarrely, she asks him to take his pants off. "*I pantaloni*," she says again, and he replies, "*Santa Maria*." By using her eyes and her lips in a way she hopes Oleg will never imagine she knows how to do, she makes Marco know what she wants and he approaches her, he approaches with relief like a gondola coming into the lagoon. "It doesn't matter," she tells herself. She wasn't here, she wasn't doing anything, she was in New York dreaming all this. Venice was on the other side of the world, a city in need of decent plumbing.

•

Then she realized he was not only Marco Polo but in fact *the* Marco Polo, who hadn't died in 1324 but had somehow managed, with that spectacular penis, to survive on one of the lesser canals, rowing around, picking up girls, giving them little antique *frissons* under one rotting bridge or another. Nobody died, nobody ever died, everyone came to Venice. If she was in Venice and Oleg was in Venice and Marco Polo was in Venice, who was not in Venice? Ezra Pound was doubtless eating bananas in cream in the Campo San Giacomo, with Henry James, and all the Doges were still around, from Paolo Lucio Anafesto to Ludovico Manin, arguing with one another about the price of pine or whether or not to fill in the Rio del Silvestro. The light was playing a trick on Marco Polo's shoulders, so that they were as blue as grapes, but he was saying he had wanted her for almost a thousand years, or something equally preposterous, it was difficult with the radio to get his syllables right in this vocal stew they called Italian in Venice, and in truth he was now using a lot of slang, words like *dodove* and *mantovizzi*. Perhaps, thought Olga, when you came to Venice it was not for the experience but for the kind of dream you could have there, not the adventure itself but the hope of adventure. Or perhaps—he was touching her face with the back of his hand and his hand was cold—Venice was gone. Long ago, the first time she had come here with Oleg, to this very Rio dei Mendicanti, this exact room, they had had their Venice, a fire glow and an explosion, a perspective with perfect balance, a sense of anticipation without memory, a triumphal march, and every visit to Venice after that had been nothing but awkwardly slipping away from this truth. Hunting for Venice, they were sinking into the lagoon along with Venice. "Does your husband know about me?" the young man suddenly said. *"Tuo marito sa di me?"*

•

Sitting with his espresso Oleg thought the thing to do was to find an undertaker and make arrangements since finding a doctor was out of the question in Venice. The doctors had all run off, like rats. He felt pain in his chest. He calculated he would have a heart attack in some neglected filthy Rio where kids throw food, the Rio del Vin. Before death, however, came shopping. He had to buy her something memorable, furniture, because she'd never in a million years expect it and

Surprise, after all, was Rebirth. In this case he wanted something she'd never forget, a monument. A chair, something hand-made, or something from another century. Then they could get extremely expensive fabric and have cushions made—not they, she. She could do cushions to honour his memory. She could get expensive fabric with the money he'd leave her, and cushions could be all over the house. The more expensive the better, nice frayed tapestry from a palazzo from the sixteenth century. A very very very very old man and a lady old enough to be his mother, as if transported from a palazzo of the sixteenth century, were sitting at the next table nibbling a couple of biscotti and a single pathetic piece of mortadella and watching him shrewdly. With difficulty he pulled out his camera and sat it on the table to grab those two old gargoyle faces chalked with the ash of time. All around him Venice was a grey shade of pink or a pink shade of grey and the air smelled of roasted goose. The sun had come out and was shining into his face. It was true he had been singing a very very very old song: he had long told himself he would sicken and die, and had told it very frequently in Venice because no setting is more perfectly suited to its tale, but today he knew in truth Venice would have him, he would become a property of Venice, because there was something between the kidney and the heart, a communication, and the message was dire. He had come all the way to Venice so that he could disappear. But now the old woman had stood up with difficulty, had taken her cane, and was walking his way. She was very near. This was not a personage one wished to speak to. Was she not the angel of death? Gardenias she smelled of, and she looked like a gardenia, that was the glory of it, or was it a camellia? One or the other, and one of them didn't smell. She was all pink in a shawl the colour of beets. "Do not!" she suddenly growled in a very handsome *Inglese* indeed, the *Inglese* of the Lake District. At this Oleg sat straight up and felt his arms detach. This, he thought, is *It*, this is *It Now*, the head hits the table, gone before he'd swallow the wine in his mouth and say "*morto*." But he wasn't dead at all, was he. She looked him a little too sharply in the eye: "Do not do this to your lens!" She touched the camera as if it were a living creature, almost kissed it, turned it round so the lens was pointing at Oleg and away from the sun. "I am what in the seventeenth century they called a forerunner. My husband," she gave a nod at the old man, who had meanwhile begun to doze, his chin upon his hand, "is something of a philosopher. In a moment he will come and sit with you, with your permission. He hates to be alone, but I must be off to sing, you see, to sing and then to cook. From an infinite distance we could tell you are civilized." Oleg didn't know what to make of this, but the pain in his chest was worsening. Could it be the drinking water? But he had drunk no water. "Without a lens cover, do not leave your lens in the sun. Off!" she chirruped then, rather abruptly, "We must all be off sometime, and I must buy five dozen eggs!" She vanished with a laugh into the hot red glare. She had a turquoise shirt and a yellow skirt, it was hysterical but also fabulous. The philosopher husband was still dozing, but now, behind him, there was the linguine boy with no linguine, walking here, walking there, silently gesticulating. The same one, beautiful like a Donatello, fragile, dark, if you touched him he would explode.

•

Eventually, as predicted, the old old man stood up and pointed his stick at Oleg and Oleg, even at a distance, blushed. It took the venerable fellow twenty minutes to cross the chasm between the two tables. He nodded chummily and took a chair. In fact his skin was green, there was no other word for it. This was a Green Man. He was dressed perfectly, a suit of brown tweed, a dark shirt as green as holly, a tie of chartreuse and gold with a little gold centaur pin, a pair of jade cufflinks. "Aha!" he began with a lilt in his voice, "You see, the last time I was in Venice—" He had a voice that was also green, slender, vegetable. "Well...," the voice seemed to expire. And now it seemed there were ramifications. "Why shouldn't I be honest, time's flying. I've come to Venice... with her...since, what?, 1927. Every single year. That's a lot of strokes of the oar. So after a while, I'm sure you'll appreciate, one Venice is another Venice and they're soon enough all of a piece. Memory isn't what it's cracked up to be, anyhow.

Don't kill for it. The last time I was in Venice, everyone in town had a nasty virus. Spread right across the city. Doors were shut, no-one in the streets, all the businesses boarded up. Hospitals—couldn't get in at all. I was on the Lido. Depressing to see the beach empty, and on the Canal Grande not a single boat, not one. I thought to myself at the time, I thought, just like Thomas Mann! Silly. But it was palpable. Alarming. Also vastly beautiful, if you want to know, all this sickness and silence. Took away the people and gave the city its own life. Pigeons took over. My wife, too, was in bed, sneezing and gagging and sweating. Awful. I was the only one. You could have dropped a coin on the street and heard the echoes for, what?, hours. I was the only one walking around." Oleg gave a little smile, flagged the waiter, and ordered a couple of Cinzani. "When I was a boy on my first trip to Venice I said I would die here," said the man. "Well, that was a hundred years ago and what did I know. Venice continues. Venice is continuity. Name's Crumb, by the way. Stayed in a little *penzione* near the Riva del Carbon, of all places. Wrote poetry all day long in the Campo San Giacomo. Love poems, sad poems, poems of exile. Boy's poems. M'father once told me, 'Venice makes people immortal' but he'd never been to Venice. I've written two thousand poems." The Cinzani got emptied. It was one of those moments that could go on forever, and yet were without content. Oleg stood awkwardly to leave, his awful height blocking the carmine sun and throwing Crumb into a black cave. "You Americans wouldn't really understand. For you, everything is here, in the moment, everything is to be possessed. But in truth, everything is coming." Oleg backed up a step, so that Crumb fell into darkness. "Gritti Palace. Room eleven. Come over anytime." There was something in the way the old, old eyes did not let go.

•

So, instead of leaving, Oleg did sit down again. "Ah," said Crumb blithely, "you surrender." There really was nothing to say, so Oleg said he was in pain. He said he had been in pain for some time. If it was a strange thing to say to a stranger, yet it was a truth. Crumb, for his part, didn't flinch for a very long time. "Pain is relative," said he, and in the same breath, "Did you bring your wife to Venice?" And then, as the answer was on Oleg's tongue, "Have you seen the dancing boy, speaking of dervishes?" Had they been speaking of dervishes? Oleg felt his throat go dry. "Young man? Black hair? Sort of a dancer? I myself have seen him for years. Never grows older. Been telling myself I'm crazy. Course, one is always crazy in Venice. This time, my wife has also seen him, I'm quite sure. He's come to both of us." Crumb was no longer smiling, and he seemed to have swum away into a place with illumination but without wind, a perspective from which one did not move. He drew his hands off the little table, to be sure. "You know, your wife undoubtedly comes here for one thing. You come for another. There it is. True with all who visit Venice. But the boy doesn't come to everyone. What is it you do? Look like a lawyer on vacation. Forgive my curiosity, at my age it's nutritional. I was once, several centuries ago, a lawyer on vacation. Decided to stop working for other people, eventually to stop working at all. My wife sings, I sit. It's lovely, sitting. Apparently one has so much money stuffed away here and there one need do nothing but sit for the next several hundred years! Sit all afternoon opening envelopes and endorsing cheques. Don't even know the people the cheques come from. Accountant assures me we will never know the extent of it. Money coming out of my ears, as they say. Not that there's enough to buy another life." With shocking agility then he stood, gave a tidy little bow, and walked off with an amazing briskness into the sunset, tipping his hat, not smiling, and quite melting into the ruby puddle that was the sun's basking place on the old dark stones. The boy doesn't come to everyone.

•

"Marco" had fallen asleep as naked as a violin, and Olga, who had wanted him to make love to her, or who had wanted to make love to him, to pluck him, or perhaps only to watch him pluck himself, who had wanted to lick his grain, had wanted him to be upon her in positions even she could not imagine, military positions, amphibious, megalomaniac positions, she who had always owned a thought to substitute for an action, she who had scenarized and agonized, now wanted nothing. She fingered his back and he did not move. Was he real? Had she conjured him, one more of her curses? She navigated gently with her finger to the bottom of his spine, telling herself she could feel him. Now he rolled over, and touched his penis with the tips of his thumb and forefinger, casually, innocently, as if it were a wine glass empty on a table. The radio was still playing, music by Nino Rota now. "I have to ask, what is your name?" said Olga. "Marco," said he, making an O of his fingers, as if of course it were self-evident, and she felt her stomach rise and thought, this is certainly enough. She was outside in the street, gasping for breath, finding a gondoliere who would take her back to the hotel, the water dark purple, the colour of wine. They were gliding past the Palazzo Businello, a dark tomb-like shape that made jabbering noises because of the million pigeons, and suddenly there in a shaft of sunset was the linguine boy in the green jacket, waving his hands, dancing with himself in silence. A chill struck her, because she wanted to stop and watch him, call out to him, but a voice in her head said, "No, he is unspeakable." This was the nonsense to end nonsense, of course, and she knew she had reached a point in her many comings to Venice, her excursions for the prize of the great kiss which is Venice, her intense need to comprehend the incomprehensible Venice, her thirst for the unceasing river which is Venice, her itch for the provocative fingertip which is Venice, when Venice had reached out and gulped her. Was it that they had come too quickly, on the spur of a moment without hesitation, without calculation, without the architecture of desire? Was it that he didn't understand her anymore? He certainly never questioned, never wondered; she was a crossword filled in and fading. She knew she would go back to the hotel room and, damnably predictable, he would have bought flowers, red carnations, dark red the colour of pony blood, and he would have booked a table for dinner. Gamberoni, Gavi, a gondola on the infernal lagoon. Yet what she wanted she was not getting, this was a truth, and for what she had she could feel no want. Now that boy in green was waving in her direction, such a wave, the smile, the hair, but he was smaller and smaller, he was becoming a dot as the gondoliere put some muscle into it against the oncoming darkness, all the Canale flickering purple and red and gold like some vast firmament above and around and beneath. That kiss—was he not throwing it to her, here, now, alone, until the end of time? "*Putana*!" grumbled the gondoliere when she paid him, his mouth an ugly hole. She wanted then, insatiably, to convince him he was wrong but words failed her.

•

She opened her eyes in fear and stood up. The bedroom of the hotel. Why had she locked the connecting door? Because the lagoon had changed in her life and she was no longer full of hope? She opened it and gazed into Oleg's room. He was not waiting, like a magnate in a suit with golden rings twinkling on dark fingers. The lights were off and the darkness had almost fallen, the room was gloom. She smelled his aftershave, thought this was the moment to run out and buy something, a bound leather notebook, or take an espresso slowly, thinking of the thousands of slow espressos one had taken that led one here, to this empty moment where everything was vibration. Or sit and read the newspaper, not in that delirious way without paying any attention at all to the words in this hour before the sun was gone yet after the energies of the day had been expended—the most wonderful hour in Venice—but empty and with weight at the same time, the hands both insubstantial and heavy, the feet flying and upon the ground. Instead she stood and fixed her eyes at the long elegant naked frame of the window and looked out at the rectangle of creeping darkness beyond which was this island, this non-city, this uncivilized prison, this cell, this holy place. In the street, would the boy be dancing again and would she go to meet him? And would his name, too, be Marco? Marco everywhere, Marco everybody. His waving hands, his panic. She told herself don't look, don't look, on pain of mortality don't go to the window. She went to the window. She looked down into the street. He wasn't there, or he was in the shadows. She tried to invent him, and invisible, he resisted her.

•

Dinner was perfect, the flowers were perfect, the ride upon the lagoon was by moonlight. He didn't know how to reach her. Her posture was all composure, the folds of her dress spread with balance across the altar of her lap, and it was a gorgeous dress, this had to be said, it had been made for her but it could as well have been made for a movie star, white organza inlaid with lagoon green, with a matching cape. Plip plip, went the water beside the gondola, plip plip. "We keep failing to solve the riddle," he said, as if trying to make a beginning of what felt like an ending. "When you've had enough to drink, you stop drinking. Don't you agree? When you've had enough to drink, you sit with a full glass and wait." She watched and watched and watched. Oleg tried very hard indeed to frame this, and you could see the veins popping blue at his temples as he worked. He sat back in the gondola and listened to the plip plip of the water. Plip plip for a long time. When you've had enough to drink you stop drinking. She watched and watched, the ravenous smile slowly setting on her face, passing onto the water, drowning. He didn't move at all, only the boat moved. And then even the boat didn't move, only the city of Venice moved, up and down in the purple darkness, up and down, up and down, the whole city, its fiery lights, its towers. Its history, its future, plip plip. Oleg, for his part, didn't flinch. Not a phoneme. Was he even breathing? Had he—everything in her head suddenly went red—had he gone under in Venice? But then suddenly in that voice which could have seduced angels, "Perhaps we should go home tomorrow," he said, "tomorrow instead of four days." He was waiting in the darkness with his lips parted, having offered the formula, waiting to see if it would open the lock. She moaned something you wouldn't understand, language but not words, and she held her breath for dear life. Before bed they had hot milk with amaretto sent up, with little chocolates wrapped in gold, perfect little geometrical nothings. He had hoped, in truth, for a treaty, that they might agree if Venice had often been wonderful and sometimes even barbaric this time it was a mistake, that you made mistakes, cleaned up, moved on, even if you didn't know how long was the canal on which you were rowing, or how much strength you had left for pulling against the thick water. But instead of a truce she was offering a look that might have cursed. He was somewhere else, thinking Crumb's wife had a coffee stain on her blouse.

•

"Venice, you know, is only a poor little spot in Italy," Crumb had told him. "People get carried away by Venice, but it is a fact the sun rises over it, and the sun sets, as with every other spot on earth." Oleg rang the Gritti Palace and asked for Signore Crumb in room 511. "No Signore, we have a person by no such name, Signore. We have no room 511. *Impossibile*." Late in the morning he handled the packing himself, Olga having piled everything she had bought in the last three hours in piles upon the bed, piles reaching to the sky. As he stood back and looked at the piles with the window light filtering in, it was as if the gifts were another Venice, the bedspread another lagoon. There was a flight at 2:30. Now the horrible pain was back, or the horrible vacuum, it was impossible to know which, so notable he thought he might never make it downstairs to the lobby, and he wondered how he could last ten hours in the air, whether he'd need to be horizontal or whether in a moment, like a fog under the sun, like an old perfume that had lingered on the surface of life, he would simply evaporate. "There is an irony about Venice, you know, Oleg, just for your information, for you to put in the file, because the one thing to say about you is, you keep files. We all know you keep files. Venice, Oleg, was the antidote." The airport of Venice was almost empty, only two or three flights were operating. What, he wondered as they handed over the bags, had one needed an antidote for? She was scanning the territory for a boutique that sold *Coloromantica*. The security screening was much too fast, like a nightmare race which has no finish line and no prize. At the gate, agents in uniform were checking one's passport. Did one step up with special excitement at the idea of going home, getting away from here before, finally, the place reached out some barnacled tentacle and snagged one into the sad lagoon of memory and tasteful tedium? "What I mean is," said she, "about

Venice being the antidote—it represented something one had to get out of one's system. The idea that everything is in Venice. The idea that Venice is life." Now there was nothing to say, although evidently she was looking for an answer, quite as if her sanity depended on it. But then she spoke again, in a voice that for a moment, while he watched the security guard's bored face, he didn't even recognize. "When I am in New York, I never stop feeling I am invisible. I am made of celluloid with my face printed on it, frame after frame. Venice, I tell myself...I think I must find a way to get an hour in Venice, ten minutes in Venice. I have moments in New York when I think for a cup of espresso and nothing else I would come to Venice. But really there is no door out of what we are. I suppose it shouldn't, but it really does make me feel much better to say that." *Was* Venice a door? It was a riddle that would surely be solved one day when they came back to Venice. The last checkpoint before the jetway was manned by a single person, who now turned to present himself. If he was intending to smile he quickly seized the impulse and pocketed it, tilting his slender head with its huge eyes and its curly black hair. His hands moved like dancers in the air while he looked at the documents they held out. "Marco," read his name tag. *"Benvenuti a Venezia!"* he said courteously, with a little bow, as they stepped past him onto the chilly plane.

Tabula Rasa

So very little did Marlowe and Olga find to admire in one another, for quite the longest time, it was inconsequential—and indeed seemed to many unbelievable—that they were friends. Her criticism of him was that his arrogance, which might have been boyish, was brutish. Now, a man has a general arrogance, this much one can take for granted; and he often finds a way to use it for good. To the general woman he uplifts himself—some say he dominates, but most men do not feel the dominance they have—and to some individuals he seems even godly. But in the face of his lover a man can surely shed his manhood in favour of something more honest. Yet, in favour of what? Many of his younger colleagues at the office, fresh out of Yale, looked to Marlowe for an answer to this sacred question and looked in vain. In the face of his lover, Olga told herself, a man becomes only a possibility. Here was a thought she could treasure. But Marlowe, to all reports, did not moult. Olga found—and she was something of a judge—that to his wife he was inconsiderate, he was stiff. (She could not know this was only the appearance he contrived to give, so that Cowrie, in her own peculiar aggression, could be protected.) From afar he never brought gifts. Money did not come out of his pockets for her, though she planted clues. "She already has," he would say. He practised, indeed, in the name of self-denial, denial, and for all his assiduousness in this it might well have been a yoga. But he held himself, in spite of all this exercise, very high; because the house on the dune, the astronomical house, that he was renting from the owner of a gallery on East 70th Street, he very commodiously referred to as his own. Certainly most people who visited there thought they were coming into his territory, by the way he stood near the woodpile to offer drinks. Cowrie shrank from him, there was no denying it. She hid in her room with Vicomte de L'Isle Adam, she hid on the telephone. If he read the newspaper with genuine aggression—not the mere typical masculine information-gathering, but utter preparation for war—she only watched respectfully, arranging scented candles, slipping through the *TLS*, brewing rosehip tea to drink in a little Japanese cup with a plate of citron macaroons. All of these aspects bothered Olga about him (not that Olga found Cowrie overwhelmingly endearing) but she did have to admit—"I have," she muttered, "fully to admit": none of them were any of her business. What troubled her personally was his excessive friendliness, as if there might, in the end, be something delectable in his relation with her. He deadheaded her hydrangeas in March. He dug her car out in December. He fetched her mail and carted off her garbage to the town landfill, bumping along that road behind the veterinarian's and coming back, always, with a smile of relief on his face to claim, "Since I was a teenager, it has been a distinct pleasure for me to dump *any* garbage. I love the feeling of letting bags go out of my hands over the pit." But even here, she knew her complaints were entirely irrational. What was there to dislike in such an Adonis, in such a Croesus, indeed; in such a Pentheus up his extremely costly imported ginger tree? Or was it a baobab? He'd insanely paid $2,000 for it and it couldn't possibly grow in Sunday, but there you had it. Something more proximate must be floating against her follicles, and when she thought and thought it resolved that she could not find it, not at all, yet Marlowe stood in place of the Invisible, stood implacable, overbearing, a little too conscious of his inherited mien, a little too openly knowledgeable about hydroelectric projects in the Netherlands and what they would do to you in the second quarter if you sold your equity, or however he put it. Even this didn't say it, or didn't say enough. She had to force herself to see that her true difficulty lay in the figure of the fact of Cowrie's complaints, seen against the ground of the fact that social intercourse with Marlowe had been nothing but distinctly felicitous. He was a charmer, he had given good wine, he told decent tales and knew when to shut the mouth (and also the refrigerator); yet Cowrie rankled. So, if Cowrie was an epigon of civilization, what could Marlowe be underneath his mask, but a Tartar?

•

Yet perhaps he was an aesthete. The thought of this, she had to swear in court, was a stimulation, but beyond stimulation it was true she had found no ticket to ride. One could recall that, sitting with his cognac, he flattered himself a connoisseur, chattered about how the very best cognacs came from Barbézieux (apparently, someone whose name and face he had forgotten had told him this once). And in that spirit, it may have been the case, Marlowe came to feel Cowrie had been, more than a redemption, a trap. She had never been a person of the body as much as a person of the spirit, and when he had married her (in the little English village of Rodmell, where blood tests were not required, and where Virginia Woolf had killed herself, and in a churchyard in the rain) it was the truth that spirit was all he wanted of the world. He had been all spirit. At the time, for instance, she had suffered the most excruciating migraines and so he walked down the road that trickled beside the yellow Ouse, all the way to the Newhaven, four miles, and then all the way back, and then all the way into Lewes, two and a half more miles, past the tawny stallions grazing at Northease, and all the way back from there, and then over to Southease, crossing the railway footbridge and passing the lines of lush mallows and up to Itford farm and all the way up to elegiac Bedlingham and back again; and then he knelt in that churchyard and prayed for her in the rain; but the headaches didn't go away at all, but she was so touched by him she fell in love all over again, except then he got a horrid case of shinsplints. Nowadays, instead of brushing her hair as she had then, and instead of falling in love with him all over again, Cowrie read. Her library had three times been reconstructed for shelving. And there were moments when she believed herself the reincarnation of Vanessa Bell. All the bookshelves she had painted by hand with great purple floppy irises, and she laid canvas upon her chairs and painted it, too. She invited queer sorts for dinner and befriended queerers. Everden Quayle was not by any consideration the queerest (although he was the queerest one remembered). She fed tiny portions of Japanese soups to them, but ate nothing herself and fed exclusively upon conversation, which Marlowe found beneath fascination. There was something wrong with her, as it were. Her books were covered in crabbed marginalia. She spoke in marginalia. She was not the sort of wife of whom one could successfully boast at a stockbroker's luncheon, over cold beef and Saint-Estèphe, or else signing a deal to make a show happen, at Balthazar. Or in the locker-room of the squash court. She did not have shape and so one could not boast of her. And part of playing with money had been coming to appreciate—as his friends in the business also knew how to appreciate—shapes. It was all, to be honest, sexual. Without shape there could be no intimation, without intimation no promise, without a promise no sense of time, no finish line, no solidity. In her somewhere she had the shape of an idea, that was perhaps true, but one didn't wish to touch her to feel its edges. It was awful to say of a wife, but to himself, perhaps, sipping that cognac, he would say that she wasn't touchable, and that she didn't promise what the other wives promised, and therefore that as an investment she could perhaps be said to have a low return. Cowrie, however, always seemed a Galatea compared to the harridan next door. The Tartar found impossible in Olga what in Cowrie would have been merely unpleasant—a way of entering a room like a queen, slowly, processionally. This came, no doubt, from being looked at too much as a girl, but Olga had not lost her girlishness and in a woman who has produced little girls, girlishness is hideous. Olga's mouth, too, had passed beyond control. Olga had given up moral responsibility. If she had given up responsibility for herself it could only be because, first, she had mislaid responsibility for everyone and everything else. The world was a palace for her, looked after by menials, in which she could roost and pronounce and become dissipated. Cowrie would never roost, she would clean, she would dab at her linoleum until it was a poem. Marlowe may have been an aesthete, but I think not; I think he was a boor masquerading as an aesthete, and he detested poems.

•

And so he went walking on the beach at midnight in a November night, because no matter what poets say there is nothing poetic about a beach, a beach is the real thing, and there in the dune was Olga, crying. Olga cried quite loudly, even hysterically—it was embarrassing. Especially embarrassing, somehow, in the notable vacancy of the place, and because she was in a shadow cast by a safety lamp that shone past a parking regulations sign. She was hunched, or neonate. He had to strain his eyes to see whether someone was curled up with her. But she was by herself, and the waves seemed to wash in only for her, and she hadn't noticed him yet. "I went for a walk to clear my mind of the entire history of my life," he said, a little politely, as he approached, and she answered, "Oh my God!" and covered her face. Then there were interminable seconds while she found some corner of her shirt to wipe her eyes and he fiddled in his pockets for a non-existent handkerchief. He crouched with her. "I imagine you want to be alone." She made burbling sounds, not at all unlike the ocean, and he stretched out his feet and began to tell her, for some reason, where he had been born. It was the queerest conversation. She became silent and listened. He said he didn't like the beach, didn't like Sunday, didn't like coming out here every weekend to be with Cowrie and the kids. He felt a bundle of nerves, he said, and every moment of the peaceful time was a burden to him because there was so much he felt he should be doing instead of this great, constantly swelling, peaceful nothing. He had never spoken to anyone so directly, so openly, or so speedily, and soon he was telling about his fears that he would never have any money to speak of, that the bubble would just burst and disappear, and that he would have trouble remembering that there had ever been a bubble, that he would spend his life scrambling over pebbles in the middle class, and about his marriage, that more than anything it was an architecture, that Cowrie couldn't be said to love him, that he no longer knew whether he loved her. It must have been half an hour he quietly prated, and the sea came in hissing, and she rocked back and forth and you couldn't see her face at all in the dune shadows from the light that was far too harsh. Then he had to breathe, and as he lay back she said, "Oleg and I fight. I tried to kill him tonight."

•

"We fight about everything, there is nothing we agree upon. He wants to save money, I want to spend it. He wants to become an academic, I want him to practice law until he's blue in the face and we're multi-millionaires. At the moment we don't have any money, and your problems seem like sardines in the sea. What we have is seven charge cards, they're all way past the limit. Our two bank accounts are each overdrafted by over $10,000. My father gives us money, along with sermons on how to spend it, and before you can turn around it's gone. We're going to Venice in three weeks and that will cost $15,000 for ten days, minimum. A day after we come back—I'm quite aware of this—I will desperately need a holiday and poor Oleg will be at his wits' end trying to figure out how to please me. I can't help it, it's like a disease. I also know that if we try *not* to go to Venice, if we try to make plans to stay out here or in the city, I will lose my mind and actually kill someone. I went at Oleg with a kitchen knife tonight. He just stood there. I don't think he cares anymore, and maybe he even hopes I'll be successful. I don't fucking know, but he fucking well better fucking come up with a couple of fucking thousand dollars by next week or we're screwed permanently. I mean permanently. We have to put a down payment on the private school for the Principessa, and we have to get a new car. I can't stand driving this heap of shit we drive for one more day. I told Oleg tonight, if you don't go tomorrow and get another fucking car, a rental, anything, I'm going to climb the walls and lose my mind. I feel continually as if I'm in a room with paper-thin walls, and outside the room is insanity, and the walls are bulging out and ready to pop. It's only a matter of time. I'm racing around and I can't stop, and the more I run the more the walls bulge out and threaten to pop. Oleg's leaving. He's taking the kids into the city first thing in the morning. He says I need a few days to calm down. I'll fucking calm down! I am going to lose my mind utterly and completely if we don't get a new car tomorrow. And if he doesn't finish a case and get a billing so we can pay the school. We probably shouldn't go to Venice. I'll tell him in the morning before he leaves. He can cancel the tickets to Venice and we can use that money for the school. It's just that if I don't go to Venice I will lose it. And fucking Oleg can't make any decisions by himself, that's what made me try to kill him. I have to do everything, and I've just reached my limit. But he doesn't take anything I do seriously. He went to bed. I told him, dream about a car." She said all this virtually in a single breath, and still sobbing but more and more drily, and then she punctuated it all with a musical little phrase: "I hear we're going to get a hurricane." Marlowe's response, "Yes, that's what I hear, too," came in an altogether absent kind of voice, but galvanization was running in his spine. She had awakened him, and he was understanding now why poets come to the beach.

•

Their two houses were directly upon the dune, a spot architects usually knew enough to stay away from in this part of the world and weekenders from the city fought tooth and nail to secure. Marlowe and Cowrie's place was modern where it should perhaps have called up the nineteenth century. Great sheets of glass fronted upon the ocean—a total idiocy in the face of hurricanes. At the hardware store, Marlowe had the luck of the city boy—which to say, he discovered that all the flashlights, all the batteries, all the Coleman stoves were long gone. At the lumberyard he was fortunate in the same way with the plywood sheeting. What he was able to secure was finishing nails, for putting the stuff up against the window frames, and a hammer for nailing them. The supermarket, too, was cleaned out. A lot of people were talking about using masking tape on their windows so he bought the two remaining rolls of masking tape, oblivious to the fact that he would have needed dozens of rolls to do his seaside windows alone. These windows were the size of tennis courts. Cowrie was pacing back and forth beside these windows, murmuring to herself that her life had gone wrong, that she had been fated, that her inspiration had turned against her in a great cataclysm of darkness and pathos and inversion—she got her exercise this way, so vast were the windows. Oleg and Olga, who should by rights have had vast windows and a kitchen by Smeg, had a place from the nineteenth century; which when it was built parodied the seventeenth century. The windows were tiny and Olga persuaded Marlowe to gift her enough of his masking tape to cover them. "You'll come here for the storm," said she. "We'll have a storm party. Cowrie has gone back to the city. Oleg has gone back to the city. There is no sense in two adults occupying two houses." This was true. Cowrie and Oleg, with the children, had gone back to the city, leaving the poodle and the Weimaraner, Louella and Bogart, with two Philippino nannies, Joleen and Alise, in two Range Rovers, black and maroon; they had gone early, on the 6:59, having risen with the sun. They had gone back to the city without peace of mind, and the train had been a minute late getting out of the station because of a problem down the line with a signal. They had occupied adjoining seats, and the children had fallen asleep again, and they had looked at one another, Cowrie and Oleg, soberly and wisely but without much to say. "Two adults occupy one house," Olga said. "If your windows break, you will telephone your insurance, or the owner's insurance. Let the owner worry about it. Let the owner worry about everything. That is why one rents. That is why rental is paradise. At any rate, it is all moot. The hurricane will bypass Sunday. In the morning tomorrow, you will have windows. We will sit with candles and I will cook soup and we will engage one another with stories of our lives and other fantastic subjects. Let the winds blow."

•

If the winds blew they blew in silence. The sky became poppy red, then bile yellow, then dark, as dark as Whistler etchings. Olga put up the heat. She did not make soup, but she supervised while Marlowe did. He used tinned materials and added parsnips and cubes of bread. "What can I say?" she kept saying. Marlowe concentrated upon the smell of the thing, and added thyme. "What can I say, what can I say?" She took a rag and began to clean. "I have an uncontrollable desire," she said with a little too much melody. He looked up, stirring. "I have an uncontrollable desire to spend money." He thought perhaps he saw something fly against the leading of the little window above and to the right of the refrigerator, a bird? "A hurricane," said Olga, "is God's way of touching the world. Everything else is his imagination, but a hurricane is direct touch. Of course, I don't know what I'm talking about." And then, as if a knife had been thrown at him, he heard her whisper, "You look as tense as a tree." Mozart's *Eine Kleine Nachtmusik* was, of course, in order, but a minute into it the power gave out.

•

As he had been every month for years, Owen was at Doc's house again. He had brought his Arriflex because tonight there would be a hurricane and that would be something to get on film. Now he was wrapped underneath a blanket, to brave premonitions of the storm. If once a month he still went out to Sunday and tended the lawns on both sides of the house, went inside and checked that everything was in order, not because Juniper had asked him to, although she was always careful to leave money, but because he felt it was his duty to the ghosts, being here tonight and photographing the storm was a duty, too. Owen had spent so much time on the island he considered himself an islander. It felt as if there were nothing of Sunday he did not know—not the surface Sunday, the Sunday of maps and legend, but the characters, the whispered provocative tales. He shot some film in the great empty house, the parlour, the kitchen, the empty medicine cabinet where Doc had written in pencil on the edges of the shelves, "Paregoric...tranquilizers...emetics...pain killers," the empty bird feeders swaying now in the rough wind that shook the cypress tree. He shot his way over to the garage, very Godard. He reached through the cobwebs and turned on the lights and walked up to Doc's suite, Arri in front of his face, very Cassavetes, and the air was still full of the stench of oil paints and all of the papers had yellowed and the furniture had gathered dust and gone rotten and cold. He shot the tall wooden cupboards with the filing cabinets still side by side like mongoloid twins, locked. One for books, one for patients. He put down the camera and stared at them coldly, thinking that somewhere there was a key. If he could only find it he could pry open this secret world of which Doc had been king. Bring back the past, since everything written here was already history. Bring back the history and open it to the light. He walked over to the high windows and looked in every drawer of the working table Doc had had built there, through pens and paintbrushes, razor blades, string, lots of coin, cigarettes that disintegrated when he touched them, rubber bands. No key. He went back to the cabinets and tried them, but yes, they were all locked. Doc's kingdom of tortured souls. There were a few of Doc's sport jackets hanging in a cupboard, and he riffled through the pockets. He took himself back into the house and went through drawers—more coins, more rubber bands, pens, pencils, scissors, scotch tape all brittle and blue—and stood finally at the shelf in the pantry that held the mustards and the chutneys, dozens of them, brown and desiccated, bottles bought dozens of years before. In the face of mustards and chutneys gone dry and solid, one gives up hope. One by one, quite without hope—in fact, in a perfect bubble of hopelessness—he lifted the chutney bottles and thought, "Gone, gone. Gone, gone," and knew that by now one was no longer young, one had gained an eye, one could see the world for what it was. Under the chutney bottles on the shelf was nothing, really: two dead flies, a penny, a paper clip, the pattern carved into the dust of a tiny key, a postage stamp pressed down onto the wood. It took several long seconds before he realized what he was looking at, the pattern of the key, and, holding the chutney bottle up to the silver flickering light that was streaming in through the windows, he saw that stuck to the bottom of the jar in a dab of congealed chutney was the key itself. With a butter knife he pried it out, rinsed it, and raced back to the garage. "Sprint," he told himself, and a young man like Owen should have been able to do that because he wasn't debilitated anymore, the debilitating migraines were gone, but he moved slowly, heavily, as if held back by an inner voice. "To crack open the files of a dead man...? Shame." But anyway the key didn't work.

•

The files of the dead man had been waxed shut, and in the winter cold the wax had hardened. He ran down the stairs and went back to the house, ransacked the kitchen drawers for a sharp-pointed knife. This he brought back and used feverishly on the wax—it took an hour—until the pink coating seal had been chipped away. But still some wax was inside the lock and he needed to bend down and use the knifepoint at close range for another hour to make access possible. The key went in stiffly, and turned only with pressure, but finally, one by one, the pair of locks popped and the drawers came open with a horrid, scrunching sound. The book files he didn't care about. Book files become manuscripts, manuscripts are published, books go on bookshelves. On bookshelves beside the filing cabinets, in fact, lay the books themselves, six copies of each, the red cover and the green cover. But the patient files were something else and he plunged into them, thick and faded, and saw that they had been organized according not to names but to code words: APPLE (broker, age: 43, Marlowe T.), SCORECARD (literary scholar, age: 39, Cowrie T.), NUTHATCH (lawyer, age: 41, Oleg F.), FIREFLY (housewife, age: 37, Olga F.), and so on. Each file had hundreds of sheets of yellow lined paper filled with his black scrawl—Owen had seen him sitting at the kitchen table writing them, hour after hour, with his tea, cup after cup, cooling until it was undrinkable and one cigarette after another burning down to nothingness in an ashtray. Here and there he took a peek from the corner of his eye inside a dossier. Phrases caught him: "...unresolved dichotomy"; "longevity or clarity...." He sat and read. He sat and read all of them, as if they were fairy tales. Some were pretty clear, some were cryptic, even completely obscure. THE SNAIL (age: 27), for example, was utterly incomprehensible from start to finish, something about a young husband terrified of his wife—but he couldn't make out any more. Only one file in the collection had an actual name on it, the very last, and the name was his. A slender file, as he himself was slender. He drew it open, holding his breath. It was empty. "Life," Doc had always said, "is a hazardous business."

•

The storm brewed and boiled. Clouds parted occasionally and let a kind of silver light streak down onto the beach. Snapping and howling sounds were everywhere, and in the darkness branches blew through the air like spears. The young man wore a torn sweater and a parka and a double layer of sweat pants. The rain upon the dune was hard, like bullets, but the wind that struck him full force in the belly was curiously silent. The enormous beach house that looked like a giant cube was dark. "Odd," he thought, circling among its labyrinthine hedges, creeping onto its verandah. Through the taped windows he saw the bulky meaningless forms of its furniture, its coffee table as big as a swimming-pool. No lights. "Where's he gone, the cellar?" He slid to the side of the house and peered through low windows that Marlowe had forgotten to tape, windows he knew wouldn't be there in the morning. The basement was a great black hole. "But that one will certainly not have gone anywhere," he muttered, and headed to the neighbouring house, the house that could have been built for Sir Walter Raleigh. There the candles were glowing faintly and even from far off he could see the movement of shadows. He let film roll from a distance and brought the camera as smoothly as he could to the face of the window. They had put a fire in the hearth—not so smart—and were eating noodles upon a pair of pink beach towels in front of it. He felt the cold rain hard on his cheek and the finger of his hand freezing on the trigger of the Arri. Mentally running down what was in his pockets he calculated there was enough film to last—if he was careful—halfway through the night.

•

Around midnight at the back of the house there was a banshee wail but otherwise nothing penetrated the great silence. Chess continued until a modified Capoblanca inversion at 1:15 in the morning. This was followed by backgammon, which degenerated into Parcheesi with a plate of cheeses and cold bread. Hungry Hungry Hippo was an excuse for Pol Roger 1986 drunk from styrofoam—all that Olga could find—and when the night was at its thickest, by the light of the stubby grey taper, they slid into strip poker. Or blackjack, since neither knew enough to continue poker beyond the initial deal. "I will tell you what I really believe," said Olga. "It doesn't matter what we do tonight. This storm will wipe out the house, wipe out the two of us, wipe out the dune. The ocean will be where you are sitting, at noon tomorrow. Come, be merry. We are so repelled by one another there can be no alternate solution." Marlowe hadn't said much, but now a thought came to his lips. "I hardly know you." Her face, at this, became grim, and her hands in the light could be seen to become purposeful. He had a five-card Charlie and she took off her shirt entirely.

•

Marlowe went upon the beach at first light. It was difficult from this distance to see the nearest trees, but they had been halved and split vertically and on the ocean side alone, as far as he could make out, their leaves were gone or salted brown. The house was intact. His place was intact as well. A red pail and green shovel had been thrown casually up against the front door—he'd stupidly forgotten the kids' beach stuff in an open bin. The beach itself had been levelled and polished like a sheet of glass. The dune crests smoothed and erased of footprints and all the marks of time. The water was the colour of a blue topaz, the sky crisp as at Christmas. The sand was hard to the touch. It was not that his marriage to Cowrie was over, he realized in this soft, patient light. It was that his marriage to Cowrie had never, in a crucial way, existed. She had gone off with the children, he now remembered, without saying goodbye, as if there was nothing material out here to say goodbye to. Her life was an academic life, a life of the mind. His was a life undecided. He had been living with her, and he would go back to live with her again, but without the illusion that had flavoured the cocktails. It was the sex with Olga that had reformed him, one could argue, but really the sex was a registration upon a map, a point from which attention could be fixed and directed; a milestone which demanded—only—cogitation. The cogitation produced the awareness. Olga didn't count, Cowrie was the one who counted, but counted as what? For Olga the sex was so self-fulfilling as to be dreamlike, and it drove her more closely to Oleg only because it produced in her a great hunger and Oleg was her mother bird. After all, satisfaction being impossible for Olga, only desire could be the produce of pleasure, and she was on the phone to Oleg within minutes. But Marlowe, on the beach, saw that he was himself little more than a flat untrammelled sheet, a tabula rasa. If Cowrie had failed to make the necessary impression upon him she certainly had a future in which to try, and her literacy gave every promise that signals of some sharpness would fly out of her. But he had been able to do nothing, could do nothing now, and felt a bonding between himself and the sand that was only perturbed caressingly by the sea. He drove into the city and made arrangements to give up the place in the country. There was a road to follow to find the light for oneself, but it lay ahead.

•

The young man who had filmed all night, who at sunrise had filmed the emptied town and the sad, sad dunes, had been filming on the beach in the morning. The two houses were on his film, and the brief, agonized liaison was on his film; he had filmed through a window every move of the two naked bodies before the fire, the man's body and the woman's body that was like a boy's. He had filmed the dune grass blowing flat in the hurricane wind. He had filmed Firefly answer the telephone and wave Apple away, and Apple leaving the house. He had filmed Apple standing in front of the waves, staring out toward England as the yellow sun came up. He had filmed without being seen as Apple went back to the big cubical house, entered it, walked around in front of the picture window that looked out upon the waves, walked out again, got into his car, and drove away. Now his batteries were all exhausted and the camera was hanging from his hand. As the roar of the waves came again and again, as the flat, mirror beach spread around him and grew bright with day, he reached into his pocket and drew out a something tiny and metallic and flashing in the light, stepped forward—clasping it tightly—into the water. He walked out, balanced himself, and out and out until he pants were wet, and threw the sacred object far, far away into the sacred sea.

Rite de Passage

Ettie Savage had put her knitting down in the nook beside her thigh. It roiled and cascaded upon the dilapidated chair like torrents in a Hokusai. "Oh God," she said, about nothing in particular, and with a great weariness. Trudy Kay, who had finished selling the Kamerman dune house at two o'clock and the Sloughton house by the golf course at 5:30 and was sitting with her knees folded beneath her a few feet away, didn't make an answer. She gritted her teeth. She leaned forward, with her hands upon her knees, coughing a little, and observed with a cold grin Katie Monahan-Prudent taking High Roller over the picket fence, over the liverpool, over the big oxer, the second big oxer, the triple bar to finish at the Classic with no faults. "I don't know; is she a good rider? Is that what good riding is?" she said in that hoarse barking mezzo-soprano Ettie thought she might well have been listening to forever, "It seems to me she's swaying back and forth a lot on that horse, she's like a parakeet or something. Is there a word for what she's doing?" Ettie stared hard into her closest remaining friend's Puck's face, which reminded her of: what?, with pigtails and a lollipop, on a tree-lined street in Brooklyn Heights, God knew how many years ago. Trudy Kay couldn't let go of it, now any more than ever. "She's—you tell me, I wouldn't know—a punching bag up there. Shouldn't she be part of the horse or something? A shoulder? A vertebra? I look at her and I don't know what I'm looking at." Ettie would have said, normally, with a rich and enchanting laugh, "She's very *very* good! And you're so very *very* funny! Katie Monahan-Prudent knows everything there is to know about the movements of that horse and she's riding in perfect harmony. This is a *fine* ride. Not just a good ride. This is a solid, graceful ride. This is a championship ride." But she said instead, without a smile, "Can you correct the colour a bit, dear? Can you get it a little less red?" The screen might have been bleeding. Then, as if to emphasize—Trudy thought at the time, because there was really no other sensible explanation—she added, "Oh God," again, rather ingenuously, and her fingers made the needles at her side click a little in the warm room that was otherwise sounding only the small hiss of the television. "You think it's too red?" said Trudy Kay, "I don't think it's red. Maybe it's yellow." She got up and fiddled with the redness. "I think it's yellow. How do you fix the yellow?" She made clicking sounds with her teeth. "See, let me tell you—that other fellow, what was his name, Ferguson?—" Ettie's lips, framed thoroughly with lines, pursed a little. "What was that other fellow's name, Ettie. Ferguson, wasn't it? *Ferguson* didn't move his posterior so much. Is that better? I've taken away the yellow." Ettie felt a dryness in her throat that she'd not felt before, the sort of thing a cup of tea would be nice for, except that she didn't feel the energy to stand up and make a cup of tea. "That Ferguson was what I'd call noble," said Trudy Kay, turning around in a circle, "I've lost my cigarettes." She had on spectacles with very thick lenses so there was something vaguely owlish about her scanning the room. She flicked her fingers. "Ferguson was my kind of boy!" Ettie spoke, finally. "*Fargas*," she said. "Joe *Fargas*. He's old school. Nowadays, anyway. He's old, old school. Though, I remember when he began. I remember way before he began. It's like yesterday. But he's old school. Do you feel like putting the kettle on, dear?" When she said this last she didn't really move, she sat in a queenly stillness, all around her the purple and the grey heather wools in gloried spirals, and a fly went up to the skylight and nosed around the barometric wires that Doc had fitted what?, 30 years ago, and that were slipping in from the roof, and one of which had come disconnected, or had Doc disconnected it? Doc would climb up and fix it, maybe tomorrow, but Doc was gone. Katie Monahan-Prudent was being interviewed now, more than boringly, so with the channel changer on her knee she selected something very different. "See," said Trudy Kay from the kitchen, her voice singing in as if from a public address system, "I'll put it to you this way, maybe this will make it clear: what's her name, Katie Monahan? She's *horsey*. Whereas Ferguson is from *Errol Flynn*. To me he's from *Errol Flynn*. That's it. She's a horse trying to ride a horse, he's Errol Flynn. Well, maybe I'm going back too far. So he's *Ronald Coleman*. But her posterior moves. From what I know about riding, her posterior should sit still and be quiet. You're not taking milk in your tea these days, are you? You stopped milk and started honey, since Doc went. But I'll never find the honey here. Wait a minute—" She went humming around the kitchen lifting and replacing bottles the lids of which were congealed in sugar. "Katie Monahan rides west coast, that's what it is. She's west coast." When she came back with the teas, Ettie was dozing a bit. The shine had come off the purple wool a little. The television showed a girl talking to a boy inside what might have been a gymnasium. The sound had been muted. Trudy Kay walked over and took the channel changer from Ettie's lap, pushed the mute button, and sat down to listen. "—never stops watching me," the girl was saying. "He waits for me to climax with Bob, and then he just fixates. And he says that's the part he likes best, watching me climax with Bob. I guess it takes all sorts." Trudy started to chuckle into her mug: "You put this on? What is this? This is certainly the strangest thing. A girl is talking about a boy who watches while another boy does it with her. That's distinctly *kooky*, if you ask me. Don't you think it's distinctly *kooky*?" It was only then that she looked over at Ettie, because Ettie wasn't one who'd sleep through a question, and that, because Ettie hadn't budged, she stood up and went over to question more intimately, and saw in the closeness that Ettie was dead.

•

Trudy Kay did something out of character then, because it was her character, even though she was herself somewhat fragile, to leap into action. She sat back, with the television on mute again, and with the mug on her lap, and she addressed Ettie Savage. "Well, well. I would never have thought it would be me talking to you. So you've gone. Just like that. It must have been a heart attack. We shouldn't have been watching the riding, not after you being on the medication. But you chose it, that's what you wanted. I don't know if I ever understood you. I don't know if I ever knew exactly who you were. We sure went through everything together. We sure went through everything. And now I'm the only one left. When you go, I always said to myself, when you go I'll be the only one left, and here I am. My Der is gone. And your Doc. And Ophelia. And the Zunbergs. And the Lakes, my God, last month. And even Paul Nugent. Everybody. I remember how we used to have barbecues on the beach, that was before you had to have a permit. We'd go on the fourth and eat lobster and watch the fireworks and tell stories half the night and Der would read his poetry and Marty Zunberg would play guitar and then everybody had kids—kids, kids, kids, kids, kids, everybody was a kid. I remember when all we did was talk about bringing up kids. But it's been a long time, it's like it's still here. We don't talk about kids anymore. You and I don't much want to talk about anything. And look at this, I'm talking to you and you're dead. Bang. I'll have to call somebody, won't I. I don't know who to call. With Der it was easy somehow, I knew what to do, but now.... I guess when you don't know who to call you call the police. My God!" And then, because at that moment it had hit her, she went to the phone and dialled o and stammered out something about an address and a telephone number and went as cold as stone. Ettie's face was perfect peace. "My God," Trudy Kay said, "You were just sitting there. You were just sitting there." The ambulance men were sickeningly efficient, because she found herself at the table staring into the garden and when she turned, that chair by the television was empty and the television was off and policemen were making arrangements to seal the doors of the house. "We were sitting and we were talking," Trudy Kay rehearsed to herself, "and then she was just dead. I don't know. I can't imagine. Bang, like a station break." A policewoman decided to escort her to her car and then to follow her all the way home, and she came in and made sure Trudy Kay had a sleeping pill and was tucked in, just like the perfect babysitter could be counted on to do.

•

The kids all came. They decided after the funeral, dining together at The Lobster Roll under a sailor's sunset, that although there were certainly a great number of steps that could be taken with respect to the house, and although some things would very definitely and very quickly have to be done as regarded the lawyer and the accountant, the very best move they could make for the time being, as The Family, was no move at all. This is how they came to that decision. Juniper, the youngest, was having charcoal-broiled tuna with glazed pineapple and Rennie, who after Harley's departure had moved into the space Harley had left behind, ate charbroiled tuna, too. Pamela Anne fresh from France—as always when she visited she was fresh from France—nibbled self-reproachfully at fried clams. Tommy, who had just bought a house in Oregon with the proceeds from the sale of his house in Pennsylvania, had fried flounder with a double order of coleslaw. The kids' kids—there were kids coming off in all directions like scintillations; except from Pamela Anne, whose many efforts to date in this respect had been unrewarded—had fries, clam chowder, tuna rolls, fries, milk shakes, fries, fries, fries, and lakes of ketchup. And they dredged these lakes with potato wedges and then converted the potato wedges to potato ketchup-hurlers, potato catapults, ketchup-coated potato battering rams, ketchup-spattered potato castles. And they projected liquid missiles by means of straws, missiles of unknown chemical composition disguised as chocolate milkshake. Through the melée came lancets of conversation. "Farm good, Jun'?" said Tommy with his mouth full, "New fields producing, you building a new barn?" And also, "France good, Pam? Dollar holding up?" and the question Pamela Anne dreaded, "What's Gareth up to?" But Pamela Anne could fence. "Tell me all about Oregon and how many swimming-pools you are planning to put in, and how many skylights, and the sports utility vehicle you bought for Alison," she said, and Tommy's wife, Alison, glowered as she always did at these warm family gatherings—her face became hot coals. "Alison, you must tell me all about Oregon and the private schools and your gardenia hedges." Alison could not fence at all. "You must still have some jet lag," she said, "we—" but there seemed nothing else. "Is Gareth coming in a few days, then?" Juniper asked Pamela Anne softly. "I've been assuming you'll stay at the house. I've basically cleaned it but I haven't moved anything." "We're *all* staying at the house," Tommy announced, "We didn't want to press in on you and Rennie. There's plenty of room at the house, we can just all camp." Alison had become besotted by the nonsensical idea she should connect with the spiteful Pamela Anne. "It's been years since we've seen you, how long has it been, three years? We were in Paris—" "Everybody comes to Paris," said Pamela Anne. "You could certainly stay with us," said Juniper, picking up a piece of glazed pineapple, staring at it on all sides, laying it gracefully at the margin of her green oval plate; "There wouldn't be any problem you staying with us. They could stay with us, Rennie, couldn't they? Except for the construction." "Except for the construction, that's right," said Rennie, who was putting salad into his mouth with his fingers exactly as Doc had once instructed everybody to do, "But of course they could stay with us anyway. Plenty of room. They could all stay with us, the kids could play with the sheep and the goats. Tommy, you could help me work through some ideas I have—"; he was trying to get a carrot missile projector out of Maxwell's hand as Maxwell was rotating it above his head. "Gareth is coming in a few days," said Pamela Anne, a little regally, "He and I have had a long discussion and we think there should be a memorial service." Maxwell leaned over to his mother and batted his eyelashes at her, and while she was gazing at him he let his fingers find the side of her oval green plate and steal the ring of pineapple. "We'll just stay a few days this time," said Tommy, "then we'll fly back out west, then in a month we'll come back and we can settle everything. Everything has to be settled." But settling was by no means unilateral: "I'll just need a few weeks here to settle everything I want to settle," said Pamela Anne, "I know what I want to settle and it won't be what you want to settle." It was hardly clear to whom this had been addressed, but Tommy paid it no heed and stood up and yawned and said it was time to go to sleep soon, time to go to sleep. "Mar-ga-*ret*!" said Alison. "Mar-ga-*RET*!" "Everybody should get everything they want to get settled, settled," said Rennie, affecting a zenny pose and squinting like Li-Po. "Pizooey!" called Maxwell, and liquefied unspecified chemicals disguised as chocolate milkshake went on trajectory for Maggie's nose. "I'll pay," Juniper said to no-one in particular. "We should arrange something," said Pamela Anne, "We should arrange something very meaningful for mama." With a magnificent smile the waitress came. "Pie all 'round?"

•

So that Juniper and Pamela Anne and Tommy could talk quietly among themselves, Alison and Rennie were despatched with the kids and a great deal of Play-Doh to fetch Gareth who was arriving at Kennedy. It took a long time to get everyone near the van, and a long time to get everyone into the van, and a long time to get all the seat belts fastened, and a long time for everyone to roll down the windows and say something to Juniper or Tommy and to wave at Pamela Anne without saying anything to her. Then there was quiet with the baaing of sheep and a breeze. "We should sell the house," said Tommy rather loudly, rapping Ettie's table in an empty space between two piles of catalogues. "We should definitely *not* sell the house, we should *not* sell *anything*, absolutely," said Juniper. "I think I'll stay four weeks," said Pamela Anne, and phoned the travel agent. "Isn't the market good out here, then?" said Tommy, moving some of the catalogues and rapping now with two hands. "It's not a question of the market," said Juniper, "It's that...it's...*look at all this*!" The furniture was coming apart, the dishes were in the sink, there were books piled up in every room, so many books they made the walls of labyrinths, the plants needed watering, the garden needed weeding, the walls needed painting, the dogs needed homes, the mail needed sorting, the bills needed paying, the clothes had to be gone through, the paintings had to be divided, Doc's papers had to be read and sorted because Ettie had never done a thing about Doc when Doc went, the stove needed fixing, the kitchen floor could use redoing, all the albums with the photographs of Sweden had to go somewhere, there were albums with photographs of Sweden, from when they had lived in Sweden as children, and the birdseed containers had to be emptied of birdseed because nobody was going to feed the birds, and the keys to all the doors had to be found, and that was only the beginning. "I don't want anything," said Tommy. "I'll just take a few books. When we sell the house I'll take my share." "I'll need the mysteries," Pamela Anne said, "And the cookbooks." "The windows ought to be washed, all the picture windows," said Juniper, who could certainly not quite see herself washing them. "Alison's pregnant," announced Tommy. "Oh, my!" said Pamela Anne, with a tone of one whose efforts in this direction, unrewarded, had been great and magnificent efforts. "I can arrange the sale," Tommy said. Juniper looked up through the skylight and saw that if it didn't clear up it was going to rain in sheets, and she prayed that yes, it would rain, that it would be a flood that ended the world and then the world would begin again.

•

Doc had torn up everything he could find from the garden, mesclun, lamb's quarters, radicchio, arugula, Boston flatleaf, twenty others, and literally pitched it into an enormous bowl with olive oil and lemon juice, capers, Moutarde de Meaux, garlic, freshly ground green peppercorns. "There are rules," he said, "in life. Life has rules. The rule for greens is you finger 'em. Greens are fingered. Pie is with a fork. Stew, properly, is with a spoon. Stilton cheese is properly with a spoon. Greens with the hand. You do not use a fork with salad. You do not use a fork with salad." While he said all this he was fingering the salad. "And you do not use a butter knife to eat soup." Spending time on a farm in the Missouri cornbelt he had learned that you butter cob corn by rolling it on a pound of butter, not by cutting a dainty little pat of butter and forking it onto your corn. He knew the rule about pancakes was, you ate them in bundles. You didn't eat a single pancake. You made a bundle and you put a pat of butter in between each pair of cakes, all the way up, and you poked through the whole bundle with your fork, and you poured syrup on top and let it drip through the holes with the melting butter. That was the pancake rule. "I believe it would be a better world if we didn't need rules," he said, "but we do, and I'm a rule-abiding man." Ettie, for her part, disattended rules for the most part, whenever it suited her; as, for instance, when she ate only one pancake at a time, or when she took a little teaspoonful of butter for her cob corn, or when she took a fork to her lettuce. They agreed about oysters—hands only. But now he had everybody fingering his salad, everybody but Ettie, who was smiling with mirth watching the show. Now the show was ended the voices faded, the salad disappeared, the table emptied and was covered with dust, the light became cold. The lettuce in the garden wilted, browned, went to seed. Wind whistled some through the cord wood stacked on the patio, old grey wood, cracked, going to stone.

•

Gareth, who was nothing if not a bundle of laughs, showed up with four massive suitcases he insisted magisterially on carrying himself. Pamela Anne had installed herself in the suite over the garage, Doc's little suite that was as private as private could be, and where the traces of Ettie were, perhaps, less up-to-date. Gareth fetched her tea and sugar cubes and stayed up there with her for some time, perhaps as much as two hours, and it became possible at one point, at least for Charlie and Maxwell, to hear, from among the jasmine plants at the bottom of the stairs, voices raised. "Gareth says he's leaving!" Charlie snuck in and repeated in a hush to Juniper. "He just got here! Is he gonna fly all the way back to France? Is he gonna go tonight?" "Shh," said Juniper. Gareth and Pamela Anne were making an entrance. Pamela Anne was demure. She sat at the dining table and read catalogues quite as if they were Jane Austen. Gareth marshalled Tommy and began assembling ingredients, from out of nowhere, for making sushi. "Ho, ho," he kept saying. They made sticky rice and Charlie and Maxwell proceeded to have a fight with it. "How am I supposed to roll this into a ball?" said Tommy, "The starch is an adhesive and this is unrollable." Gareth was aglow with a huge and brittle grin. "You are supposed to be an expert," said he, "Ho, ho, ho." Rennie, having driven madly in pelting rain from the airport, was dozing on the couch beside the chairs in front of the television. He was roused to run out and pick up first-class raw tuna. "There was a tin of *wasabi* stowed away here last time," Gareth said, picking things out of the pantry; watermelon pickles, rhubarb conserves from Scotland, pickled ginger, eleven coagulated mustards; smoked oysters in brine. "Last time," called Pamela, "was six months ago. He thinks his treasure is still sitting here from six months ago." "Found it!" said Gareth. The tin was a little rusty from the sea air. Prying it open with a churchkey he inspected for roaches. "Pristine." "There's no way to ball this," said Tommy definitively, in the tone of a man who has designed skyscrapers and made his own *petits fours*, "Rice is like glue." Charlie and Maxwell, at a corner of the table, were using the sticky rice to build an Eiffel Tower. Juniper looked over at Ettie's chair and saw that the wool and needles were still sitting there, waiting for continuation.

•

Maxwell was snoring in the parlour in the crib Ettie had always kept for him and that he had not quite outgrown, and Alison and Tommy were upstairs watching "Nature" in bed with Maggie sleeping like a teddy bear between them. Pamela Anne and Gareth had retired evanescently to their aerie over the garage. Under them in darkness lay a twelve-foot skiff Tommy had once built all by himself but never got around to painting. Rennie had driven over to the farm to feed the animals. Juniper sat with Charlie in the semi-darkness of the living-room, with the dogs like little boot jacks sitting silently before them. "I know why Grandma died," Charlie said suddenly, and there was a surprising sound of a dog scratching himself on the wooden floor, "I know what happened." Juniper had been thinking about a photograph her mother had shown her, of her grandmother, with an unknown gentleman, in a long white summer dress, and in a wide white summer hat with ribbons, standing in a garden on an overcast afternoon, holding by leads two princely Irish wolfhounds. All of the eyes—the grandmother's eyes, the gentleman's eyes, the eyes of the dogs—were glowing in sepia, and with a ferocity that Juniper could not quite understand, not *seize*, as if an event had just a moment before occurred which now, almost 70 years later, eluded her. "I had a dream last night," Charlie went on. "A man was standing in front of a house but the house was becoming him. His eyes were becoming the windows and his mouth was becoming the door, and as he got older the house looked more and more like his face. Finally he turned around and went into himself and he died." "What?" said Juniper, because the dogs had been trying to tell her something, not the dogs on the floor, who were still again, but the dogs in the picture. "What?" "She turned around and went into herself," Charlie said. Juniper touched him a little coldly and stood up and went through all the drawers of the side table and all the drawers in her mother's bedroom and all the bookshelves in every room of the house, but she couldn't find that photograph. That was when she knew she had no mother, and this house, which had been Ettie's realm, was only a building like other buildings in this startling world.

•

On Wednesday afternoon while Pamela Anne was at the post office and everyone else but Pamela Anne was at the beach Gareth emptied the kitchen and painted it white. The effect was quite stunning, as beforehand the walls had been burnt sienna; and the fumes, as he had availed himself exclusively of oil-based enamel, were insurmountable. To counteract, he lit a joss stick and stuck it over the back door where it was smoking indifferently as Pamela Anne walked in. "Should I have the catalogues transferred?" she said, "There are a lot of catalogues. Will they send catalogues out of the country?" She began fingering through Williams-Sonoma and Smith & Hawken and JCrew and White Flower Farm, L. L. Bean, Hammacher-Schlemmer and Wicker Warehouse and Hancock's of Paducah and Neiman-Marcus and Ethan Allen and Stokes Seed Co., Haddonstone, and Country Curtains and The American Blind and Wallpaper Factory and Jan Dressler Stencils and Baccarat and Hormel Foods and Forest Glen Winery and See's Chocolate. "I could transfer at least some of them. Maybe I'll do that. Or everything? What do you think? Mama wanted me to have the catalogues." One or two dozen catalogues arrived every day in Ettie's mail. The ones from the last month were piled in boxes beneath the dining table and current ones were piled up to prevent people from dining. No-one had told anyone to stop the catalogues from coming. "I could write a form letter, the same letter to all of them." Gareth said, "Personally I don't approve of catalogue shopping, you see. Personally I think it's immoral, or at least decadent, or maybe both. But you must live by your own lights. Or you will. You will anyway. You will do anyway what you crave to do. Have you mailed off all the bedsheets?" he was descending to the wine cellar to rummage for an hour in the dankness, "Have you loaded up all the books you want? Because the luggage will be full." She'd spent the day wrapping and mailing packages to herself in Paris. She didn't know what else she could do. He came up in 40 minutes with three bottles of Château Puijoule Contraire 1954 and set them like offerings upon the dining table. "She has six dozen of these down there," he said. He picked up the phone and dialled a number that he found by squinting at a smeared hand-written list taped to the wall. "Can you tell me what you'd offer for a Château Puijoule '54?" Why did he bring up three?, Pamela Anne wondered, why not just one? Gareth's eyebrows had become apses, and he was letting forth a long low whistle. "I don't see," he told her, putting the phone back into its cradle a little harshly, "who else besides me has shown any interest in that wine cellar." Of all moments she chose this one to announce to him, "I think I should like to have another go at babying, if it's all the same to you."

•

A week to the hour after the death, Trudy Kay brought herself for a look-see. It wasn't because of erosion that she muttered to herself, or because of loneliness, which amounts to the same thing, but in truth Ettie was there listening. Ettie was at her side. "What am I looking at, hm? What do I expect to see?" she was already mumbling as she pulled into the driveway. "Who the hell do I think I am?" She wandered around the garden, which was set out with tricycles and baseball equipment and giant mammal-sized clumps of Play-Doh a little like a jumping course. Nobody had seen to the weeding of the perennials, or to the mowing of the lawns, and many of the flowers were distinctively ready to be picked but nobody was picking them. "They're all just moving in," she said, "They're all just ensconcing themselves. What are these, morning glories?"—the flowers she was fingering were hibiscus—"What's this?"—angelica, luminous and kiwi green—"I love Sweet William!"—it was phlox, but behind the phlox, where she wasn't looking, was a broth of Sweet William. The bird bath needed filling but as Trudy Kay had no place in her heart for birds she just walked past it. "Well well," was all she said. "Well well, Ettie. I know you want somebody to keep an eye on this for you. You can trust me. Who better to trust with a house!" Then she caught herself against the pear tree and began to cry, because this was Ettie, from long before the Island, long before real estate, long before gardens and the Sunday Ladies Improvement Society, long, long ago in the channel of her own heart. She let the kids bring her in for a cup of tea, and give her cookies, and she talked about the old times, and the kids blushed sorrowfully as if they remembered and missed what kids cannot possibly remember.

•

In a month Trudy Kay came again. It was the heart of fall. The garden was a symphony of brown flecked with stubborn shoots of green. The winds were getting stronger, rattling the picture windows, scattering the leavings of bird seed into the drying lawns. The kids were gone with their kids, except for Juniper who stopped over once in a while to collect bills, tidy some papers, make phone calls. But Juniper was the one who had not moved away. Juniper took care of everything. Trudy Kay saw that the rooms had been more or less denuded. The paintings were gone. The books were thinned. The master bedroom was as clean as a whistle. The linen closet, except for two torn sheets, had been emptied. But the oddest thing about the house was that it hadn't in the slightest sense lost the taste of Ettie Savage. She was here as much as she had ever been. She was here now. So, to tell the truth, was Doc, but always stepping around behind her, carrying his cup of tea but forgetting to drink it. So was Doc. And no-one would evict either of them. Ettie, in particular, was in the beams. Trudy Kay put on the television, why not?, and watched "Days of Our Lives." She made herself some tea. "All I have left now is time," she said openly. "I wait and I look around and I think about people who don't bear thinking about anymore. My God, who am I talking to?" There was a pitter-patter. She looked down. It was one of the dogs. "You here? You here? What are you anyway, some kind of a terrier? Where's your brother? Where's the other one?" The dog smiled and sat at her feet. "Who feeds you? You stay here all by yourself?" She found the channel-changer and pushed a button. The Olympic equestrian trials were on. Katie Monahan-Prudent was clearing a big oxer on High Roller, and then a triple bar, and the wall, and a vertical, another vertical. "I'm sorry, but I think she rides like a hippopotamus," Trudy Kay said to the little dog. He shuffled at her knee and watched what she was watching. "See? She's really a hippopotamus. See those hips? Gosh, you're an observant doggie. I never saw before how observant you are." He was watching her sympathetically, waiting. "It's October now, and soon it'll be winter," she said, "Everything will be snow. I hate snow. Don't you? My God, I'm conversing with a mutt." The dog looked up. "Do you hate the winter as much as I do? We'll be lucky to get through the winter, you'll see what I mean, and then it will be spring again and you can go running after rabbits." She looked at him and he walked away through the patio doors and into the yard where the leaves were on the ground. When she left, she left the television on for the dog to watch. Juniper'd take care of it. Juniper took care of everything.

•

Juniper was coming into the drive with milk and butter when she saw Trudy Kay's car parked next to Tommy's skiff. She caught her breath. It would be another song and dance about the real estate market and "You should get this place cleaned up" and "We should bring some people in" and "You have no idea what we could do with a place like this" instead of the perfection of silence, the birds dancing on the other side of the windows, an hour to breathe. Trudy Kay was coming out now in fact, her head down, her teeth clenched against the future. But the head came up and across a gulf the older woman stared at the younger. "Beautiful girl!" Trudy Kay thought to herself, "What a vision!" Juniper was squinting in a flood of sunlight, and the sky was blue on her cheeks and long golden hair, and the two clouds alone in the sky were white as ice-cream. But then, all in brilliance, and with a shock, what had been waiting its long measure to strike Trudy Kay, produced itself. It struck the old woman so that she had to gasp with it: "*Look at you*! I can't remember...I can't bring back *anything*...Where am I...Where is this? *Look at you*! I know that face. I have seen that face before. Where have I seen that face? Years ago. Charming, optimistic, inspired, happy, tragically bright? Yes, *that* face!" It was true, then, what she had always suspected and sometimes feared, that the past was the future and that death was life. It *was* the same face! Of course it was, and had always been the same face even if Trudy Kay hadn't perceived it since those first days in Brooklyn Heights when once everything had been golden but then she had forgotten her ability to forget time. The face had always been there waiting to become itself. Now whatever line made the pattern had finally, as the geese were flying, been etched. The world was slowly swimming, patiently going nowhere. The circle had started all over again.

MURRAY POMERANCE is the author of *Magia d'Amore*, *An Eye for Hitchcock* and *Johnny Depp Starts Here*, as well as the editor or co-editor of numerous volumes including *American Cinema of the 1950s: Themes and Variations* and *Enfant Terrible!: Jerry Lewis in American Film*. His fiction has appeared in, among other places, *The Paris Review*, *The Kenyon Review*, *New Directions*, and *Descant*, and he has been anthologized in *Prize Stories 1992: The O. Henry Awards* and *04: Best Canadian Stories*. He lives with his family in Toronto.